SEEKING VALHALLA

SEEKING VALHALLA

A RETRO SCIENCE FICTION NOVEL

ERIC G. SWEDIN

THE BORGO PRESS

MMXIII

SEEKING VALHALLA

FIRST EDITION

Published by Wildside Press LLC

www.wildsidebooks.com

DEDICATION

For my uncle, Curtis Hunt,
dead in an automobile accident at age
seventeen, yet who inspired me posthumously
with his science fiction paperback collection

SEEKING VALHALLA

CHAPTER ONE

Major John Carter learned to hate the Nazis the day that he stood in Dachau before a pile of emaciated corpses. He had been fighting the Germans since D-Day, crawling from Normandy across France, Belgium, and into the Fatherland, but that was soldier against soldier, a struggle between professionals. Now he learned to hate, a visceral feeling that came from deeper inside his brain than intellect, from the same fundamental place that a man craved food, survival, and the affection of a woman.

That spring day in 1945 was like most spring days in Germany: pleasant temperatures, blue skies, the trees showing life after a harsh winter, and the promise of rain in the air. The smell of death didn't belong.

Other members of his Ranger company were helping the survivors, supporting them as they placed one foot slowly in front of the other, carrying them if need be. The prisoners' collarbones supported the rags they wore like odd tent poles, and their bony arms looked more like sticks than things belonging on men. Doctors from the medical battalion had set up a receiving station near the camp gate and were slowly administering water and food, careful not to let the starving men eat too quickly, lest they bloat and die.

The main gate to the camp was wrought iron, with three words welded into the metal: *Arbeit Macht Frei.* "Work Brings Freedom." Irony turned into mockery, all reflecting only bureaucratic savagery.

"There's more over here, Major."

Carter turned to look at Master Sergeant Carson Napier. The sergeant had been with him for two years, since they had first trained together in Georgia. A rock of a man, with a squat sturdy frame and a cunning intelligence behind eyes that now streamed tears. In contrast, Carter stood just over six feet tall, with a lanky body and wavy light brown hair, and the bearing of a Virginia aristocrat.

"Lead on, Sarge."

They walked past rows of barracks, made of poorly cut pine planks, each forming a single large room. A solitary stovepipe in the middle of each building provided the only heat. In some places, boards were missing from the walls, perhaps used as firewood to survive during the winter. They came to another barracks, better constructed than the others, with planks that fit tightly against each other. Three stove pipes showed that this building was heated properly. A tall fence of wire mesh surrounded the building, with barbed wire coiled across the top.

Napier led Carter through an open gate, past the empty guard boxes. Two of his own Rangers stood casually but alertly near the door to the building. They didn't salute, but stiffened their backs in a way that showed respect for their superior. Rangers were the elite, and fought because they were proud to fight; they didn't go in for that formal horseshit.

The sergeant opened the door for the major, waiting for Carter to step inside before following him, standing behind him as a loyal aide. Carter was surprised to find the interior well-lit from numerous windows; the other barracks he had looked into were more like caves than proper buildings. A row of single beds lined each wall, with proper mattresses, blankets, and pillows on them.

Clustered against the far wall were the inhabitants of the building. Young women, all with long hair, some blonde, most dark-haired, and even one redhead. They wore white night-gowns and white slippers, and looked so fresh that a man ached to look at them. He noticed that all seemed to have large breasts straining against their nightgowns. The poor girls were obviously terrified. Glancing around, the major noticed that a few had remained in bed, huddled under their blankets, some with covers over their heads, and others peering out fearfully with eyes that seemed too large for their faces.

"Why are they so afraid?" Carter asked.

"Don't know, Major," Napier replied. "They won't say a thing."

"You found them?"

"Jenkins did, sir. He came and found me. You figure this is a brothel, sir?"

Carter's eyes searched more carefully. "Could be. I've heard that the guards liked to have their pick of the prettiest."

"And these are certainly pretty enough."

"True, but this doesn't feel like a brothel. It's too...pristine."

Carter had finished his degree in Classics at Yale only two years ago, just before joining up. He had always had a gift for languages. Professor Jones had said that he was a prodigy, a once-in-a-generation talent. Carter didn't care to think of himself as some sort of language genius—that went against his upbringing—but he enjoyed the taste of new words.

He spoke in German. "Young ladies, we are not here to hurt you. Please do not be afraid. Is there anything that you need? Water? Food? Please speak to me."

The redhead spoke up. "You are not Nazis?" Her German was heavily accented.

"We're American soldiers, miss. Please don't be alarmed. What is your name?"

She detached herself from the other women, pushing away hands that tried to keep her in their cloister, and walked down the center of the room, her head held high and her eyes alight with awareness. She didn't look to be a day over sixteen years old. Carter noticed that her nipples were pushing against the linen of her nightgown, perhaps from nervousness, and studiously tried to keep his eyes on her face.

"My name's Aoife McLaughlan. I'm from County Clare."

"You're Irish?"

"Yes."

"You speak English?"

"Enough. My family spoke Gaelic and I know a bit of German."

Carter switched to Gaelic and saw a pleased glow come to her eyes. "How did you come to be here?"

"I was kidnapped," she said.

"Kidnapped?"

"A group of soldiers came ashore from a submarine and tried to grab my sister and me on July 8, 1941. I fought them and my sister got away, but they brought me here, and I have lived in this barracks ever since."

"And these other women?" Carter indicated them with a wave of his hand. "Also kidnapped?"

"Aye, we come from all over Europe. Some from Sweden, Norway, Finland, Denmark, Poland, France, Belgium, Holland, England, Scotland, Wales, Switzerland, even Iceland." She sounded like a schoolgirl reciting all the countries in north-western Europe.

"Who took care of you?"

"The matrons did," she spat. "Bitches, every one of them. But no one hit us if we obeyed, and we've always had enough food—not like those poor souls out there." She pointed towards a window covered with dark paper. "We didn't like to watch them. It was too sad."

"Where are the matrons?"

"They fled with the guards. They said that you wanted to rape them and they said that you wanted to rape us too."

Major Carter stiffened. "We hang men who do that."

"Good."

"What did the Nazis do with you here?" Carter asked "Why did they want you?"

"Not what you're thinking, I should say," she said, fury in her voice. "We are all virgins here and have remained virgins."

"No doubt." The major felt his face flush.

"We were all kidnapped and fattened up and kept here until our turn came."

"Your turn?"

Her voice faltered. "To be sacrificed."

"Sacrificed? I don't understand. Taken somewhere else?"

"Yes, taken somewhere else. To the temple of Odin."

Carter paused, mentally checking the meaning of the words. Had she really said, "temple of Odin"? Odin, the chief god of the Vikings?

"You were to be offered as sacrifices to Odin? As in—human sacrifices?"

"Yes." She was completely serious. "I have seen it with my own eyes."

Yesterday, Carter would not have believed her, but after coming across Dachau that morning, he was able to believe. "How did you come to see this?"

"They took me there once. Along with another girl. Her name was Elena, a pretty blonde from Prague. I think that they had planned to sacrifice us both. I was so scared that I vomited all over myself. For some reason, that made me impure and they only killed her." She swallowed, her eyes wide and distant. "They made me watch."

"Could you take me to this temple?"

She slowly nodded, her green eyes wide with trust.

CHAPTER TWO

The Bavarian forest in the full bloom of spring could not erase Dachau from his mind—nothing ever would. One does not forget a train full of corpses stacked like firewood or the haunted looks in the eyes of tens of thousands of prisoners, some so far gone that they couldn't even feel grateful at their liberation. One does not forget the sight of a man lying on the ground where he fell, his chest heaving as he sucked in air, his eyes vacant.

The light-colored trunks of beech and the grey bark of oak flashed by as Napier drove the jeep along the paved road under a canopy of green. Carter sat in the passenger seat, his hand resting lightly on the .30-caliber machine gun mounted just in front of him. The girl from Ireland sat in the rear seat, a place normally filled with backpacks, duffle bags, and other gear. Napier had left those behind in a neat stack at the company's bivouac outside the concentration camp.

Aoife spoke in English for the benefit of Napier. "I remember that small house that we just passed. The road is just up here. See it?"

As Napier slowed down, Carter looked behind them. Two trucks followed them, six-by-six Studebakers painted army green, carrying two sections of Rangers of eleven soldiers each. Carter didn't care for acting as scout. It was bad tactics to have the command element lead, but he feared that the girl would be terrified if he and the sergeant were not with her.

A dirt road snaked off between the trees. Napier drove slower and Carter stood up to get a better look, bracing himself against the machine gun mount. Ideal place for an ambush. Besides the cover from the trees, the rolling ground made the jeep flow up and down along the road like a skiff at sea. The Third Reich might be collapsing, and her soldiers surrendering in droves, but die-hard believers still fought with skill and tenacity. Before an advance party of army soldiers had stumbled on Dachau, the Ranger company had been attached to the 45th Infantry Division, moving in position into attack Munich. That city had not surrendered, and these woods could be crawling with stragglers, deserters, and small units still under discipline.

"Please stop," Aoife said, laying her hand on Napier's arm.

The sergeant rolled the jeep to a stop. "What's wrong?" he asked.

"The temple is just beyond that rise. I don't want to see it again."

"Fair enough," Carter said. "Turn off the jeep, Sergeant."

The major leaped down from the jeep and signaled back to the truck driver behind, twisting his thumb and forefinger to indicate turning off the truck engine, and twirling his finger to order the troops to dismount. Soldiers in green piled out, automatically spreading out into the surrounding trees, veteran instincts demanding that they secure the area.

"Miss McLaughlan, I'm going to leave a soldier with you and take the rest of my men forward."

"I volunteer, sir," Napier said quickly.

Carter looked at his sergeant. The soldier looked away, a pink flush working its way across his cheeks. Normally Carter wanted the former coal-miner from Utah to be with him at all times. The sergeant was his rock, as close to him as his younger brother back home in Virginia, always reliable, and had saved his life twice, once on D-Day and once in a snowy town in Belgium that Carter could not remember the name of. He decided that the sergeant had earned some leeway and nodded curtly.

"Corporal Finney," Carter called to one of his section leaders. "You will take two men and scout ahead."

The young man from New Jersey waved a salute and headed forward with two men in line behind him. Carter arranged for the two sections to advance through the woods, keeping off the road. At least it was spring, with only occasional patches of snow to be found in shaded spots.

Taking his M2 carbine from the jeep, Carter walked up along the edge of the road. Small purple and white flowers grew in clumps next to the dirt ruts, like little presents from the spirits of the forest, and Carter took care to not step on them. It just seemed wrong that anything so pretty should be destroyed. As he topped the rise, he looked back to see Napier engaged in earnest conversation with the girl.

In front of him was a small hollow. The trees had been cut back to make room for a walled enclosure. Stone pillars reached up about fifteen feet, with wooden palisades between the pillars. The corporal and the two scouts stood before a gate—not entering, just looking. Another road joined the first, just before the gate; from the wear on the ground, it looked like it was used as much as the other. Carter followed the second road back with his eyes and saw that it disappeared into a thicket of spruce, heading west. Carter sniffed the air: no smoke or any smells out of place. Some birds twittered in a nearby tree. It all seemed peaceful and safe.

Carter trotted down to join his men. The grass growing between the walls and the forest had been cut so that it was only a couple of inches high, like the lawn that Carter had played on as a child back home.

As he drew closer, he noticed that the wood forming the palisade had geometric shapes inscribed on it, and the gate itself was inlaid with a carving of an elaborate tree. Carter had specialized in Greek and Roman classics, but two classes from Professor Lundgren on Nordic languages had intrigued him enough to enable him to remember much of the content. His mind shifted gears, dusting off old information and finding fresh meaning in what his eyes saw. The geometric shapes were obviously Nordic runes. He didn't remember what the shapes meant; his talents ran more to the auditory side of languages. The tree on the gate was obviously Yggdrasil, a giant ash called the World Tree, with a small deer at the base nibbling at its branches. This tree connected all nine worlds of Norse cosmology, from the abode of the gods in Asgard to the middle realm of Midgard where humans lived, down to Niflheim, the cold land of mists and ice, where Hel, the daughter of Loki and the giantess Angrboda, ruled.

"Shall I open it, sir?" the corporal asked. Finney had already been a sergeant twice. He was a reliable man on the battlefield, but a drunk on leave, which had cost him his rank both times.

Carter looked back and saw that his troops were approaching, maintaining their distance from each other, not clumping up like amateurs. "Second section, reconnoiter the surrounding woods," Carter called out. "First section, follow us in."

Finney hauled at the ring set to the side of the gate, leaning back to take the weight of what must have been a full ton of wood. He fell as the gate opened smoothly on oiled hinges. Perfectly balanced, Carter thought, as he stepped back to let the gate drift open. Good German engineering.

The wall enclosed about four acres—a garden with trimmed grass, groomed walkways of white gravel, manicured bushes, and oak and beech trees to give shade. Someone had been taking care of the place, perhaps even that morning. From the inside it was obvious that the walls formed the shape of an octagon, with eight stone towers. Stone pillars, covered with runes, some as tall as a man, were scattered about, seemingly at random, yet Carter suspected there was order to their placements. Dominating the center of the space was a giant oak tree, reaching some forty feet into the air, with a base ten feet wide, and thick branches standing firm under the weight of lush foliage.

The men scattered to explore the small buildings built against the inner walls, some of dressed stone, others of carved wood. Carter was drawn to the giant oak. He was reminded of Irminsul, meaning "great pillar" in the Old Saxon tongue, a precursor to modern German. Irminsul was a great tree that represented the connection between heaven and earth, a center of worship for the Saxons who lived in Germany in ancient times. Charlemagne, in his campaigns against the Saxons and the Danes, captured the temple and burned the tree. He intended to destroy the old pagan religions.

As he drew closer, Carter saw iron rings hanging from hooks driven into the tree about eight feet above the ground. The tree bark underneath the rings was patchy and discolored with dark splotches. In a small shrine nearby he found human skulls arranged on shelves. In a flash, it all came together. The virgins from Dachau being brought her, tied to the rings, scraping the bark off the tree with frantic motions, sacrificed, and their skulls kept as trophies, or perhaps offerings. The whole idea left him feeling sad; so much of the rage he would have liked to feel had been exhausted by the morning at the concentration camp.

A screech from a bird jerked his eyes upward. Two ravens burst from the giant tree and circled around, screaming their displeasure. The dark birds alighted on one of the stone towers and perched there, intently watching the American soldiers. A chill went through Carter as he recalled the ravens of Odin, Huginn and Muninn, meaning "Thought" and "Memory," who traveled the world, acting as spies for the Norse god.

"Sir," one of the soldiers called from a nearby building. "You've got to see this."

Carter shook himself, making his whole body move, as if this would slough off the malaise that he felt. He trotted over to the building. It was narrow in depth, with wide doors that the soldier had pulled open. Arranged on shelves were silver bowls, steel knives, and small boxes of gold coins. The bowls were of exquisite manufacture, with runes and stylized Nordic faces embossed on them.

The soldier's eyes gleamed. "Can we liberate some of these, sir?"

Carter allowed himself a small smile. A roundabout way to ask if looting was allowed. While Carter found looting to be unseemly, not the act of a gentleman, he knew that many of his soldiers took pilfering as their due as conquerors, as it had been for millennia.

"I recommend that you don't," Carter said. "This a cursed area, and these are cursed items. They will only bring bad luck. Over there, women were murdered by the Nazis as human sacrifices to pagan gods."

The soldier's eyes went wide as he pushed the doors closed. Carter was surprised with himself at the words that had burst out. Brought up as a Methodist and now a deist, he was not a superstitious man given to believing in rabbit-foot charms, or any of the little rituals that many of his soldiers clung to. But confronting the evidence of such raw evil made a man think in a more primitive way, of spirits and curses, of basic emotions and fundamental values.

The doors of the building held a wonderful wooden cutting of the great serpent Jormungand, who encircled all of Midgard, with his head eating his tail. Inside the serpent was a map of Europe. A great swastika showed the location of Germany. He was intrigued to find three more smaller swastikas, one in Poland, another in Austria, and still another further north in Sweden. Another great swastika, as large as the one in Germany, was located at the very top, near the North Pole. In the Holy Land, the British colony of Palestine, a cross lay broken.

Glorious music suddenly poured from the trees. Carter dropped to a crouch, looking around like a trapped animal, his carbine at the ready. He looked up at a nearby tree and saw a speaker, painted in camouflage brown, nestled in the branches. There were speakers in other trees and in recessed cavities inside the buildings. A sound expert had laid everything out so that the grove vibrated with the music. It was Wagner; *Ride of the Valkyries*, if he wasn't mistaken, certainly something from the Ring Cycle. He had heard that Wagner was Hitler's favorite composer. The Ring was based on ancient epic pagan stories, so it all made sense.

"Captain—I mean, Major," a soldier called out. Carter had only been promoted a couple of weeks earlier, and not everyone was used to the new rank. Carter himself wasn't used to it. Normally a captain commanded a company, so he was supposed to move up to battalion staff, but he had asked to remain with his company. The war against the Germans would only last a few more weeks at most, and he wanted to finish the war with his men; he would submit to staff work when they were transferred to the Pacific for the invasion of Japan.

Carter walked over to the soldier and was shown the interior of another of the buildings that huddled up against the temple wall. Two phonographs sat on a table, with one rotating the record on top. More records were arranged vertically in shelves, and underneath the table was a stack of car batteries connected together.

"No Tommy Dorsey, sir," the soldier said, leafing through a sheaf of records. "Just more like this lady screaming music."

"That's called classical music, Jenkins," Carter said. "Let's turn it off. We're still in a war and that's like a foghorn attracting the enemy."

Jenkins picked up the phonograph arm; the sudden silence felt eerie. Carter slowly rotated, observing his soldiers rummaging through the buildings. The ravens still watched them. There were a lot of valuable goods here and this temple had obviously been important to high-ranking Nazis.

So where were the guards?

CHAPTER THREE

She was the prettiest girl he had ever seen and Carson Napier struggled to keep his eyes off her. He was intensely aware that she was sitting in the jeep next to him; the tension grew so intense that he lurched out of the jeep and stood nearby, trying to glance at her furtively, but finding her eyes on him every time that he looked.

Napier searched for the right words to open a conversation. He was no good at chatting a girl up and all the lines that he had heard his friends brag about as being a surefire way to charm a lass didn't seem to make much sense. Maybe he should just talk to her.

"I heard you speaking another language to the major," Napier said. "He called it Gaelic?"

"Aye, it's what I spoke at home."

"I'm from Scotland myself. Or I should say, my parents were. Edinburgh. I was born there, but was taken to America when I was still a baby. I don't remember anything of the old country."

She smiled at him and he thought that his heart must be visibly pounding against his shirt, like a jackhammer out of control. "I have cousins in America. They live in Boston. Where did you live?"

"Price, Utah. That's a long way from Boston."

"What was in Price?"

"Coal mines. It's hard work and dangerous. Kids even used to work in the mines, but new laws changed that so I didn't start until I was fifteen. Worked with my dad and my older brothers.

There was an Irish family in town, the O'Reillys. Good enough people. The father worked hard, but he only had daughters, no sons to help him in the mine, so they had to live on only his wages. That's hard. They were always in debt to the company store. Of course, that's how the company liked it, when you owed them so much money that you couldn't quit your job. There were lots of different people there. Lots of Finns, Poles, Czechs, Serbs, even a couple of German families. There was only one other Scottish family—my Uncle Ian, Aunt Beth, and my cousins. It was like a little Europe, just a soup bowl full of immigrants. There were a lot of people I liked there, but the work was hard and I wanted to see more of the world than more tunnels of the mines. When Pearl Harbor happened, I was pretty happy. No, that doesn't sound right. I felt bad for all those families that had lost sons and fathers. Something like twenty-five hundred Americans died. That was sad. I took a bus to Salt Lake two days later and joined the army. Best thing I ever did."

He paused for breath. He felt like he was chattering mindlessly, dumping out information because he was terrified that he wouldn't have anything to say. "Enough about me. What about you?"

"What about me?" she smiled widely as she watched him.

"Where'd you grow up?"

"On a farm. Not an estate, I'm no daughter of a lord. It was big enough for our dairy herd. I lived in town so that I could go to school. The nuns were strict, but I miss school."

"I didn't get enough schooling," Napier said. "Just up to eighth grade. But I read a lot, mostly magazines and comic books. The major says that I've got a big vocabulary."

"They gave us books and magazines at the camp. Mostly in German. It kept us distracted as girls were brought, and as girls were taken away, never to return."

"It must have been hard to find a reason to survive," he said. "You must have lost hope at times."

"I prayed," she said simply. "My faith in Jesus kept me alive."

"I believe in Jesus Christ."

"Are you Catholic?" she asked.

"Presbyterian."

She looked disappointed. "My cousin Claire married a Protestant from Ulster. Our priest refused to give her communion and told her that she was damned to go to hell."

"That's not very friendly," Napier said. "I know of a nice couple from Silver Ridge, back near my hometown. She was Catholic and he was a Baptist. Her priest let her keep going to mass as long as they both agreed to raise their kids as Catholics."

Her smile crinkled her face, bunching up her freckles on her cheeks into two dimples in a manner that he found utterly charming. "That sounds more reasonable," she said.

"Do not move!" The harsh voice with the obvious German accent startled Napier into obedience. His body tensed and he clenched his fingers into tight fists as his eyes searched frantically for who had spoken.

The German officer entered the edge of his vision, wearing a black uniform with the black swastika on a red armband. He was a small man, no taller than Napier, and on the slight side, barely able to fill out his uniform. His pistol was still in his holster, but the two SS troopers behind him, with their MP43 assault rifles pointed at Napier and the girl, gave weight to his command.

Napier felt a cold calm come over him. The first time that he had gone into battle, coming under fire in Sicily, he had frozen in panic, unable to move his weapon to return fire. None of his fellow Rangers had noticed, or perhaps they just never said anything, but that act of panic frightened him more profoundly than anything else he had ever experienced. He had resolved to never panic again, and surprisingly, the power of mind over action, he never had.

He did not panic now. Keeping his eyes on the Germans, so that they could not follow his thoughts by watching his eyes, he remembered where his carbine was—propped up between the two front seats, with the safety on, at least a good six feet away. Going for it would be almost certain suicide, since he respected those grease guns that the Germans carried, but the real problem was that Aoife was sitting right next to the carbine. She would certainly be caught in the crossfire. He couldn't have her death on his conscience and so resigned himself to submission.

The officer walked around the jeep, taking care to not block the lines of fire of his soldiers. Napier watched him. The Nazi peered at the girl and spoke quickly in German. She paled and tears rolled down her cheeks.

"What's going on, Aoife?" he asked. "What'd he say?"

Her voice quavered. "He knows who I am and he's going to take me."

"Over my dead body!" Napier exclaimed, taking a step towards the jeep.

His head exploded in pain.

CHAPTER FOUR

Aoife cried out in dismay, scrambling across the driver's seat of the jeep and onto the ground next to the soldier. She buried her hands and face into his chest. She heard his heart beating, steady and strong, so reassuring. His uniform smelled sweaty and musty, as if it hadn't been laundered for weeks, but she liked the scent of this man. As her initial alarm subsided, she heard the German officer order one of his men to get her.

Her father had always said that she was a quick-thinking lass. He did not always mean it as a compliment, especially when she got in trouble, but he was proud of her good marks in school. Aoife slipped a bracelet off her wrist and slid it onto the American's wrist, whispering an enchantment that her mother had taught her, binding his imagination to the bracelet and to her. It was a most curious piece of jewelry, made of three inter-twined golden hairs, and so fine and flexible that it was lost in the arm hairs of even a fair-haired girl like herself. Her mother had given it to her after she had become a woman.

Rough hands pulled her up. She looked into the German's blue eyes and saw only hard evil. He pawed at her breast as he stood her on her feet.

"None of that," the officer barked. "She's to remain a virgin."

As they dragged her through the forest, away from the jeep, she stubbed her toe on a rock and cried out. Slippers were better than bare feet, but not by much. The soldier yanked her arm to keep her moving.

After only a couple of hundred meters, they came upon

another road. A group of German soldiers, wearing camouflage uniforms and carrying short, stubby weapons, waited for them. She counted nineteen of them. The officer stopped to give them orders while the first two soldiers dragged Aoife further down the road.

Her mother had always told her to pay attention, whether when baking a pie, listening to her teacher, or just watching the sea come in and out on the rocky headland near her home. A good rule of life, she always thought. Life was full of surprises when you paid attention.

To her surprise, she realized that the two soldiers were twins, or at least brothers who looked identical. They were big men, well-proportioned, with blond hair and blue eyes. The matrons at the camp had enthused enough about Aryan ideology for Aoife to see that the twins fit the bill. It had probably kept them out of fighting on the front, assigned to the temple.

They reached two trucks parked on the road. One of the men found a piece of rope and tied her hands together in front of her, being unexpectedly gentle to make sure that the rope was not too tight. She figured that she could get out of the bonds if she had five minutes or so to work on them.

The officer came striding up the road. As he approached, Aoife paid attention. Before, the officer had been defined by his black uniform in her mind, but now she looked at his face and realized that she had seen him before. In a different uniform.

As the priest who had sacrificed her friend Elena.

CHAPTER FIVE

SS Colonel Hans von Krohn constantly moved back and forth in the passenger seat of the truck, peering up out of the windshield or the door window. He could only see part of the sky, and was completely blind towards the back of the truck. Fritz was supposed to be watching outside the back of the truck. Driving during the day was just foolish, with all the American and British Jabos, low-flying fighter-bombers, armed with rockets and cannons, that ranged over Germany with impunity, shooting at whatever struck their fancy.

Just that morning, Krohn had seen a Jabo chasing an old woman in a farm field, swooping in again and again as she stumbled across the furrows, too far from trees or a building to find shelter, her dress flapping against her shins. Finally a burst of cannon fire cut her down and the airplane climbed up into the sky, like a raptor seeking other prey. Krohn did not condemn the pilot—he could see the sport in the hunt—but it pained him to see his fellow Germans dying as their Fatherland was ripped open.

A slight man with a limp that disqualified him from front-line duty, the result of a childhood accident with a horse, Krohn knew that the heart of a warrior beat strong in him. As a high priest to the god Odin, he contributed to the war effort with his temple. On the first day of the war, September 1st, 1939, in the old Christian calendar, the sixth year of the Third Reich, he had offered up to Odin his first bride. She was a fourteen-year-old girl from Czechoslovakia, but of Polish extraction. He had personally investigated her genealogy to make sure.

In just over a month, the German legions had overrun Poland. Krohn wrote a private letter directly to Reichsführer-SS Heinrich Himmler, the bespectacled head of the SS, communicating his belief that the bride-offering had encouraged Odin to directly help achieve the victory. Himmler was always interested in Krohn's work and approved the funding and secret orders necessary to collect more girls.

The launch of the Norwegian campaign in April 1940 was so secret that Krohn was unprepared when he heard the news. He commandeered a transport aircraft and flew to Oslo as quickly as he could, found a comely virgin, and flew her back to the temple. Though she acted terrified, he knew that she was secretly honored to become a bride of Odin. After only two months, Norway belonged to Germany. Truly a day for joy, since Norway was an Aryan nation, of the purist Nordic stock, not like the Poles, who as Slavs were fit only for servitude.

Only a few days later, Himmler passed the word that the Low Countries and France were about to be invaded. Krohn scrambled to find offerings from each of the countries. France itself was so large that it presented difficulties. From his historical studies, he knew that France was really not a single ethnic nation. He needed girls from the Franks, Bretons, Basques, Normans, and Alsatians. He failed to find a Norman girl, but the others died in a glorious ceremony. After the success of conquering France in only six weeks, a task that Germany had failed to accomplish after four years of trying in the First World War, Krohn's faith in his program of offering brides to Odin was confirmed.

After France, Krohn embarked on a vigorous program to find virgins from every possible country and region that the Führer might decide to add to the Reich. He housed them at the nearby concentration camp and took care to ensure that they received the best treatment. Success followed success, and Himmler presented Krohn with a Totenkopfring, a ring with runes and a skull on it, only granted to the most honored SS officers.

"Go to my house," Krohn now told Karl. The twin grunted his obedience. When they first came to him, Krohn had been irritated by how few words the burly twins from Stuttgart seemed to know. He had came to realize that they were bright enough and knew the words; they just didn't like to talk, though at times he had seen the twins hold long whispered conversations with each other. Krohn decided to allow them their seeming insolence after he realized that they were as loyal as the best shepherd dog a man could ask for.

Still no planes. Probably because of the trees, or maybe the Americans were so sure of victory that they had already started to celebrate and the pilots were drunk. How had it come to this? The first two years of the war had been one success after another, military victories on a scale never before seen in history, and Krohn knew that Odin had played a major part. Then came December of 1941 and the reverses before Moscow.

Desperate to recover German fortunes, Krohn had stained the snow with the blood of dozens of brides. He had plenty of girls from Russia and the Ukraine, sent to him by SS units that roamed behind the advancing German armies, getting rid of Jews and other undesirables. Even with the entry of America into the war, German fortunes recovered in the summer of 1942, and Krohn thanked Odin.

Then, in the winter of 1942, everything started to go wrong. Rommel lost in Egypt, the Americans invaded North Africa, and worst of all, the German Sixth Army surrendered at Stalingrad. Krohn had been summoned to an emergency meeting at Wewelsburg Castle, the ritual home of the SS. With other scholars and officers, Krohn watched a grizzled old woman, perhaps even a gypsy, draw from her bag human bones, mostly from fingers and worn from long use. She cast them onto the Black Sun mosaic set into the floor of the Marble Hall. Looking up at Himmler with her rheumy eyes, the oracle pronounced the end of the Reich.

Krohn heard later that she had been sent to the camps for her audacious prophecy, though Himmler did not seem to doubt her. That day began the many plans for the National Socialist movement to continue even if the Allies defeated the military forces of the Reich. Krohn participated in many of the efforts, especially the Norwegian project. Krohn also redoubled his efforts to placate Odin with more brides. Even after sending eighty virgins to Odin in 1943, the military reverses continued. The skies brought death and ruin from British bombers at night and American bombers during the day.

Krohn asked himself, why had everything gone sour? Even as he continued to offer brides, he came to the conclusion that the leaders of the Reich must have lost faith. Hitler himself had always seemed lukewarm to many of the more interesting implications of occult knowledge. Perhaps it was the heart of Hitler that was to blame. Perhaps Hitler was not the great leader that the Aryan nation truly needed.

Krohn kept such ideas to himself.

CHAPTER SIX

The crackle of submachine-gun fire alerted Carter that the guards had returned. Four of his men came rushing through the open gate, heads down low, running as if they expected a bullet to find their backs at any moment.

Carter's eyes swept the temple, counting his resources. One section, plus four men. Most of the men were crouching down, looking up at the walls, waiting for guidance.

"You three BAR men," Carter roared. "Take cover behind some of those rocks and shoot anyone who comes through that gate—on second thought, hold your fire until you're sure it isn't one of us. We still have men out there."

BAR men carried the Browning Automatic Rifle, a twenty-pound beast of a weapon that looked like an oversized rifle. The high rate of fire exhausted the twenty-round magazines in less than a second. Many of the Americans envied the Germans their MG-34 light machine gun, which accepted belt-fed ammunition and could lay a curtain of fire. The three BAR men, two from the section inside, and one a survivor from outside, ran over to hide behind rune-covered stones. Their helpers, carrying canvas packs full of extra magazines, scurried after them. Veterans knew that moving quickly kept them alive.

"Everyone else, rally to that big tree," Carter called out as he ran back to the giant oak.

Even as the adrenalin pumping into his veins urged him to choose fight or flight, Carter's intellect had retained control and he analyzed the situation. It was unique in his experience. The temple with its walls was like a fort defended by soldiers in a Western movie, with Indians on the outside. Of course, these Indians were much better armed. Carter didn't read Westerns, but Napier liked to read all those pulp magazines: adventures, Westerns, mysteries, and science fiction. He suddenly remembered the sergeant and the girl, back up by the jeep and trucks. He hoped that they were safe.

The men clustered near Carter under the tree, keeping a wary eye back on the open gate. The temple was like a fort, but it didn't have ramparts for defenders to look over. In many ways the fort was actually a trap. The real problem was that he had no idea what was happening outside the walls.

"Peterson, get up that tree and give me a report on what's happening," Carter said. Peterson was a small, wiry youth known for his wiggling ability. He handed his carbine to a friend, stepped into two pairs of waiting hands, and was hurled up into the branches. He grabbed hold of the lowest branch, some ten feet in the air, swung his legs up, and moved further up into the tree quick as a kid in a schoolyard.

"You," Carter pointed to one of the men who had run in through the gate. "Report."

"SS, Captain," the man gasped, more from adrenaline than from the short run. "Came out of the trees. They have submachine guns."

"Where's the rest of your section?"

"We were scattered around. I assume that everyone else went to ground. I think that someone was hit, but I can't be sure." He looked down at his feet. "They caught us by surprise and we just ran."

"How many of them?"

The soldier shrugged his shoulders. "A bunch?"

After the initial patter of fire, the air had become quiet. Carter was concerned that the Germans would come over one of the walls, using a ladder or felled tree trunks to gain access. They might even have some heavy weapons support. He regretted not sending some scouts up the other road. For all he knew, a Tiger tank could be lumbering down that road towards them. The coming end of the war had cut into his paranoia, which gave him his edge, making him slack off.

"Scatter around, men. I want eyes on every wall, keeping watch. You see a German pop up, you shoot him."

As the Rangers moved, Carter looked for a radioman. No such luck. The radio was back in the jeep. They didn't even have a corpsman with them. It was like going into battle without underwear.

"Captain—I mean, Major," came a loud whisper from above him. Carter cupped his ear and looked up. "There's another door, sir. It's directly to the rear, behind a building. I can see Krauts gathering behind it."

"All men, except the BAR men, with me," Carter shouted, running towards the back of the temple. There were three buildings up against that wall, long and low like the other buildings in the compound. Carter searched the grass and saw the faint discoloration of a trail that led around the building to the left. The door wasn't used enough to wear a path into the grass, but often enough to make that crucial track.

Raising his hand to hold everyone else back, Carter crept around the building with his carbine held ready at his shoulder. This building was not flush up against the wall, and the regular-sized door in the outer wall was blocked from view, though the building was low enough for Peterson to see the door from high in the tree. The door had a simple latch. It was an ideal entry point for the Germans to get inside the temple and surprise the Americans.

Not if I surprise you first, he thought grimly. There was not a second to lose.

Carter hurried back to his men and whispered urgently, "Everyone take out one grenade. Move silently. No noise at all. At my signal throw the grenades all at once over the wall. Then we attack."

The Rangers crowded in the narrow space between the building and wall, each with a metal pineapple in his hand.

Carter checked each of the men, looking in their eyes when he could catch their attention. Some were too fidgety to look at his face. Carter held up three fingers. The men pulled their grenade pins and arched back like amateur baseball pitchers getting ready to throw at a home plate in the sky. Carter brought down one finger, then another. The wall was only twelve feet tall, but the alarming image of one of his men not throwing hard enough and having the grenade bounce off and land back among his troops flashed onto the stage of his mind. No time for worries. He dropped the last finger.

Ten grenades flew over the wall as cheap improvised artillery. Another ten quickly followed. They heard alarmed shouts in German, then a rapid series of explosions that left the American ears ringing. The sturdy wall visibly shivered.

Carter pushed the door open and quickly stepped out, crouching with his carbine ready. His men hurried through the doorway after him, ready to shoot at anything that moved. Their haste was unnecessary. Man-sized clumps of hamburger lay crumpled on the blood-soaked ground. One of the clumps had the jagged edges of his ribs sticking out, like an anatomy lesson gone awry. The German troopers wore grey and green camouflage uniforms, with silver-on-black SS collar tabs that showed conclusively that they belonged to the elite private army of the Nazis. He had never made the connection before, but now Carter saw that the sharp-edged SS symbol was modeled on Nordic runes. On one nearby soldier, next to his SS collar tab was a small metal pin of a grinning skull on two bones. He had only ever seen that insignia once before—on the guards at Dachau.

He counted fifteen bodies, but he couldn't be sure, since some of the bodies were clumped together and Carter didn't care to look too closely. He never looked at the faces of the enemy dead, because all he saw was young men like his own soldiers.

"Half of you with me." Carter pointed to the right. "Half of you with Finney." He pointed to the left. "We'll catch them in a pincer movement."

With five Rangers following, Carter charged for the corner of the temple wall. He wanted to retain the initiative and knew from experience that keeping a step ahead of the enemy came from quick decisions and fast action.

He slowed to a stop, took his shaving mirror from his shirt pocket, checked to see that the sun wouldn't broadcast his presence with a reflected beam of light, and used the mirror to peek around the corner. No one there. Around the corner, and running again, trying to not make a thundering noise with boots on dirt. He heard firing break out in front and discarded the notion of trying to be quiet.

A glance behind showed him that Ferro was with him. The little Italian was a crack shot, especially with the scope on his M1903 Springfield rifle, and left-handed. "Ferro, you get the corner."

The Italian rushed ahead of the pack, reached the corner and swung his rifle around. Shooting with the rifle butt at his left shoulder allowed him to use the wall to cover most of his body. He fired, withdrew, worked the bolt, went back to the corner, aimed, fired again.

Carter leaned out for a moment to get a quick glance and stepped back. The Germans were crouched behind trees, returning fire at Finney's group with their submachine guns. The heavier burp of the BAR men joined in. They must have moved up and were shooting out of the open gate. Carter felt a surge of pride at this display of Ranger aggressiveness, without needing commands from an officer. The two sections worked like a construction crew that had built the same building over and over and everyone knew their jobs.

Carter and the rest of the men with him ran out from behind the wall to the flat ground that surrounded the temple, dropped to the grass and added their fire. Caught in the crossfire, the Germans died quickly, and so the American fire slowed, then just a few pops, and silence.

Carter pulled himself up and looked at his men. "Anyone hit?"

No casualties among his group of soldiers. Carter trotted along the temple wall. Two BAR men emerged from the gate, followed by Peterson, who must have climbed down out of that tree pretty fast. Finney brought his men up. "Anyone hit?" Carter asked the corporal.

No casualties there.

The Rangers went through the dead, making sure that there was no one faking it, then fanned out to find their own dead from earlier in the battle. They found Private First Class Billy Joe Fernández, from Baton Rouge, Louisiana, crumpled on the grass near a shrub. He had survived a leg wound at the Battle of the Bulge and returned to the unit only two weeks ago. Another few days and the war would not have claimed him.

The rest of Rangers caught outside by the attack emerged from the forest in ones and twos. Normally they would have had to suffer being the butt of jokes about surviving by running faster than German bullets could fly, but the death of Billy Joe had washed out any humor that the Rangers might have felt.

"Half of you follow me," Carter said, starting up the road that they had come down. "We need to find Napier and the girl."

Approaching the jeep cautiously, Carter found his friend curled up on his side near the jeep. There was no sign of the girl.

"Spread out, see what you can find," Carter ordered. "Be careful, there might still be Krauts around."

Setting down his carbine, he examined Napier. The tough soldier was still breathing, with a nasty mess of blood and matted hair on the back of his skull. Carter felt the wound gently, getting his fingers covered with blood. A good-sized lump, but no softness or give in the bone, so he assumed that the skull hadn't been cracked.

A Ranger returned to report that he had come across a German truck on a nearby road, hood still warm, but no enemy soldiers around. From the looks of the tracks on the ground, there had been another truck there.

The obvious conclusion made Carter feel sick. "They must have taken the girl."

CHAPTER SEVEN

Carter was torn. He wanted to accompany his friend back to the medical corps at the battalion bivouac, but what about Aoife? The image of the big tree, the rings, and dried blood, kept intruding in front of his eyes.

Rapid orders followed. Carter took two men in the jeep. One of the trucks was to be driven down to the temple, and the rest of the men took the other truck to transport Napier back to the bivouac.

Carter normally let Napier drive the jeep—an annoying consequence of rank, because Carter really enjoyed being at the steering wheel. As a child he had ridden horses competitively, continuing a family tradition, leaning into the horse as if they were one organism as they jumped over poles and water. The jeep consumed gasoline, not hay, but its four-wheel drive was as versatile as a horse. Carter had seen lots of horses during this war, many of them dead or dying. Many farms in Europe still used horses, not tractors, and he had been surprised to find that both the Italian army and the German army still used horses. He had not seen a horse in either the American or British armies, except for a few in England that senior officers used for recreation. Perhaps this one insight told much about the industrial struggle of factory output between the Allies and the Axis and why the Allies were on the verge of victory.

As Carter drove by the temple to get to the other road, he found his Rangers laying out the dead Germans in a row. Now that spring had arrived, burying the dead quickly was always a good idea, before putrefaction turned the bodies all gooey.

A quarter of a mile up the second road, they came across the German truck. Carter stopped for a moment and stood up to get the lay of the land. Putting the jeep into gear, he drove around the truck, bumping over the rough ground and over a half-buried log, and accelerated as he regained the road. The trees rushed by faster, forcing Carter to concentrated on staying in the two brown ruts among the blur of green.

Ferro sat in the rear, with Carter's carbine in his hands and his own rifle jutting up between his knees, its scope resting against his thigh in order to keep it protected and aligned. "You think that maybe you are going a little fast, sir?" the Italian from Boston asked.

"We need to catch them before the road meets some other road and we lose them."

"What about mines, sir?"

Carter slowed for a moment. The standard tactic was to drive slowly enough to be able to see if the ground had been disturbed, which only worked if the mines had been recently laid. He hated mines, with a passion born of raw fear; six of his men had been maimed by them, and two others had died. In one of those sick twists of logic that war thrived on, antipersonnel mines were designed to wound and cripple, not kill. A wounded man delayed a military unit, as his comrades stopped to care for him and get him to medical attention, while a dead man did not slow the unit down. Of course, an antipersonnel mine would probably not wound them in the jeep, but roads didn't have the small AP mines, they had bigger mines to destroy vehicles. Outside Cherbourg, he had seen a jeep hit an antitank mine. Not pretty. The mine had ripped up like a molten geyser from hell and left only charred metal and men.

"They wouldn't have put a mine on this road," Carter said as he pressed on the accelerator. "The Germans would have expected their squad to overrun us back at the temple, since they had the element of surprise. Mining this road would have just as likely have caught their own, as us."

"Life ain't logical, Major," Ferro said. The soldier sitting in the passenger seat, his hands clutching the grips of his .30-caliber machine gun, nodded his agreement with Ferro. He was new to the unit, a greenhorn replacement brought in from the paratrooper pool. Carter could not remember his name. Carter understood that no one wanted to die in the last days of a war—where's the fairness in that?

Carter responded with determined words. "We don't have time to stop."

CHAPTER EIGHT

The chalet had belonged to a Jew. When Krohn had showed up in 1937 and demanded the deed to the home, accusing the old man of getting the money for the summer home by betraying the Germans during the First World War, the Jew had shown him an Iron Cross and indignantly explained that he had earned it on the front, in the trenches, just as the Führer had. Krohn had smiled tightly, hiding his surprise that any Jews had fought during the war, and coldly insisted that he wanted the chalet.

Of course, laws had been followed. The Jew had signed the deed over for a cheque drawn on a Swiss bank for what amounted to a tenth of the true value of the chalet. The Jew then disappeared, using the money to flee the nation. Krohn would have arranged for the man's arrest, but this was five years before the Final Solution began, and Krohn didn't have time to complete the required paperwork.

Krohn moved into his new home as he supervised the construction of the temple, ensuring that only workmen of pure blood applied the best of their skills, building always in the traditional manner, using only hand tools invented thousands of years ago.

He loved his chalet, the wooden floors worn shiny by years of use, a grand fireplace in the center room that lit the room up magnificently on cold winter nights, reminding him of how he imagined Nordic warriors must have felt in their longhouses thousands of years ago. In fact, he had built a longhouse behind the chalet for his soldiers to live in, but for himself, he preferred the red bricks and iron stoves of his own chalet. As a realist, he recognized that his romantic views of the past had limits when it came to personal comfort.

As was his habit, to know the true and pure history of all things, he researched the history of his new home. He was not surprised to find that it had been built in 1843 by a pure-blooded German, a tax collector from Munich. It had stayed in his family for generations and only fell into the hands of the Jews in 1923, when inflation had destroyed the wealth of so many good Germans.

"Fritz, stand guard," Krohn ordered as they drove up to the chalet. "Karl, bring the girl in the house."

She didn't struggle, but obediently followed, with Karl's hand on her shoulder. Krohn appreciated that; he despised it when the girls struggled. Could they not see the honor that he had bestowed on them? In quieter moments, sitting in his library with the phonograph playing some Litz, schnapps in his hand, he admitted that the other sex bewildered him. They always seemed to act differently from what his scholarship told him to expect.

He had been married for three years, to a beautiful peasant girl with blonde hair, full breasts, and hips that promised healthy children, of the purest blood, not a hint of any flaws. What a miserable experience. She had refused to be obedient, ignored the Nazi doctrine that he had tried to teach her, and worst of all, failed to become pregnant. The doctors said that she should be fertile; he suspected that she had used some peasant poison to bind up her womb tightly, the kind that medieval witches used. There were many sources of ancient wisdom, not all of it good.

After he cast her out, sent her home to her parents, and arranged for a divorce, he had burned her possessions. A year later he found that he had missed one trunk of clothes and had never gotten around to destroying it. The passion to burn had ebbed.

Pulling the trunk out of a closet in the guest room, he flung it open. "Put some of these clothes on," the colonel ordered.

She seemed to balk at his instructions, twisting her fingers around each other, glancing at him and back at Karl, who stood at the doorway, another of those sloppy grins on his face.

"Now, quickly!" Krohn barked. "He won't touch you."

Grabbing a large valise, Krohn left the bedroom and hurried to his library. Floor-to-ceiling bookcases covered two walls of the room, filled with books and stacks of papers. He paused, overcome with emotion, almost ready to weep. How could he leave all this, the result of twenty years of collecting, a treasure trove of the most obscure knowledge?

For a long moment he was paralyzed by indecision. The coming of the end of the war had moved from the abstract to the real the day before, when his platoon of guards had been ordered to Munich to help defend the city against the approaching Americans. General Kapp was a fool, like most of them, not a believer in how Odin could save the Reich, seeing only twenty-two more soldiers to add to his doomed effort to defend the city. Krohn obeyed, for obedience was the hallmark of a good officer, but he was relieved when he reached the city with his men to find the general's headquarters in flames, having been hit by Jabos.

Where was the Luftwaffe? He had seen those wonderful new jet fighters, a testament to Aryan intelligence, able to fly so fast that the Allies could not shoot them down, but with many of their airfields overrun, and no more fuel, the Luftwaffe was finished. That fat man Goering was finished too. He had never been a true believer, always unwilling to render honor to the ancient gods.

Krohn had watched as General Kapp was carried out of his headquarters, still breathing, but with blood staining his face and a hole in his skull that showed gray matter chewed up by shrapnel. No need to remain in Munich any longer. Krohn turned the two trucks around and left town. Because the Americans ruled the skies, normally Krohn would only have traveled at night, but he sensed that everything was falling apart. Perhaps the Bavarian Redoubt plan would not even be implemented, where the best German units would find shelter in the forests and mountains, extending the war even with most of Germany overrun, until Churchill and Roosevelt came to their senses and realized that the Bolsheviks were the true enemy. No, not Roosevelt—that archfoe had died just two weeks ago. Now it was that man Truman, and who knew what his inner thoughts might be? How could a man from Missouri become president of the most powerful nation on Earth? The Americans made weak decisions because they were a decadent people; but in his more sober moments, Krohn acknowledged that the Americans knew how to churn out weapons at an insane rate. He had read a classified report from the Abwehr that estimated that the Americans would build over 100,000 airplanes in 1945 alone. Germany had started the war with only 3,000 airplanes of all types. The mind boggled at the number: 100,000. But it was not numbers of planes and tanks or men that won wars—those were just the tools. It was spirit, blood, and the gods that brought victory.

Odin had helped them win many victories, but not enough. Krohn knew that he was not to blame, but he wondered whether his brides to Odin would have carried the Reich beyond the mistakes and the lack of faith if he had understood the ancient ways better. He strongly believed that he could still save the Reich, even in defeat; he just needed time. What did he need from the library? Truly need, not just want?

He went to the safe. Sitting on four legs shaped like lion's paws, the black beast weighed over five hundred kilograms. Spinning the dial, he opened it and looked at his choicest treasures. On top was a typewritten manuscript, a book that he had been writing and revising carefully for years. He had hoped to have it published in 1946 by Nordland Verlag of Berlin, the SS publishing house. An editor there had been quite enthusiastic. The manuscript went into the valise.

Next he grabbed three envelopes of money. One contained German reichsmarks, probably soon to be useless; the next contained Swiss francs, always useful; and the last contained American currency, nice and crisp, counterfeited by the Abwehr just last year.

What else?

A handwritten copy of the interrogation by an inquisitor of a heretic in Cologne in 1241. The cleric had been looking for heretics and found a man who still worshiped the old gods. The original document had been lost, but was copied many times, always by hand, never printed in a pamphlet or book. Krohn had received this copy from Himmler himself. The answers to the cleric's questions, probably encouraged by torture, were a gold mine, including one long entry that described the sacrifice of virgins to become brides of Odin. Krohn could still recall the summer night that he had read those words, at the table of a rustic home on a large farm that the SS owned, feeling an electric charge at the thought of reviving this most sacred of rituals. How many centuries had Odin waited for new girls?

Two heavy books, weighing over a kilo each, printed in Lübeck in 1521, so rare that Krohn knew of only two other copies, one in the SS library at Wewelsburg Castle and other purported to be under lock and key at the Vatican. It had always irritated Krohn that the Führer had decided to respect the farcical international rules and treat the Vatican as its own nation, not sending troops into that warren of churches and monasteries that occupied less than half of a square kilometer. Krohn had fantasized about being with SS research teams who pushed the black-robed priests aside and went into the archives. As they say in westerns, that would have been the mother lode of all mother lodes.

These two volumes, *Tales of Peasants*, recounted stories that the author had recorded from among the peasants of northern Germany, Denmark, and Sweden. Written in an old dialect of German, reading them required a dictionary and sustained concentration. The stories were often only dimly remembered, having been washed by hundreds of years of Christianity. Many were useless, but that made the gems gleam that much brighter, knowledge making its way through the years directly up from the source.

A folder contained pictures of rune stones in Sweden, stark black and white, haunting images that told so much to a man who could read the runes. No one could read every one of the runes—that knowledge had died out—but Krohn was pretty good at it. All went into the valise.

The book *Sacred Geodicy: Leys of the Ancients*, published in Dresden in 1883, dictated where sacred buildings should be built. The leys, lines of force crossing the surface of the Earth, intersected at certain points of extraordinary power. The Vatican was built on such a nexus, which was not surprising, since the ancient Romans had known that place to be special. Jerusalem was another such nexus, as was Wewelsburg Castle. The Temple of Odin was built on a minor nexus, not as powerful as others, but one of the strongest in Germany. A master dowser from East Prussia, really just a peasant farmer, descended from a long line of peasant farmers, had done the work with two freshly cut birch rods, held out in front of his body as he walked. He refused any payment, explaining that the reichsmarks would compromise his gift.

On an inspired guess, Krohn took the farmer to Braunau am Inn in Austria. The farmer found many strong ley lines, though they lay confused across the landscape of the small town. Krohn was privately pleased. He had expected the birthplace of the Führer to be like that.

The next book was by the Austrian mystic Guido von List, *The Secret of the Runes*, the Leipzig edition published in 1908. He had revived Wotanism, worshiping the ancient German god Wotan. Krohn identified Wotan with Odin. Much of the information came from the Icelandic sagas, since von List had discovered that the Vikings who settled that northern island had been refugees from northern Germany, fleeing the Christian priests. This particular book was special to Krohn. He had read it when only fifteen years old and it had given him direction ever since. He often quoted long passages from it and fancied that he had memorized every word. As much as he cherished those worn pages, he put the book back. He could always find another copy.

"She's dressed now, Standartenführer," Karl said from the doorway.

Krohn twisted around, irritated that the soldier had violated his inner sanctum. None of his soldiers had ever even been in the house. Only his housekeeper was allowed into the house and she was forbidden to enter the library. Krohn stifled the angry outburst on his lips; times had changed. This would no longer be his home.

"Get some handcuffs from the storage shed and confine her hands. Get another set of handcuffs and attach her to the door of my car. That should free you up to go get whatever you and your brother want to take from the longhouse. Oh, and take your winter gear."

"We are going on a trip, Standartenführer?"

"A very long trip. A trip to save Germany."

CHAPTER NINE

Fritz Steinhauer stood near the trees at the edge of the clearing in front of the chalet, relieving himself. As he drew circles on the ground, he whistled softly to himself, a tune that he heard sung for the first time a couple of weeks earlier in a café in Munich. He and his brother had earned leave for one day. They walked the twenty kilometers into town, spent all their money, and managed to walk back, blurry-eyed from drink. Fritz couldn't remember the lyrics—he always had difficulty getting words to stick in his brain—but he always remembered a tune.

There had been a prostitute in Munich, whom he shared with his brother. Pleasant memories there. And that girl, the one now in the chalet, the redheaded bride of Odin that the colonel had insisted that they take. Just thinking of her led to a frustrating erection.

Buttoning up his camouflage pants, Fritz picked up his Sturmgewehr. After so many years of carrying a bolt-action rifle, this new Storm Rifle gave him such visceral pleasure. He would love to have used it in the real battles that he had fought. The last enemy soldier that he had seen, the first in seven months, was that short American that the colonel had not allowed him to kill. Fritz was not a dumb man; he understood the need to be quiet, but why not use his knife on the man? As happened too often, that clever idea only occurred to him later.

The sound of a vehicle coming down road from the temple jerked up his head. He rushed over to a mound of dirt, pressed his body to the ground and laid his Sturmgewehr on top, sighting down the road.

Carter noticed a clearing ahead and instinctively eased the pressure of his foot on the accelerator. He noticed sparks flying off the hood of the jeep at the same time that he heard the rapid rattle of a machine gun. Part of him puzzled over why the fire sounded so odd; not from a light machine gun or from a submachine gun, something new that put too many bullets in the air too fast for his comfort.

Slamming on the brakes, Carter skewed to the left, placing the jeep to directly face the incoming fire. That positioned the engine block as a shield and made it easy to fire the .30-caliber machine gun directly back. As soon as they ground to a stop, dust and grass flying, Ferro stood and emptied Carter's carbine towards the bad guy.

Where was their own machine gun? Carter looked to his right and saw the slack face of the greenhorn, pasty cheeks, mouth gaping open, his shirt soaked with blood. Tugging out the field dressing from his first aid pouch, Carter pressed on the man's chest, desperate to stop the flowing blood.

Ferro finished with the carbine, stood up in the jeep, leaned over the two front men, worked the release on the .30-caliber, and let loose. Carter glanced up to see the signature of the bullets down the road—flying bark and clumps of dirt. Ferro hosed down the entire area that the enemy fire had come from. Carter raised his arm to shelter his face from the falling spent shells and links, and leaned over to use his body to shield the greenhorn. The noise reverberated through his skull.

Inexperienced in working the .30-caliber, it was not surprising that Ferro failed to conserve ammunition by making shorter bursts; after half a minute of steady work, he had used up the 250 rounds in the belt. As the machine gun clicked on an empty chamber and the forest grew calm, Ferro grabbed his sniper's rifle and leaped from the jeep. Carter trusted that the veteran Ranger would take care of matters.

For Carter, the forest sounded eerily quiet because his ears were still ringing from being too close to the machine gun. He desperately did not want this greenhorn to die. Pulling the man forward so that he could reach the first-aid pouch on the green-horn's webbed belt, to get the field dressing there, Carter found the man's back an even worse mess. Blood covered the back of the seat, and the twisted bullet, spent by its passage through the greenhorn's body, lay on the seat.

Carter pulled out the field dressing and applied it to the back. Normally he would have scattered the sulfa powder in the pouch also, but there was no time for that.

"Captain, the Kraut cleared out. I found the shells at his ambush site. There's a house over there."

"What?" Carter could barely hear the words from Ferro.

The Italian repeated himself more loudly. Carter nodded. "Give me your dressing."

The green bandage went into Carter's hand and he applied it to the man's back, struggling to get the tape to hold in the slip-pery blood. Normally there was a larger first-aid kit in the jeep, but the contents had been used up after a firefight two weeks earlier and not replaced.

Carter stood up, ripped open his shirt and quickly pulled it off, dumping out the paper and pencil in the front pocket, leaving the new major insignia on because it would take too long to pull off the pins. He wrapped the shirt around the green-horn to hold the bandages on.

"Sir."

Carter looked up and saw Ferro handing over his own shirt, masses of curly chest hair peeking out from his green t-shirt. Carter added the Italian's shirt. Only then, having bound up the wounds, did he take the time to see if the greenhorn was breathing.

The shallow breaths came short and quick.

"He's still alive." Carter knew that he was shouting, though his words sounded normal to him. Excitement and deafness do that. "You take him back as quick as you can. I gotta find the girl."

Ferro hurried to pick up the major's carbine, handed it to the officer, placed his own rifle in the back of the jeep, and started the jeep up. Carter moved away and watched as the Italian turned around and drove back up the road even faster than Carter had been going when he complained earlier.

As soon as he emptied his magazine into the American car, Fritz was moving quickly, running back to the chalet, bent low as he heard return fire start. He reached the door to the colonel's house and burst in. He paused long enough to look back out the doorway, put a fresh magazine into his Sturmgewehr, and shout, "Standartenführer, the Americans are here."

The colonel came down the stairs in a loud clatter of boots on wood, displaying near-panic. When he saw the twin, he paused, and a measure of composure returned to his features. He spoke quickly, like a veteran officer on the field, not a man fresh from training camp who still made sure that his trousers were creased. "How many?"

"Just three in a small car. I think I got one."

"Good. We will leave in my car."

Carter put down the carbine and wiped his hands on his pants, trying to get the greenhorn's blood off his palms and the back of his hands. Such a damned mess. Placing a fresh magazine in his carbine, Carter moved forward into the woods, crouching to make a smaller target, but not so far down that he couldn't see.

A man relied as much on his hearing as his sight and Carter's hearing was absent. He knew from experience that it would take hours for his hearing to completely recover and that he would have a ringing in his ears for at least a day.

Through the trees, Carter could make out the brown and red color of a building. He approached carefully, thinking how reckless he had become on this day, creeping around miles away from the support of his troops. The situation around Munich had become very fluid and he had no idea where other American troops might be found. He had assumed that there was only a few German soldiers here, but on what evidence? For all he knew, there might be dozens over there. His only consolation was that the ambusher had taken off—not the act of a man who had much in the way of help.

Hiding sideways behind the trunk of a tree, Carter took a long look. Just three buildings: a chalet, a storage shed, and what looked like a Viking longhouse. He recognized it from a picture of a reconstructed longhouse in Denmark that he had seen in a *National Geographic* magazine—a thatch roof, smoke holes, and walls made from rough-hewn wood, looking like shingles mounted vertically. There didn't seem to be anyone around.

The sound of a car starting came clear. Acting on instinct and in retrospect, just damned foolishness, he burst from cover and bolted across the clearing towards the corner of the chalet. He held the carbine across his chest, swaying back and forth as his feet pounded across dirt and then mown grass.

He reached the corner of the chalet, pushing his back up against wood painted a deep red. Peeking around, he saw a black car, civilian, rolling down a driveway that merged with a road beyond. He saw a flash of red hair through the rear window.

He aimed his carbine, knowing that the act was futile because he wasn't going to fire and risk hitting her. The car turned onto the road and disappeared.

Carter spit on the ground. "This damned day is just cursed!"

CHAPTER TEN

He smelled the smoke first. Coming around the chalet, he saw smoke trickling out of an open door. Looking inside, he saw broken glass on the floor and a merry fire licking along the floor and up the walls of a kitchen. The Germans must have thrown an oil lamp onto the floor before fleeing, intent on burning the home rather than let it fall to the Americans intact.

Carter ran around the house, tried another door and found it locked, pumped half a magazine of bullets into the door near the handle, spraying splinters, and kicked it open. He was in a parlor, with furniture made mostly of fine woods and not much padding. He could smell the smoke, but not see it in this room. He tried the first door. Bedroom. Not interested in that. The second door opened into a library. Sunlight streamed in from large windows, making the center of the room glow, but the bookcases on the walls remained in shadow.

It had been over two years since he had been around so many books and the scholar in him was intrigued. As he quickly walked around the room, the smell of smoke came to him at the same time that he noticed the open safe by the wall. The safe was half-full of papers and books, including some that had spilled onto the floor. Carter had obviously interrupted the occupant of the house in the process of grabbing his treasures.

Carter ran back into the parlor, threw his carbine out the front door, wincing at the disrespect that he was showing his weapon, went into the bedroom, ripped off the top blanket and rushed back into the library. The smoke was getting heavier now and he coughed as he scooped all of the contents of the safe onto the blanket. He folded the edges of the blanket over the top, wanting to tie it closed, but there was no time. He picked up the bundle into his arms and hurried over to the door to the parlor.

The fire had spread from the kitchen and was licking along the ceiling, tendrils of flame reaching out like a hungry monster. Holding his head low, Carter ran across the room and out the door that he had kicked in.

Waddling over to where the lawn reached the edge of the forest, he dropped his booty. He turned to find that the fire had engulfed the house, sending a plume of grey smoke high into the sky. It was frightening how fast a fire could move; he shivered, amazed at the reckless risk that he had taken. On just a whim.

Checking his carbine to see if he had damaged it with his neglect, he found only grass stains, though he suspected the sights were probably off now. Walking around the burning house, he found a water pump that emptied into a trough. The water looked clean enough and he drank deeply, placing his lips on the surface of the water, like the unwise soldiers in the biblical story of Gideon, washing the smoke out of his throat. He splashed water on his face and rubbed his hands in the water, watching the blood from the greenhorn soldier form streaked clouds.

The door to the longhouse was ajar, almost an invitation. Carter went inside, his carbine leading the way. Bunks lined the walls. From the amount of military gear in the room, it was obvious that soldiers had roomed here. Probably the unit that his soldiers had just wiped out at the temple. He counted the bunks. Twenty-four spaces, but three of them were obviously not being used, holding rolled up mattresses among stacks of gear. His troops had killed nineteen back at the temple, which meant that only two remained, plus whoever lived in the house. Thinking back, he realized that there had only been three other people in the escaping car besides the girl.

Carter walked past the two cast-iron stoves in the center of the room and opened the door on the far side of the room. This was an eating room, with two tables, benches, a stove, two sinks, an icebox, and cabinets. Everything was smartly taken care of, with no clutter or even a dirty dish in the sink. Another door led further along the building. Carter opened this and found a room bathed in light from two large windows.

A carved wooden statue dominated the room. It was obviously Odin, with a raven on each shoulder, and the grimace of a warrior. On a small table before Odin were two daggers with Nazi insignia on their handles, and wooden bowls with some water in one, a hardened crust of bread in a second, and a piece of dried meat in the third. Several stacks of bones, probably from small animals, completed the offerings. Benches with runes carved into them faced each other across the room. A Nazi SS battle flag was pinned to the wall above the door that led from the room.

A shrine. Even after finding the temple to Odin, Carter was surprised to find this.

The final door led out the other end of the longhouse. Carter exited and walked past a pair of outhouses back to the burning house. As he came around the corner, he found that the fire had reached the lawn and was creeping towards the pile of papers and books from the safe. He rushed over, laid down his carbine, gently this time, pulled the blanket out from under his loot, and used it to beat the fire down.

Picking up his carbine again, Carter walked around the house, seeing if any other forays had been made by the fire. He could just imagine the forest catching fire and becoming a raging monster that threatened his Rangers back at the temple. Fortunately, the lawn proved to be a decent firebreak.

When Carter rounded the house back to the side nearest the road that ran into the forest and back to the temple, he found a middle-aged woman watching him. She wore a simple dress with pale flowers on it and dark leather shoes that looked like they had been repaired many times.

"Who are you?" Carter asked in German.

"Frau Smuller. I am the housekeeper."

"You lived in the house?"

"No, I live down the road with my husband. I only came here to work."

"Who lived here?"

She looked at him with suspicion and he imagined the thoughts going through her mind. She shouldn't pass information on to the enemy. The war was lost. "My son was killed at Anzio."

That answer surprised him. "I'm sorry that he died. Too many people have died in this war. Do you have more sons?"

She shook her head and looked down at the ground, tears running down her cheeks. "He was my only one. He was married and I have a grandson. He is all that is left now."

"The killing is coming to an end. The war is about over."

She looked up and touched the cross at her neck. "Praise the Lord."

"Yes, praise the Lord."

She looked back at the fire. "I don't have a job anymore."

"I'm sorry about that. I didn't start the fire."

They watched the fire together for a while. Both stepped back when part of the roof collapsed, sending out a gout of flame and a geyser of sparks. The death of house reminded Carter of his purpose.

"Frau, I came here because I am chasing the people who I think lived in that house."

"Only one man lived in that house," she said. "The other men lived in the longhouse."

"You cooked for them?"

"Only the Standartenführer."

"Who was this Standartenführer?"

The question brought only slack cheeks and closed lips from her. Carter sighed, reined in the frustration that threatened to erupt, and explained all that he had found: Dachau, the virgins, the temple of Odin, and the kidnapping of the red-haired girl.

"I don't believe you," she said. "You are telling lies. Dachau was for criminals, not young girls. The Standartenführer was a good man, a good German. You are trying to defame his name."

"Standartenführer who?"

She shook her head.

Carter grabbed her arm, pulled her face close to his, and hissed, "What is his name?"

"Hans von Krohn," she squeaked.

"That's better." He asked more questions and learned that she had worked for von Krohn ever since he had divorced four years earlier. She seemed to genuinely know little about the colonel or what he did.

"Where do you think that he has gone?"

"I have no idea."

Carter released her and she fled, dress flapping against her legs. Feeling a sense of helpless frustration, he checked his carbine, realized that the magazine was half-empty from shooting at the door, put in a fresh magazine, and walked around the burning house to see if the fire threatened to expand. The thatch roof of the long house seemed to be an open invitation to the sparks, but so far it hadn't caught. Coming back around, he stopped at the pile of papers and books. The housekeeper had not returned, nor had she sent any friends.

He sat down and began to go through them, practicing his German reading skills.

CHAPTER ELEVEN

The airfield was a mess. The skeletons of burned airplanes stood as stark reminders of who ruled the sky. Bomb craters littered the runway and surrounding area, leaving shattered trees poking splintered fingers upwards. The hangars, machine shops, supply sheds, and barracks were all wrecked by concussion and fire. Not a single building spared.

At one end of the airfield, among a cluster of tall pines was a single remaining airplane. Thousands of the venerable Junkers Ju-52s had served the Third Reich well, but few of the airplanes were left anywhere. This three-motored airplane still remained because of the camouflage netting stretched from tree to tree, including having a few trees poke up through the center. Krohn was even more impressed when he drove closer and got a better look. The fuselage of the airplane was tucked so tightly between two birch trees that he wondered how they had avoided damaging the tail.

The three men of the aircrew sat on kitchen chairs, probably scavenged from the ruined buildings, drinking out of metal cups. Krohn pulled the car deep into the woods and got out. He felt a twinge of regret as his men unloaded the trunk of the car. The BMW had served him well and he was attached to it. He closed his eyes for a moment. How could he pine over a car to be left behind when he had burned his home, with all his books? Even his journals. He had been so rushed that he had failed to finish filling his valise. That hurt on a deep level, as if he had lost a part of himself.

"Standartenführer, I am Lieutenant Holst," the pilot said as Krohn walked over. "We await your orders."

"We will fly out tonight, Lieutenant." Krohn pulled a folded map from his pocket. "You have a full load of fuel?"

"Almost full, sir. Not another drop left at this field."

Krohn handed over the map. "We are flying to an airfield in Denmark. There will be more fuel there waiting for us. Can we make it?"

The pilot opened the map, twisted his lips in concentration. "I need to make a few calculations."

"Very good."

The twins carried the small amount of baggage to the airplane before returning to share coffee with the aircrew. Krohn heard them talking about the girl, who had sat down beneath a tree. The twins explained that she was their prisoner, nothing more, which pleased Krohn. The sacrifices were kept secret because not everyone, even good German airmen, were ready to understand where the real root of the Third Reich lay.

The pilot returned, offering him a cup of the coffee. Krohn sipped at it. Cheap coffee made of some root. Ever since the Allied blockade began six years ago, preventing merchant ships from coming in, the only real coffee had come from carefully preserved personal hordes.

"We can make it, sir," the pilot said. "Having only four passengers will help a lot, but it will be tight. We have to fly at night and low to the ground, which takes more fuel."

"Flying high is too dangerous?"

"The Americans and British completely dominate our skies. Radar will detect us and their night fighters will get us. Flying high or low is dangerous."

"Everything is dangerous nowadays," Krohn said. "Do you have a recent report of how close the Americans are? How soon before this airfield is overrun?"

The pilot shrugged. "Last report from this morning was that they were fifteen kilometers away. We just have prayer and hope."

"Prayer to any of the gods could be useful," Krohn said. "How long before it's dark and we can leave?"

"Three hours, sir."

More chairs were found and Krohn sat apart from the other five men. He watched the girl. She was not like the other virgins, sobbing to the point that they became hysterical, thrashing about, screaming, tears flying from their faces. This girl was like a caged animal, always alert, missing nothing with those green eyes. He had no doubt that she would bolt if given the least chance. She intrigued him as no woman had for some years. She stared back at him; neither showed weakness or submission by flinching or looking away.

"Standartenführer," Fritz called. "Men are coming."

Krohn stood and joined the others. He counted the large group of men approaching across the airfield. Sixteen. They all wore officer uniforms, mostly the black of the SS, a few with the blue of the Luftwaffe, and one with the grey of the army. He noticed the red stripes on the trousers of the army officer, indicating that he was a general staff officer.

"Fritz, Karl, follow my lead and be prepared," Krohn said in a low voice.

The man leading the group of officers stopped before them and the other officers clustered behind, like goslings in a gaggle of geese.

"What is your name, Standartenführer?"

Krohn looked at the man's collar tabs. The twin leaves of an SS Oberführer, a brigadier general, outranked a simple colonel. He saluted with outstretched arm. "Standartenführer Hans Krohn, Oberführer."

"This airplane belongs to you?"

"I have been assigned this airplane, yes."

"I require it for myself and my staff."

"To go where, Standartenführer?"

"We are flying to Geneva, where arrangements have been made with a monsignor in the Vatican to smuggle us to South America. You may come with us, if you wish, though I don't believe that there will be room for your men. Maybe we can make room for your mistress."

"Mistress?" Krohn turned to look at the virgin. She looked back straight at him, unblinking, expressionless. He knew that she understood German and was puzzled by her reaction. No fear there. He looked back to the general. "Yes, she is with me, but she is not my mistress."

The general shrugged. "Regardless. You will hand over the airplane."

"I have orders from Himmler himself authorizing this airplane for my own mission," Krohn said.

"What is that mission?"

"That remains secret, Oberführer. I am sorry, but you will have to find some other means to run away."

The general flushed. "That is insubordinate, Standartenführer. You will hand over the plane now."

"Fritz, Karl, cover them."

The twins obeyed, moving to each side of their own officer to have clear fields of fire, their assault rifles leveled. Krohn saw some of the officers reaching for their holsters.

"Do not move!" Krohn shouted. "Those Sturmgewehr each have thirty rounds in a magazine. Your Lugers won't help you."

"How dare you aim your weapons at officers of the Third Reich!" the general screamed. "You will immediately put down your weapons."

Krohn pulled his own pistol from his holster and shot the general in the face. He fell back with arms and legs splayed. The other officers looked down at him with dumb expressions.

"You are not worthy to be an Aryan," SS Colonel Hans von Krohn spat.

CHAPTER TWELVE

"We've been finding these death camps the farther we push into Germany. We found another at Buchenwald and the Brits and Canadians found one at Bergen-Belsen. The Soviets have found even more. It seems that they were concentrated in the East." The division G-2 spoke like a school teacher and after the war would return to his job teaching history at a high school in Cleveland. "Just for your information, Dachau was the original concentration camp. It was built only months after the Nazis took power and was where SS guards were trained for the camps that engaged in more serious work. You have probably heard about the gas chamber that was found. It was for killing the inmates, but apparently was never used. Interrogations have revealed that the gas chamber may have been used to train the men and women who used the real gas chambers in the extermination camps in the East."

"That's just barbaric," one of the gathered officers said.

"Yes, no doubt. We also have further information about the locked boxcars full of dead that we found. The guards have told us that those inside were Polish prisoners being sent in from the East to avoid being liberated by the Soviets. The guards let them all die of thirst."

"What an awful way to go," another officer responded. "No wonder our boys were so angry."

Carter stood at the back of the room, listening intently. His ears still had an annoying ring in them and his throat felt abused by the smoke from the fire. He had already heard that American soldiers had promptly executed dozens of SS camp guards after they found the train. It was not his Rangers that had taken justice into their own hands, but regular army soldiers. The 45th Infantry Division was composed of National Guard units from the American Southwest, but the middle-grade and senior officers were men from the regular army. Most of the officers looked at the Ranger company attached to their division with a mixture of envy and annoyance. At one time or another they had all voiced the standard complaints: any good infantry unit could do what the Rangers did; that the Rangers drew off the cream of the crop, making it harder for the rest of the infantry to do their job; and that the Rangers took all the glory, leaving the hard work for the real soldiers. Another source of friction came from the fact that Carter's commission was in the reserve army, while many of the officers in headquarters had regular army commissions. Coming from Virginia, Carter had a sensitivity to social distinctions bred into his bones, and he was constantly reminded in subtle ways that his gold oak leaves were somehow inferior to the same insignia on a major with a regular commission.

"Yes, our boys were angry, but we must maintain proper discipline, even if we ignore this incident of shooting the guards." The G-2 looked down at his notes. "On other fronts, we have received news that Army Group C has signed a surrender document. It takes effect in two days. That means all German troops in Italy will be out of the war. As you can see from this map, most of Germany had fallen to us or the Soviets. All that's left is this pocket in the Alps, a pocket around Berlin, and a pocket up by the Danish border. The battle of Berlin is still going on and we hear the casualties on both sides are pretty high."

"We should have gone for Berlin," one of the officers said, loudly enough for everyone to hear.

"Yeah, then American boys could be dying instead of the Russians. Leave Berlin to them." This officer was one of the battalion commanders. Carter didn't know him personally, but had always enjoyed his acerbic wit.

"Regardless," the G-2 said, reasserting control as if his students had become unruly. "Let's talk about Munich. Yesterday we picked up radio broadcasts from a group called the Bavarian Freedom Fighters. They called their radio station Free Bavaria Radio. The transmissions ended earlier today and the best reports we have is that a coup inside the city has been suppressed by loyal SS troops. When we move in tomorrow, I expect only pockets of organized opposition. We need to be on watch for snipers and fanatical kids from the Hitler Youth. Same old drill, we all know it."

Major General Robert T. Frederick stood and everyone turned their attention to him. "Thank you, Major, for that report. Now listen up. I've been talking to Corps about what we found, and in the next few days we are going to take all the adult residents of nearby towns and force them to tour Dachau."

This led to a groundswell of approving noises. "We will be leaving the medical battalion, three infantry companies, and the Rangers to take care of the camp. Colonel Walter will be in charge of that operation. The G-3 will issue orders for everyone else for our move on Munich."

Carter had learned to talk to his superiors and come to their headquarters only when absolutely necessary. He was not a career soldier and intended to return to the university as soon as the war was over, but while the war was going on, he found the real war at the front much more pleasant than bureaucratic infighting in the rear. Staying at Dachau suited him, though he didn't want to go back into the camp.

General Frederick continued. "Our division has taken almost 21,000 casualties in this war and has been in combat almost 500 days. We only have a few days left. Let's be careful and get our boys home."

The meeting broke up, men shuffling out, lighting up cigarettes. Carter positioned himself near the door to intercept the G-2 officer.

"Major, you said that we've been finding these camps. Has anyone found anything like the temple that I reported?" Carter asked.

"That was an odd report, John. Very odd. I haven't seen anything like that in the intel reports, though we have instructions to quickly report anything really odd like that. I'm going to pass it up to Corps tomorrow."

Carter nodded his thanks and stepped out into the evening air. It had rained a little and high clouds had come with spring rains. The setting sun reflected against the clouds, turning the entire sky pink, like a runny watercolor. Near the setting sun were more sharply defined orange hues. What a glorious reminder of God's wonders on a day that had seen so much of the Devil's handiwork.

The 45th Division had taken over the country mansion of some member of the Krupp family. Building the railroads and arms for Germany had yielded handsome financial rewards. Carter would have enjoyed a leisurely exploration of the house; he had overheard that there were more than forty rooms. No time for that, though.

Ferro waited for him at the jeep. The Italian had driven back to pick Carter up at the Krohn country chalet. He had tried to clean off the seat, but Carter knew that there must still be dried blood in the nooks and crannies of the seat and jeep, joining dirt accumulated from France and Belgium. Ferro would serve as his driver until the return of Napier, so the diligent solider kept his sniper rifle in the rear seat.

"Did you find Sergeant Napier?" Carter asked.

"Yes, sir. I can take you there."

"Please do." Carter climbed into the seat. "What about the greenhorn?"

Ferro started the jeep and pulled out into the stream of vehicles leaving the mansion grounds. Everyone had their lights on to prevent accidents. "He died, sir. About an hour ago."

"Dammit," Carter said in a weary voice.

They drove through the darkened streets of the town. Carter had no idea what the name of the place was. He had looked at the map only that morning and knew at one point the name of the town, but right then he just couldn't retrieve it from his tired brain cells.

"What was his name?" Carter asked.

"Clayton, I think, sir."

"Is that a first or last name?"

"Don't know, sir."

Carter sighed. "Find out his name. Collect his personal effects and his gear. I have to write the letter." Carter leaned forward as a dog raced through the jeep's headlights, concerned that they might hit the mongrel. The dog disappeared into a dark alley. "I hate telling parents that their son is dead."

"Better you than me, sir," Ferro said.

The medical battalion had commandeered a hotel for its hospital. Carter found Napier on the second floor, in his own room. Coincidentally, a white-smocked doctor was there, checking on the sergeant. Carter knew of the doctor, who had also served in the First World War, yet his seventy-year-old hands were still steady enough to wield a scalpel.

"How's my sergeant, Doctor?" Carter asked as he looked around the room. The hotel decor was undamaged: nice sheets, a painting of a mountain lake on the wall, washbasin in the corner, and a faded spot on the wall where a Nazi poster had been hanging.

"He has a concussion. I recommend that he stay here for a few days to rest," the doctor said. "I think that the war can spare him."

"I think that the war can spare all of us, Doctor."

The doctor patted Carter's arm as he passed by on his way out. "I agree, son. And soon it will all be over."

Napier spoke first, slurring his words slightly. "Did you get Aoife back?"

"I'm sorry," Carter groaned with guilt. "I chased them, but they got away."

Napier looked devastated. "What will happen to her?"

"I don't know." The words hung in the air. Both of the men

had seen enough of this war to know that bad things were more likely than any good things.

"I wanted to save her, sir," Napier said. "I really did. I liked her. But they had the drop on us."

"I know that you did your best." Carter patted his friend on his shoulder. "You always do."

"Why didn't they just shoot me?" Napier asked. "That would have made me feel better."

"I guess they didn't want to spoil their surprise attack on us in the temple," Carter said. He started to explain how the attack had been foiled, but he noticed that Napier was starting to drift off to sleep.

"I should be going," Carter said.

"Wait. Before you go, take a look at this," Napier said. "A nurse let me use a mirror to see it."

Napier leaned forward and showed Carter the back of his head. The regulation crew cut had been shaved to the skin, the ends of five stitches protruded from a swollen bump the size of a triple-A egg. The bump and surrounding skin was blue and mottled from bruising.

"Looks nasty, but better than a bullet hole in your head," Carter said.

"Most things are."

CHAPTER THIRTEEN

The Junkers Ju-52 took off at dusk, weaving down the field to avoid the bomb craters and debris. Krohn had left the brigadier general lying on the ground, still alive, choking on his own blood. He liked the idea that the general's blood, mixing with the soil of the Fatherland, might act as a sacrifice for the man's cowardice.

The other fifteen officers sat nearby, where they had been guarded by the twins until takeoff. Krohn had locked their pistols in the car and had no intention of allowing them to find other weapons. The twins also searched them and filled a bag with money, jewels, and even three small bars of gold.

Krohn looked out of the window as the transport circled the field. Some of the officers on the field were shooting up at the airplane with their pistols. Not much chance of hitting them with such short-range weapons, but he imagined that it helped with the frustration.

Turning in his seat, Krohn's eyes met the eyes of the virgin for a moment. She sat across from him, handcuffed to the metal bars that formed the frame for her canvas seat. She did not blink.

The pilot headed the airplane north, flying just five hundred feet off the ground. Night came quickly. Faint illumination came from a dim red light near the rear exit door. Krohn looked out the window. High clouds hid the stars and the full moon. It was so dark that he couldn't see anything. They could fly into the ground, or a hill, or a building, without any warning.

Krohn hoped that this would not be his last view of the

Fatherland, so dark that nothing was visible. Of course, that was fitting in its own way, for darkness truly had descended on the nation that he loved. Perhaps his mission would redeem all that seemed lost, but even if he succeeded, he suspected that it might be at the cost of his own life. That was a sacrifice that he was willing to make, just as willing as all the sacrifices that he had made already. He glanced over at the virgin, but could only see her outline, her hair so full and feminine. So many sacrifices.

Krohn touched the Thor's hammer that he wore on a chain around his neck. As a child his mother had insisted that he wear a cross, and he had learned to pray to the Christ, but as a man he had claimed a man's religion, not the religion of children, women, and weaklings. Odin and his son Thor were warriors, not pacifists who turned the other cheek.

The dark outside the window drew his eyes back. At such a time, he supposed that a lesser man felt fear. Of course, fear was just weakness. The time of a man's life was determined by the length of his thread on the tapestry woven by the three sisters, the Norns, who sat at the foot of Yggdrasil, the world tree, dictating the destinies of men. Even the gods had to submit to their design.

Gently rubbing Thor's hammer between his fingers, Krohn accepted his fate as the airplane flew on through the night.

CHAPTER FOURTEEN

The bath felt heavenly. It had been two weeks since Carter had washed with more water than his helmet could hold. The soap had been looted from the Germans and the lye was so strong that his eyes watered just from lathering his body. He scrubbed the dirt and blood from under his fingernails, using an old toothbrush that he carried for just that purpose.

While Carter was out at the temple, his second-in-command, First Lieutenant Hartwell, had taken care of the Ranger company. A pair of houses had been requisitioned, the owners sent to live with neighbors. A master bedroom had been set aside for Carter.

When the water turned too cold, Carter surrendered and stood, water and suds streaming off his lean body. He toweled off and reached for his clothes. The clothes that he had worn for a week smelled like his father; perhaps the Carter family had a unique scent, a family odor strong enough to become part of the fibers. He found his duffel bag and pawed through it, pulling out clean clothes. Three weeks ago he had paid a Belgian woman two dollars to do his laundry. She had done a fine job and he found a clean shirt and pants.

Carter was not the type of man that paid much attention to his emotions, finding introspection often just too confusing, but putting on fresh clothes seemed in some subtle way to erase many of the stains of the day.

The first order of business should have been cleaning his carbine. He still felt guilty that he had mistreated his trusty tool, but the thought of getting his hands oily after such a pleasant bath repelled him. Just this one time he would be negligent; the war was about over anyway. It's not like the carbine wouldn't work, although he supposed that it could jam, though.

Second order of business: he had to write the letter. Ferro had brought the information, so that could no longer be an excuse to delay. Besides, he had learned that waiting just made him miserable. Lighting a lamp, he found his typewriter, put in a fresh piece of paper, and let his soul ache.

This was his thirty-fourth letter. By now he had enough stock phrases, full of regret, thanking them for their sacrifices, duty and honor, that the letter wrote itself. The only hard part was that Carter had made it a personal rule to always be completely honest about how a man died, even if it was a stupid accident, or an artillery shell from his own side. At least this time he could write that the Clayton had died trying to rescue a young woman. Carter even wrote the humiliating words, that the rescue had failed, though through no fault of their son.

Since he was miserable already, he decided to write a report on the day. He had reported verbally, but the army ran on paper, as much as it ran on fuel, food, or ammunition, and a thing had not truly happened until it was committed to paper. As he typed his terse narrative, he wished that he had some whiskey to act as a balm. No doubt there was liquor somewhere in the house, but he had promised himself that he would never touch the stuff again. His father had been heavy drinker, a bottle a day; and had handled it well, keeping up his law practice and the family estate going, but he had died when Carter was in college because his liver couldn't take it anymore. After that, Carter looked at himself, at how often he got drunk on weekends, and how he wasn't nearly as functional as his father when he had a buzz on, and decided that the family tradition would end with him. Not even beer. Never again.

The report finished, he found that even though it was after ten, he was still alert. The blanket full of papers from the Nazi house sat in the corner of the room. He settled down to read more of them. He had already identified several bound volumes with neat writing in them as the journal of Hans von Krohn, apparently written in a style with future publication in mind.

Carter ended up reading for hours, having the most surreal experience of his life. At two in the morning he came across the entry for 28 October 1943, which was particularly long, a good six pages:

> Today a package arrived by courier from Wewelsburg. Friedrich sent it, sure that I would find it interesting. He is a good friend. Inside was a very old manuscript. Friedrich's letter explained that he had found it in a Lutheran church in Tromsø. The church was only four hundred years old, but apparently it had inherited several trunks of material from a local monastery, which had been active when Norway was Catholic, before Luther changed all that. Imagine the excitement of finding such a treasure trove, to be the first to touch and read documents forgotten for hundreds of years.
>
> The document tells the oddest story. Written in Latin. This is a translation.
>
> In the year of our Lord 1311, some fishermen from the village brought to the abbot a man half-mad from cold and starvation, his beard encrusted with salt and his eyes so bloodshot that they were red, not white. They had found him in a small boat made of leather bound to a frame of wood. The abbot is renowned for his healing skills, a talent given to him by our Lord. At first the man seemed to recover. He told us his name was Einar and his manner of speech was odd, using uncommon words that some of us hadn't heard since we were children.
>
> Einar believed in the old gods and their Satan-inspired pagan religion. He said that he not only worshiped Odin but said that he had also been Odin. He also claimed to have died many thousands of times.

Most of the other monks either ignored his stories as the ravings of the mad, or as demon-inspired, designed to lead us astray. I was young and foolish and curious and so I listened.

Einar said that he had been born in the same year as Harald Fairhair. Einar's father, Ragnar the Hunter, was chief of their tribe. When Harald fought to create the larger kingdom of Norge, Ragnar opposed him. Einar's brothers fell in battle, and after they lost, the tribe was sent into exile. Because their women were kept as slaves by Harald, the exiles were only men and boys, forbidden to return to their homeland.

They sailed north, seeking a valley of green among the ice, a place of legend. They reached the place, starving, their ship encrusted with snow and icicles, pulling on their oars out of desperation. There they met Loki, the trickster god, who gave them food, mead, and warmed them around his fire.

Ragnar and his men wanted to go back to Norge but Loki enticed them to go to Valhalla instead. There they fight all day, and the dead are raised up at nightfall to go to the great hall. They drink mead and consort with Valkyries all night, and then fight again all day. He who is the last standing becomes Odin for the following day. Einar maintained that he had truly been Odin many times, with ravens that showed him what was happening everywhere else on the earth.

He said that the earth is a great round ball, much bigger than we realize, with many people living in far-away lands and even inside the earth. He said that not all people look the same: some are dark, some brown, some have slanted eyes; others are very short in height and lived in hot steaming places with many trees, and there are tall, black people that drink the blood of their cattle. He told many other amazing stories.

I looked up Harald Fairhair in the library. He really existed. He was the first king of Norge, about four hundred years ago. His name came about because he sought the hand of the daughter of a neighboring king, who refused him until he would become king of all Norge. He vowed to not cut his hair until he had achieved that goal and won Gyda in marriage. Just because part of a story is true does not make the whole true. That is a truth that I have learned.

The abbot taught Einar the story of Christ and called him to repentance. We put him to work in the gardens and fields. He grew older faster than a man should. As he wasted away, growing older before our eyes, he consented to baptism. The water was sprinkled, he managed to eat and drink of the Eucharist, and only an hour later, last rites were performed. We buried him as a Christian.

CHAPTER FIFTEEN

The smell of cooking brought Carter downstairs. He found Corporal Ferro in the kitchen, with half a squad of men sitting at the table, watching the Italian at work with rapt attention. Carter doubted that they would have been as interested even if it was one of those French cabaret shows where the dancers had misplaced their clothes.

"Italian meatballs, Captain," Ferro called out. "Made like my mama makes. Meat and cheese—they have real cheese here—and just the right spices. Garlic, pepper, oregano, and some basil."

"You found all those in the house here?" Carter asked. "They must have been hoarding them since before the war."

"I already had oregano and basil," Ferro said. "My mama sent them."

Carter laughed. "We all haul around odd things." He walked over and took a long sniff of the steam coming from the pan. He hadn't been hungry a moment ago, but now he was ravenous.

"Does anyone know where Colonel Walter's HQ is?"

"Just across the street, sir," Ferro said promptly, not looking up from his careful work. "He already sent a runner and asked you to drop by at noon."

Carter retrieved his carbine and joined his men in the kitchen, clearing a small spot for himself at the table to strip and clean his weapon. The smell of gun oil, mixed with the cooking, felt right on a deep level. These men were his family, and even with the war ending, he knew that they would hold a place in the internal landscape of his life that no other people could ever replace.

The company's executive officer came in, shaking rain droplets from his helmet and jacket. Lieutenant Hartwell was a nondescript man that most soldiers wouldn't have looked at twice, if it weren't for the silver bars on his soldiers. Hartwell illustrated the point that a leader can be completely devoid of charisma, yet still function effectively because his soldiers had learned to respect the rank, not the man.

"Our unit is providing HQ security," Lieutenant Hartwell reported. "Half of our guys are still out at that place that you found."

"What about the barracks with the girls?" Carter asked. "Are we still guarding that?"

"Yes, we still have a two-man detail there."

The conversation descended into the minutiae of running the Ranger company. A Ranger company had only sixty-eight soldiers, unlike a regular infantry company, which had another hundred soldiers. Despite the listed strength that they were supposed to have, the ranger company was like other companies in that they were undermanned, with only forty-eight Rangers after yesterday's casualties.

Promptly at noon, his belly still pleased with a large helping of meatballs and dark bread, Carter left his headquarters. The sun had come out, driving away the rain, leaving the world feeling baptized and clean. Carter stepped around the puddles as he crossed the street. In spite of the feeling that the world was getting better, Carter did realized that the rain must have turned the dirt of the concentration camp into mud, adding to the misery of prisoners already too close to the edge of the chasm between life and death.

He also remembered the red-haired Aoife—a girl on the brink of womanhood. He would learn to mourn her with all the others he had seen disappear in the war.

An orderly showed him into the library of the mansion that

Colonel Walter had requisitioned as his headquarters. Walter was a gnome of a man, so short that Carter wondered if some Army regulation had been deliberately overlooked. He served as the engineering officer for the division, running its combat engineer battalion, and everyone respected him as the most organized man in the division. Back home he ran a civil engineering firm.

Bright light from a wall of bay windows provided good illumination for two large tables covered with diagrams and reports. Through an open door, four orderlies sat at tables, furious fingers working typewriters. Men who could type only went into combat if they wanted to, since the 45th Division had no WACs like higher headquarters did. While the colonel finished a conversation with two of his officers about where latrines should be dug, Carter glanced down at some of the papers. One was a medical circular explaining how to feed the liberated prisoners, and another was a tally of survivors, some 32,000.

Colonel Walter ushered his officers out and closed the door to the typists. The heavy wood muffled the sound so that now it sounded like bees at work.

"Welcome, Major Carter." The gnome offered his hand. "I read your report on that place you found in the woods. Awful stuff. Nasty stuff." He paused, brow furrowed as he sought for the right words. Carter could sympathize; he had not found the right words himself.

"Satanic stuff," Walter pronounced.

Curious thought. Carter mulled it over, nodding slightly in acknowledgment. The idea had not occurred to him, since his own Christian faith didn't have much of a role for Satan. The darkness in the souls of men was a sufficient enough source of evil, without needing a supernatural force goading them on. Nevertheless, Carter could see why other people would see the human sacrifices that way. Certainly early Christians had viewed the pagan practices of their northern neighbors as demon-inspired, worthy of destruction. Though his academic detachment had returned, having abandoned him the previous day in the face of such horror, he thought that perhaps the Christians had been right. Burn them out.

"I'm thinking of asking our chaplain to go to that place," Walter said. "Bless it, curse it, do an exorcism, whatever it takes."

"That won't be necessary, Colonel."

Carter jerked his head around. He had failed to notice the other man sitting in the corner in an overstuffed chair, hidden in the shadows created by the angle of the bay windows. The man stood up, a lithe movement that displayed the grace of a gymnast or ballroom dancer. As he came out of the shadows, Carter saw that although his hair was completely white, his face was unlined; he couldn't have been much over thirty. The man's white hair was longer than regulations allowed, long enough to have a wave to it while not touching the ears. The face did not match the hair, looking to be about thirty years old, with no lines around the eyes. He stood about two inches shorter than Carter's six feet, was of medium build, and carried an unlit pipe in his hand. He held out his other hand to Carter.

A dry, firm handshake. Soft hands. Not a man used to manual labor, as Sherlock Holmes would have deduced.

"Ah, yes, Major, this is Colonel Edgar Rice," Walter said by way of introduction. "SHAEF sent him to talk to you." Supreme Headquarters Allied Expeditionary Force was Eisenhower's headquarters; any higher command was found only in London or Washington, D.C.

"I think that you have found something quite fascinating," Rice said. "I'd like to see it."

"You are detailed to take care of Colonel Rice," Walter said. "Have your lieutenant take care of the Rangers."

"Yes, sir."

As they were leaving, Rice turned back to the engineering officer. "Will the truck be there?"

"In an hour, Colonel," Walter said. "Two at the most."

Carter had no idea what the two colonels were talking about, but a lower-ranking officer got used to that. That's how the

Army worked.

Once outside, Rice took Carter for a walk in the garden behind the requisitioned house. Rain still dripped from flowers and leaves, sparkling on the lawn, but the walkways, made of rounded stones, were already dry. Whoever lived in the house had obviously cared for their yard.

"If I may ask, sir," Carter said, "what's your interest in the temple of Odin?"

"Ah, you recognized the deity?"

"Yes, I remembered the details from a college class."

"Tell me more about yourself, your background, your education, your interests."

Carter quickly summarized his life—Virginia, Yale, his interest in languages and history, and his dedication to the Rangers. He felt like he was putting himself up for sale, and spoke quickly, using as few words as possible while remaining accurate. His grandma had always told him that bragging was reserved for imbeciles and men who were scared inside.

"Very interesting, Major," Rice said. "And what do you think about what you found? Do you think that it was of the Devil?"

"It's evil, sir, but I don't see where the Devil is involved," Carter said. "It's just another example of the insanity that Hitler and the Nazis visited on this world."

"It's not that Hitler and his henchmen are more insane than so many other megalomaniacs in history," Rice said, waving his unlit pipe. "He is just much more effective, so methodical. That is what our modern world has become: a relentless drive for efficiency, to make more things at lesser costs—more clothes, more cars, more dead people."

"I suppose so," Carter said. "Again, if I may ask, who are you and why are you interested?"

Rice stopped and lit his pipe, puffing a few times get the tobacco glowing. He tapped the pipe stem on his teeth, reminding Carter of a professor standing in front of a class, ready to hold forth on arcane knowledge.

"I am an Occult Science Officer, Major."

"Excuse me?" Carter said, trying to put the words of that title together in his mind in a way that made sense.

Rice laughed softly. "I'm with intelligence, G-2, and I am in charge of taking care of the needs of occult warfare."

"Are we fighting an occult war?" Carter asked, trying to keep the skepticism out of his voice. He wondered if the man was an imposter, using forged papers.

"Yes, we are," Rice said. "Right now, though, it's time to see your temple."

Carter found that his men had set up camp outside of the wooden palisade, with two men walking a perimeter while the rest played poker near a campfire that had burned down to ashes, leaving with a thin stream of smoke that wafted up through the trees. A row of fresh graves showed that they had cleaned up after the battle. One of the graves had an American helmet on it. Billy Joe was buried there. Carter swallowed sharply, hiding his shame behind wooden eyes. He had completely forgotten that Billy Joe Fernández had been killed. How could he remember the greenhorn, and write the necessary letter, and forget Billy Joe?

Carter walked over to the muddy grave, removed his hat and stood for a time. He recalled that Billy Joe had been Catholic. Not a lot of Catholics back in Virginia, so most of what he knew about the Catholics came from movies. Weren't last rites supposed to be performed? He made a mental note to ask the chaplain to come out here and do what was necessary. The best that he could do was offer up a short prayer, not so much in words, but more a feeling that he hoped would convey to God that Billy Joe had been loved by his friends and would be missed.

After checking on his men, Carter went into the temple to find Colonel Rice. The colonel was carefully looking at the gold and silver vessels, rubbing his fingers over their designs, even sniffing them. It looked odd.

"Have your soldiers taken anything from here?" Rice asked.

"I gave orders that there be no looting."

"There are a lot of gold objects here," Rice said. "The temptation would be hard to resist. Can you be sure? I would like you to search each soldier and make sure."

Carter locked eyes with the colonel and gave him what he hoped was a withering stare that would make the Gorgon proud. He had not decided yet if he liked this officer or not, but the scales had definitely tipped to one side. "My Rangers follow my orders," Carter said in a low voice, "and I will not question their integrity."

Rice spoke as if he were addressing a strident student. "I appreciate your loyalty to your men, but I have to make sure. At least reiterate the order to them and request that any looted objects be returned. No retaliation, no questions. I just want to be positive. These objects may have latent power and I don't want them wandering away."

"Latent power?" Carter looked around the temple, wondering if Rice had seen something that he hadn't seen. "Wandering away?"

"I could give you a direct order to command your men to turn over any loot, but I think that would just be a waste of breath."

Carter didn't answer.

"Look, here, Major," Rice said. "I realize that you are the result of a skeptical university education, and that healthy skepticism is one of the great intellectual achievements of Western Civilization, but there is more to this world than what is found in Western science. Old traditions still have power. Their sacred artifacts still have power. Or at the very least, they *might* still have power. We have to be careful, we have to be certain, to destroy that which is evil."

"Does General Eisenhower know what you do?" Carter asked.

Rice smiled. "Whether you believe in my mission or think that I am a fool is not very relevant. I need your cooperation and my silver eagles trump your gold oak leaves. Please go find out if your men have looted anything."

Carter straightened his back, saluted and said in spoke crisp, clearly enunciated words, "Yes, sir."

Carter left the superior officer to continue poking around the temple and returned to his men sitting near the fire. The men looked up from their playing cards, a deck that one of the men had bought in Paris with scantily clad women on the backs. A blanket spread on the ground served as a table and kept the cards from getting too dirty. Their unshaven faces, knuckles still crusted with dirt, and the weary slump in their shoulders were so familiar to him. He loved these men, every one of them, not in the way that a man loved a woman or a parent, but in the way that brothers loved each other, a loyalty that remained unspoken.

"We have strict orders that nothing was to be looted," Carter said, watching intently. "I know that I already gave orders to that respect, but I have just been ordered to make sure that nothing was taken."

A chorus of denials came as expected, but Carter noticed that Finney spoke his words a beat slower than the rest. Not really surprising. If anyone would have succumbed to the argument that just one gold bowl didn't matter, it would be the corporal from New Jersey.

"Finney, hand it over," Carter said, gesturing with his palm.

The corporal reached for his pack and withdrew a small bowl embossed with men, bows, and spears in their hands, chasing deers. "I didn't mean to lie, sir," he said as he offered the bowl to the major.

"I know, some things just happen."

Finney looked back down at his cards.

Carter sighed. "The other thing too, Finney. You just can't lie worth a damn."

Finney put his cards down and reached into his jacket pocket, pulling out the handle of a knife, made of silver, with inlaid gold and small red gems.

"Look me in the eyes, Finney," Carter said. "Tell me that's all that you have."

The soldier looked up, his eyes watery, and said, "That's all, sir."

"I believe you," Carter said. Two years of experience had shown Carter that Finney just couldn't speak an untruth when he had to look at a man, an odd trait for a man whose only ambition in life seemed to be a petty criminal.

"You know us too damn well, Captain," Peterson said, chucking his cards onto the blanket in a dramatic gesture. "You probably know who was going to win this hand."

Carter looked down at the pair of threes. "Looks like it wasn't you."

He left his soldiers laughing as he returned to the temple. Rice was kneeling on one knee before one of the stone with runes on it, copying the Nordic characters in a notebook.

"Can you read the runes?" the colonel asked when Carter walked up.

"No, sir."

"It says: 'Hans von Krohn, priest to Odin, loyal Aryan, SS Order Circle of the Raven, sacrificed to his god here. May victory come swiftly.' Of course, the SS runes are just made up, so they are mixing old and new."

"Krohn is the SS bastard that I chased, the one who kidnapped Aoife."

"A pity that he got away."

Carter bristled. "More than a pity for Aoife."

"Yes, quite so," Rice stood up and closed his notebook. "We need to find this Krohn and destroy him."

"And the girl?"

"Yes, and find her."

"Damn right."

Both men looked toward the entrance of the temple as they heard the sound of a truck's engine. "We have a couple of a tasks to complete before we begin our quest," Rice said.

The bed of the truck was filled with five gallon metal cans of gasoline. Rice issued orders and the Rangers lugged the cans around, splashing the fuel on the poles of the palisade and on the buildings inside. Carter participated with relish, soaking the base of the giant oak, where so many maidens had lost their lives.

The air stank of evaporating gas fumes. As the major walked out of the temple, he noticed that Rice had dumped fuel on the stone markers; the liquid ran down the runes, following the shapes of the letters as if they were miniature streambeds.

One last fuel can was used to soak a line in the grass from the truck up to the gate. The men clustered around and watched the colonel take a book of matches out of his pocket. He scraped one across the box and tossed it into the grass. The flame didn't race as Carter expected, but leisurely worked its way down the line of diesel, like an exuberant dancer sashaying on her way to a ball.

The flames lapped up the gate, with its magnificent carving of Yggdrasil, setting the World Tree on fire. In his gut, Carter was sure that there was some subtle symbolism in that act. Wasn't the world in Norse mythology supposed to end in fire? Or was it ice?

The flames spread down both directions of the palisade. The heat caused the soldiers to step back. The driver of the truck jumped in and drove his truck up to the top of the hill, then returned to watch with the others. Carter felt the fascination of the fire. He had seen a lot of fires in the past year, though the most impressive had been a village in central France that the Germans had set on fire in an effort to create an obstacle to the American advance. It had worked; the houses in the village burned for a whole day. While it was impressive, Carter had felt sorry for the villagers who stood outside, watching as all their possessions were destroyed. The Rangers had helped as best they could before they joined the division for a further advance.

Carter remembered the two artifacts in his pocket. He walked over to Rice. "Sorry, sir," he said, handing the bowl and knife handle over. "One of my men did a bit of looting."

Rice took the objects and threw each one into the fire. The Rangers looked at him as if he had lost his mind.

The giant oak tree in the center of the temple burst into flame all at once, as if it had struggled to avoid its fate and suddenly failed. The flames shot several hundred feet into the air, spewing glowing cinders and ash. The soldiers stepped back further.

The heat from the fire was ferocious. Carter had hoped that the surrounding forest, soggy with last night's rain, would be sufficient to contain the fires. Now he realized that the heat of the fire was toasting the moisture out of the surrounding trees and foliage—the fire was going to spread.

"I'm going to put a call into headquarters," Carter said to Rice, shouting to be heard over the flames. "See if we can round up the local German firefighters and get them out here."

Rice looked at the major. "Burning this temple will take away its power and take away the power of all those sacrifices." He mused for a moment. "I guess that you can put in the call. By the time that they get here, everything will have been destroyed."

Carter nodded his head and went to find the radioman. He learned later that the request for fire trucks sent Colonel Walter in a tizzy. He had to find the town burgomaster, find the firefighters, give them gasoline to run their three fire trucks, which hadn't had fuel for half a year, and send them out. Two hours later the firefighters had arrived. They were all old men, since the young men had been taken by the war.

The Rangers wanted to stay behind to help the firefighters. Carter consulted with Rice on this request. They both knew that the Rangers wanted to search the ruins for lumps of gold and silver. Rice said, "Let them take the metals. The power of the objects are gone."

Ferro had driven the two officers in the jeep; he looked a bit dismayed as they prepared to leave, no doubt envious of his fellow Rangers, who were staying to root through the ashes.

"Let's go find this Krohn," Carter said.

"We will," Rice said. "But he has already flown away, so we must prepare for our quest."

"Flown away, like in an airplane?"

"Yes."

"How do you know this?" Carter asked.

"I have a guide that tells me many fascinating things."

"What guide?"

"You will see eventually, but not now," Rice said.

"Where did Krohn fly away to?" Carter asked. "Is Aoife with him?"

"He is heading north and she is with him. She is important to him."

"How are we going to follow him? We don't know where's he going, do we? We don't have a plane. The war is still going on."

"I have ordered a plane to be made ready. We will leave tomorrow."

"I can't leave my Rangers to fly off somewhere."

"Oh, yes, you can," Rice said. "I have decided that you are to be reassigned to me."

"I'm not interested in intelligence," Carter said. "You guys have tried to get me several times in the past and I'm still not interested."

"I can see why we were interested," Rice said. "College education, skill with languages, obvious brains. This time, though, it's not a request."

"I don't want to leave my men."

Rice sighed and pulled an envelope out of his inside breast pocket. "This is an order signed by General Eisenhower himself. It gives me the authority to requisition any resource that I need and reassign anyone who I need to reassign. It is a very magical piece of paper. I am reassigning you to be my aide."

"At least let me bring along my sergeant," Carter said. "As a driver, bodyguard—whatever you call it."

"Very well," Rice said. "We can use the extra man. Right now, though, we have one more task to take care of before we leave."

CHAPTER SIXTEEN

Aoife stood on the edge of the airfield, feeling the sea breeze on her face, inhaling the salt air deeply. Across that sea was England, and just beyond that was her home of Ireland. She so much wanted to run across the heather and down to the beach. Not so much a beach really, mostly mud, but close enough. She wanted to touch the water.

The twin standing near her made that option impossible. He had his gun taken apart and spread the pieces on a blanket as he meticulously cleaned each part. She knew that he didn't need a gun to control her. If she ran, she had no doubt that he could catch her. He was not some slow animal, but a coiled spring, like a jungle animal, ready to move faster than any human could move. Full of menace. Occasionally he looked up and stared at her. Her skin crawled under the fixed gaze of his eyes. She knew what he and his brother wanted to do—knew that there would be no love, not even a trace of kindness, only hurt.

They had been in this remote place all day. When they arrived as dawn was breaking, the airplane had been almost out of fuel, or so she overheard the pilots saying. The airfield was little more than a stretch of mowed grass. There was a single hangar and a cluster of small wooden buildings. The airplane now hid in the hangar, like a sparrow afraid that a hawk might see it.

In the buildings they found some tinned food and two bicycles. Apparently the garrison had abandoned their post. The Nazi officer, Krohn, had clearly expected more than this to greet him. He took a bicycle and rode away in a foul mood, with one of the twins trailing him. He had not returned and she hoped that he failed in whatever he wanted to do.

"Fräulein, go get me some water."

Leaving the seashore, Aoife went back to the building where she had eaten that morning in the same room as the men. She was not used to being around men. Even at Dachau only the SS matrons had come into the barracks. These men didn't even give her any privacy when she had to squat, making a show of averting their eyes and cracking jokes, while she arranged her skirt as well as she could to retain her dignity.

She found a cup and dipped some water out of a rain barrel. As she walked back, passing the aircrew dozing in their chairs, she thought of spitting in the water, but was afraid that someone might notice. And what was the point? Her saliva was not poison.

Setting down the cup next to the soldier, she returned to watching the sea. She wished that she was like her great-grand-mother, Briana. Aoife's only direct experience of the formidable woman came from carefully scrutinizing a faded photograph of the woman, taken over fifty years earlier: strong features that seemed familiar when Aoife looked in a mirror, wearing an elegant gown that buttoned up to her neck, with a rosary in her hand. Aoife had been given that rosary the day after her first bleeding; it remained at her home in Ireland.

It was said that Briana had been blessed with a more powerful share of the gift than had been seen for many generations. Aoife's Aunt Caitlyn had once whispered to her that one night when she was a young girl she had sneaked out at night to the place where the sacred fire was lit, and saw Briana standing before the fire, her robes at her feet, her naked breasts sagging with age down to her navel, calling on the goddess that no one but their family worshiped anymore. As the fire burned down, Briana threw something into the fading flames that caused sparks to fly up. When the sparks cleared, Briana had transmogrified into a bird; not a eagle or other great bird, just a sea bird, like the gulls that make so much noise along the beach. She flew away.

Aoife wished that she had the gift to transmogrify. To become a bird. To fly back home.

CHAPTER SEVENTEEN

The farmhouse looked like it belonged on a postcard: freshly painted window sills and doors amid grey stone walls, a paean to the rustic values of the German farmer. The roof was made of slate. Several cows grazed nearby, as did two draft horses.

Carter ordered the jeep to be brought to a stop several hundred feet from the farmhouse. He was not fool enough to drive right up. He picked up his carbine. "Ferro, cover us."

The corporal stepped out and knelt, sweeping back and forth with his sniper's rifle. Occasionally he looked through the scope to see a suspicious shadow or shape better. Carter moved out in crouch, keeping close to cover. A low fence of stone and logs; a haystack; a small shed. He was vaguely aware that Colonel Rice followed at a slower pace, gripping his .45. Carter didn't like working with someone he didn't know; for all he knew, that scholar had no idea how to shoot and would just as likely put a bullet in the back of Carter as hit what he was aiming at.

Two shots from the farmhouse disturbed the quiet air. Someone screamed.

Carter rushed over to a fence in front of the house, mostly green foliage along a wooden lattice. Wouldn't stop a bullet, but provided him some concealment. He knelt and kept the front door covered. Rice tumbled to the ground next to him, squirmed to a sitting position, and pointed his pistol through a break in the leaves.

The sound of a woman crying in the house tugged at Carter's sensibilities. He was debating what to do when the door opened and a man stepped out.

He wore shabby civilian clothes, with gaunt cheeks and unkempt hair. The handle of a revolver protruded from his waistband. He took a bite from a large sausage and tucked a loaf of bread under his other arm, stepping out into the yard.

Carter suspected a robbery. "Halt! Don't move," he shouted in German, stepping up to show himself, his carbine at his shoulder, aimed and ready.

The man froze, then relaxed when he saw Carter and resumed chewing on his sausage. A woman came out the door; older, in her sixties, wearing a dress and apron. Tears streaked her reddened face.

"This man just murdered my husband and my son," she wailed. "Arrest him. Shoot him."

"What do you say to that?" Carter asked, keeping the conversation in German.

"I would say that they deserved to die," the vagabond said. "At least the old man did. He was an SS officer and in charge of the guards at Belsen. He deserved execution."

"Who are you?" Rice asked. He had come up and was standing next to Carter, his pistol held casually, pointing down at the ground next to him.

"Abe Rosenberg, sir." He took another bite from the sausage and spoke around the food. "I have papers that the British gave me two weeks ago. I'm a Jewish refugee."

"Belsen?" Carter said to Rice in English. "I heard that name last night. It was another place like Dachau."

"Yes, sir, just like Dachau," Rosenberg called out.

"You speak English?" Rice asked—not really a question, since the answer was obvious.

"Yes, sir, Colonel. I believe that you are a colonel?"

Rice nodded.

"Belsen was just like Dachau, except by the time that the British came, almost everyone was in such bad shape that I guess that about half of us died after being liberated." The man repeated himself. "There were forty thousand in the camp and half of us are dead."

"You seem to be in good shape," Carter said.

Rosenberg looked straight into Carter's eyes, unafraid of the carbine pointed at him. A brief flicker of hate disfigured his face, just for a moment, and then he smiled. "Yes, Major—I believe that is your rank." Carter nodded. "I was lucky. I was captured in Poland and marched to Belsen in the snow, but was only there for a week before the British came."

"I see why you killed the father," Carter said. "But what about the son?"

"He was a soldier, really a deserter, I think. He got in the way."

"He tried to protect his father?" Rice asked, walking up to Rosenberg, circling around to keep out of Carter's line of fire.

"Yes, sir."

Rice took the revolver out of the waistband of the Jew and retreated a few steps. "I want to see your papers."

The blue card came out of his shirt pocket and he handed it to the Colonel. Rice looked it over and asked, "How can we be sure that is valid? Pretty easy to forge."

Rosenberg dropped the sausage and the bread on the ground. "I am a Jew!" he shouted. "I will prove it."

Carter almost shot Rosenberg when he reached for his trousers, but paused long enough to be astonished as the refugee unbuttoned himself and pulled down his pants to his thighs. "See," he shouted. "I am circumcised. It is my death warrant."

This did not convince Carter. He knew that Jews were circumcised, but he himself was also circumcised. It was common in the States, a matter of medical hygiene. He didn't know if non-Jewish men in Europe were circumcised. Regardless, he didn't care to be looking at another man's equipment.

The woman had been watching all this talk in a foreign language in silence. She stepped forward and demanded, "Why are talking to this Jew? Arrest him. Execute him. He is a murderer."

"Tell us about your husband and son, Frau," Carter said in

German. "Were they in the Army?"

"The war is over," she cried. "There is no more Army. There is no more Germany."

"Your son was a soldier?"

"Yes, in the Army. He came home only two days ago." She started to cry, not the tears of anger like before, but tears of loss.

"Your husband was in the Army, too?"

"Yes."

Carter persisted. "The Army? Not the SS?"

She looked up sharply. "He served his country. What does it matter how he served it?"

"Did he work in a camp guarding Jews?"

She did not answer for a long moment, her face blank as she stared at Carter. "He was wounded in the first war, in his feet, so he couldn't serve in the regular army in this war. Our Fatherland found another use for him."

"In a concentration camp?"

"I don't know that word," she said.

"Did he work in a place that starved Jews to death?"

"We are all hungry. The bombers have made sure of that. They attack women and children, not soldiers. They bomb the cities and the trains. Even if farmers can grow food, we can't get it to where it is needed."

"Of course he worked in Belsen," Rosenberg cried out, addressing the woman. "I saw him there with my own eyes. I found his home address in the camp records. How else could I have found you? Don't explain away the evil in his heart."

"My husband was a good man." Tears were streaming down her face as she turned to the Jew. "The war is over. No one should die anymore."

The war wasn't really over yet. Carter had no doubt that dozens of American G.I.s had died just that day, taking Munich, pushing further into Germany. Maybe even hundreds or thousands had died. Certainly, in Berlin, where the battle still raged, thousands had died. Yes, the war was over by any rational assessment, but the German government had still not surrendered.

"Wait here," Rice said, going into the house.

The woman sat down on the ground, pulling out tufts of grass as she sobbed. Carter felt sorry for her. Everything in her life had ended, but was her pain any worse than the other victims of this war? The Jew buttoned up his trousers, retrieved his food, and resumed eating.

Rice came out of the front door and walked over to Carter. "I found an SS uniform. One of them must have been an officer. Story sounds plausible."

"You're the ranking officer," Carter said, relieved to say those words. "What do we do?"

Rice turned back to the Jew. "Tell me, are you a rabbi?"

"No, sir." The man looked puzzled.

"How is it that you know English so well?" Carter asked.

"My father sent me to live with relatives in New York City when I was eight years old, so that I could learn English. I came home at fourteen. He wanted me to grow up to run the family export business. Our biggest customers were in America."

"Are you descended from rabbis?" Rice asked.

Carter looked at the colonel out of the corner of his eye. What was all this preoccupation with rabbis?

"My grandfather was a rabbi, from a long line of rabbis. My father was the oldest son and was trained as a rabbi, but he thought that business was much more interesting. He had also gone to the university in Warsaw and had become an unbeliever. I am also an unbeliever. And look what little good it did for us. We were killed as Jews even if we didn't believe. All of us dead."

Carter nodded his head in agreement. Irony had ceased to surprise him. The moral confusion of war made irony so common that one came to expect it, and to expect its twin, absurdity. God must be very frustrated.

The Jew's final statement was, "All that's left is vengeance."

Rice stepped closer to Carter, placed his hand on the barrel of the carbine, and motioned for Carter to lower the weapon.

"We're taking him with us," the Colonel said. "He needs to find redemption."

CHAPTER EIGHTEEN

Under other circumstances, Krohn might have found the small Danish village quaint, a testament to the Nordic peasant. A Lutheran church dominated the center of the village, with two pubs, a small hotel, and several stores clustered nearby. Perhaps several hundred people lived in the village, mostly farmers who tended their nearby fields and cows. There was no evidence here that a war was going on.

After circling through the village once, Krohn cycled up to one of the pubs. He had not ridden a bicycle since his days at the university, and his legs objected when he finally stopped and stood. Motioning for Fritz to follow him, Krohn pushed open the door to the pub. He noted that the twin carried his assault rifle cradled in his right arm, looking casual, but ready to deploy his lethal fire in an instant.

Even this early in the morning, the pub was half full. Didn't anyone work? A radio was playing in the corner, a news announcer speaking in Danish. The buzz of conversation stopped as everyone turned to look at Krohn and his soldier. The colonel straightened his back, conscious that they saw only his black uniform; he could feel their disdain, even hatred.

"I am looking for the commandant of the airfield," Krohn said in German.

The blank looks of deliberate indifference or even barely concealed hostility led Krohn to assume that he would have to become more assertive to get information out of these peasants. To his surprise, the woman behind the bar spoke up, "He's over at the hotel. Room six."

Two minutes later, Krohn pounded on the door of room six. The hotel only had eight rooms and the proprietor had explained that only two rooms were being rented. He stood at the end of the hall, wringing his hands, as if he had betrayed a customer by talking to the SS colonel.

The door opened and a gust of vinegar and alcohol hit Krohn in the face. He blinked away his irritation and pushed his way in, following closely by Fritz. The Luftwaffe officer fell back before the black uniform. He was probably a young man, certainly younger than Krohn, but his gut hung over his grey trousers, stretching his undershirt to capacity. A plate of sauerkraut and bratwurst sat on the nightstand behind him, alongside three wine bottles, two of which were empty. Bleary eyes and three days of whiskers completed the picture of a defeated man.

Krohn expected to find a Danish girlfriend with the wayward officer, but the room was empty except for the drunken German and his bad breath. "You are the commandant of the airfield?"

"Yes, sir," the man said, stumbling about, finding his shirt and trying to find the sleeves where his arms were supposed to go. "Oberleutnant Seidensticker, sir."

"You have standing orders to wait for a plane coming from Munich?" Krohn demanded. "Orders to have fuel ready?"

"Yes, sir." He found the arms and pulled the shirt on backwards. "But the radio said that Munich had fallen, so I thought that the orders no longer applied."

"What radio?"

"BBC."

"You listen to the enemy and believe it over the report of our own radios?"

The senior lieutenant looked at Krohn as if he were an idiot. The SS officer felt his face flush. He often listened to BBC himself to find out the real progress of the war. Dr. Goebbels's propaganda was necessary for the masses, but a man needed the truth in order to make good decisions.

"And you decided to abandon your post?" Krohn asked. "I

should court-martial you on the spot."

The lieutenant stopped trying to get his shirt to cooperate and looked at the colonel with fear that caused his eyes to sparkle. "The war is over," he whispered.

"The war is over when the last loyal German stops fighting!" Krohn roared. "I have not stopped fighting and neither will you!"

"Of course, sir."

"Where's my fuel?" Krohn was still shouting.

"Gone, sir."

"Gone where?"

The lieutenant swallowed hard, his Adam's apple bobbing like a yo-yo. "I, uh, I, uh, sold it, sir."

Those words hit Krohn with a jolt of despair. He resolved to summarily shoot this traitor when the man had outlived his usefulness. "When? To whom?"

"Yesterday, to the store in town."

"Do they still have it?"

"I don't know."

"Let's go," Krohn demanded.

The lieutenant conquered his shirt, found his jacket, and led them out of the room. The hotel proprietor scurried away. The store was not far away, a building of whitewashed stone, though it was closed. Odd for a Monday. Krohn looked back at the pub that they had visited just a few minutes ago and saw that it also looked closed. He didn't like that.

Behind the store, they found a Czech truck, with the German Luftwaffe cross painted on its doors and its bed filled with metal barrels. Krohn walked around, tapping on each barrel. Only the two at the back were empty.

"This is property of the Reich that you had no right to sell," Krohn said to the hapless lieutenant. "We are taking it back. Get up with the barrels, we need every hand that we can get."

Krohn drove while Fritz sat in the passenger seat, his assault rifle pointing out of the window.

"I always thought that the Danes liked us, sir," Fritz said as they left the empty streets of the village behind. "These didn't like us."

"The Danes are like any other Nordic people," Krohn said. "They respect strength. Right now the Reich doesn't look strong, but we will. I assure you, we will. This war is not lost."

The first shot shattered the windshield in front of Fritz. Krohn let his foot off the accelerator, unsure of what to do.

"Drive!" Fritz screamed. "Drive as fast as you can!"

Krohn jammed his foot on the gas and the truck leaped forward as if it had been goosed in the rump. Fritz sprayed a clump of trees as they hurtled past. Amid the sound of the assault rifle magazine being emptied, Krohn thought that he might have heard some more shots coming their way. Hard to tell. Everything was happening so fast.

Then the ambush was behind them and the graveled road in front of them seemed to be clear. Fritz opened his door and leaned out to look back past the truck bed. After a moment, he slammed the door shut and slapped a new magazine into his weapon.

"That Luftwaffe officer jumped out, sir," Fritz reported. "He stood up and then fell down again. I think they shot him."

"Good," Krohn said, his eyes intent on the road, worried that the Danish farmers had dug a trench or something that would stop him. "At least he died with a little purpose."

"I apologize for shouting at you, sir," Fritz said. "Proper tactics is to drive through ambushes, not stop."

Krohn put aside his wounded pride; he was a scholar, not a field officer. At least he had not screamed in terror. "You acted appropriately," he said curtly.

Aoife sat at a table in the hut with the aircrew, eating canned beets. The soldier was outside standing guard. The beets had been too ripe when the factory had sealed them up and instead of being firm on the teeth, they quickly became a slurry as she tried to spear them with a two-pronged fork. They didn't taste good either, though the smell that would have indicated that they had gone bad was absent. The war had taught her that food was food and you ate whenever you had the chance. The guards at the camp had not starved them, like the other prisoners that the virgins occasionally caught glimpses of, but the food had not been as good as what the guards ate.

The copilot had emptied his pockets on the table as he rummaged through them, looking for a can opener. He was obviously a packrat, with pencils, two folded maps, a metal flask, a screwdriver, three bolts, a watch, a compass, a pair of dividers for marking distance on a map, a penknife, many odd pieces of paper, and two can openers.

Karl opened the door. "The colonel is back with the fuel. Everyone needs to help."

As the men pushed back their chairs and filed out, Aoife loitered for a moment. When she was certain that no one was watching, she reached out and snatched the penknife. A small object, only about three inches long, made of shiny steel, with a black swastika on it. She slipped it into a pocket of her skirt.

"Keep up with us, girl," Karl demanded when she emerged from the hut. She followed and sat on a bench as she was told. The aircrew and two soldiers bent to the task of pumping the fuel from each barrel, using a hand pump. Krohn stood to the side, glowering, checking his watch. Occasionally he left the hangar to check the road that he had just come back from.

From the conversation, Aoife gathered that there might be Danish partisans about. She prayed that they might come, but didn't get her hopes up. When everyone was doing other things, she slid the penknife out of the pocket and put in on the ground behind the bench, covering it over with dirt. If they searched her, she didn't want to risk their anger.

Two hours of work left the five men with soaked shirts and arms that hung at their sides as if they had been working the oars on a slave galley of ancient times. Aoife had gotten bored watching them and wished that she had a book to read. At the camp the guards occasionally gave them books or magazines to read, which the girls devoured. After so many re-readings,

Aoife had memorized most of what they had: Nazi propaganda, Western novels from America (which seemed oddly popular with the Germans), insipid newspaper writing, and French romance novels.

Krohn ordered that all be made ready for departure. Aoife watched the aircrew leave to collect their baggage. For long minutes she waited for a commotion to erupt over the missing penknife. When nothing happened, she waited for a moment of neglect and retrieved the penknife. Wiping the dirt and grit off it, she slipped it into her waistband, rolling it tightly up in the loose cloth there.

CHAPTER NINETEEN

Napier didn't believe in dreams.

Back home in Utah, one of his friends had a grandmother who liked to tell everyone about her dreams. An old woman, bent over so sharply that she needed two canes to help her walk like a wounded insect, she often cornered Napier when he visited and told him her strange stories. Napier knew that he was supposed to be polite to his elders, so he pretended to listen. Most of the words just slid by. Then one day she told him that she had dreamt that Arto the Finn would die in the mine in a fire. The next day Arto died on the third level, from a rock fall, not fire, and Napier never visited his friend's house ever again. As time passed and the memory faded, Napier decided that the old lady had just been lucky (if you call it luck); that if you predict enough things, eventually you will hit on something.

How could anyone believe in dreams? It was obvious that dreams were just odd stuff that happened in your mind when you were asleep. Adventures, mysteries, and dramas, all rolled into one, fighting monsters one moment and making love to a damsel another moment, then playing baseball with his friends right afterwards. Napier had heard about a Jewish doctor from Vienna who had even stranger ideas about dreams, so Napier had looked up the psychiatrist's book at a library in London while on leave and tried to expand his mind by reading a chapter from it. He came away even more bewildered. Sometimes he wished that he were educated.

This was the strangest dream that he had ever dreamt. He

was aware of lying in the hospital bed, thrashing against the sheets, feeling confined, yet not alarmed because they were just sheets, not ropes. And Aoife was in his dream, just as redheaded and pretty as he remembered. She wore a peasant dress, or what someone might think a peasant would wear if they could afford colorful cloth instead of just grey.

Her hands were manacled together and she sat in a canvas seat in an airplane. Napier could feel the noisy vibrations from the three engines of the plane. There were men in the plane with her. That officer that he had seen, and the soldier who had given him this headache. Another solider looked just like the first. One of those odd effects that dreams sometimes had, where all soldiers looked alike.

Napier smiled to himself and saw his smile on his face on the hospital bed. What a strange dream. He was like a director of a movie and the critic, observing and criticizing.

She was asleep, occasionally rocking when the plane hit a pocket of air that caused it to lurch. She looked so damned beautiful that his heart ached.

Without opening her eyes, she looked at him, and pleaded, *Come quickly, come and rescue me.*

Napier woke with a start, fully alert, aware that the sheet was tangled around his legs.

He absently rubbed his wrist and wondered if he should believe in dreams.

CHAPTER TWENTY

The sight of the woman startled Carter. A woman dressed as a pilot, with a fur-lined leather jacket, gloves bulging in the jacket pockets, baggy pants, men's shoes, and an officer's cap pulled down over her hair. A brown curl escaped out from under the cap above her neatly plucked eyebrows. The twin silver bars of a captain on her collar showed her rank.

"Major, this is Captain Angela Wright," Rice said.

She offered her hand to Carter and he shook it, surprised to discover that she had fine, feminine fingers, not the meaty fingers of a man or a woman who wanted to be a man. The fingers matched her slim, athletic build.

Rice introduced the other members of the group. They had driven to Augsburg early that morning and it was not yet nine o'clock, with the skies fair, perfect for flying. A C-47 Skytrain transport sat on the pavement behind Wright, painted in green camouflage, a large engine built into each wing. Each Pratt & Whitney radial engine had fourteen cylinders. Some of the nearby buildings were intact, broken windows covered with lumber or tarps, being used by the American Air Corps ground personnel. The rest of the buildings were burned husks.

Carson Napier took his turn shaking the pilot's hand. He still had a bandage wrapped around his head, but seemed chipper enough. The doctor had said that normally he would have disapproved of the sergeant leaving the hospital so soon, but he needed the beds for survivors from the concentration camp.

Abe Rosenberg shook her hand. He now wore green US

Army clothes, though without rank or any insignia; they were the only clothes that Ferro could scrounge up.

"Captain Wright is the last WASP," Rice said.

Carter was still confused. "WASP, sir?"

"Women Airforce Service Pilots," Rice said.

"I had no idea such an organization existed," Carter said.

"It did until December 20th of last year," Wright said, bitterness and resignation mixed in her voice. "We were allowed to fly when there was a shortage of male pilots, but now that's all over. Our commander asked if we could be certified as regular army pilots for one day so that we would all be eligible for the GI Bill, but Washington said no. So everyone packed their bags and went home. The colonel asked that I be retained as his personal pilot. Colonel Rice gets what he wants."

"I had heard about women pilots back home, but not over here," Carter said.

"I ferried one of the transports over to England, flying via Iceland. Women were restricted to training, ferry duty, and flying as targets."

"Targets?"

"We tow the target for other pilots to shoot at or for ground troops to practice hitting."

"What if they hit the wrong plane?"

"Then you hope you don't die," she said, her voice completely deadpan. "Someone has to do it, and we women pilots will take any duty that we can get. It's not like we wanted to pick up a gun and shoot the enemy; we just wanted to fly."

"Though the Soviets have let their women fly as fighter pilots," Rice interjected. "They even let them fight as troops."

"That's just wrong, sir," Napier said. "Woman are for protecting, not for doing the fighting."

"I suppose you wish that we had never gotten the vote," Wright said to the sergeant, an edge in her voice.

"No, ma'am," Napier said. "My mom was proud to be able to vote for a president for the first time."

"I would love to talk politics all day," Rice said, "but I want to get to Scapa Flow before dark. Angela and I will preflight the aircraft, if you gentlemen will load the luggage. Please be careful with my things. Treat them like they're made of fragile glass."

The three men unloaded the gear from the back of the truck. The Jewish refugee had nothing, while Carter and Napier both had their duffel bags and carbines. The colonel's luggage included three suitcases, two medium-sized trunks that felt heavy enough to be completely loaded with books or papers, and a long cylindrical tube of the type used for holding maps. All went into the plane.

The C-47 aircraft was the military version of the commercial DC-3, an airplane that was already the most successful aircraft in history. Its range of 1,600 miles was three times the range of the German Ju-52 transport. With its green camouflage paint, one expected the interior to be militarily utilitarian, ready to carry twenty-eight troops. Because this particular aircraft was used by generals and politicians, the innards were more like the DC-3 airliner, with wooden paneling, carpeting, and even a small toilet and washroom. Instead of canvas seats along the length of the fuselage, facing each other across the aisle, there were plush leather seats facing forward, just like pictures of commercial airliners that he had seen. Petite curtains were draped to each side of the many small windows that lined each side of the fuselage.

"A woman on a plane is bad luck, sir," Napier said, avoiding looking at Carter as he said this.

Carter looked at his aide. "Carson, you just made that up right now."

The short westerner shrugged, refusing to answer.

"I'm sure that she will do a good job," Carter said.

"We can hope," the sergeant said. "A plane's like a ship, and you know that women are bad luck on ships."

"If that was the case, sergeant," Carter said, "then no women would have ever crossed the ocean."

Napier shrugged again, as if withdrawing in on himself.

"She's as strange as a woman in a coal mine. I don't like it."

Rice reappeared wearing a fur-lined leather jacket similar to Wright's. He carried a sack of sandwiches and thermoses of hot chocolate for everyone.

"Are you a pilot, colonel?" Carter asked.

"Yes. But Angela is much better, so I'm just the copilot."

"Where did this plane come from?"

"General Eisenhower lent it to me, along with Angela," Rice said. "I have flown all over Europe in this rugged swan, taking care of my work. Don't look at me like that, Major. I don't want you to think that my relationship with Captain Wright is anything but proper. She's not my mistress. She is an excellent pilot who allows me to indulge my own love of flying without complaint. Besides, we have another crew member—our radioman."

"How long before we reach Scapa Flow?" Carter asked.

"If we can keep up our maximum cruising speed of 160," Rice said, "we should be there in about seven hours. If we have headwinds or other weather, it will take longer."

The woman pilot returned from a nearby building, with a young man walking with her. As he approached, Carter could see horn-rimmed glasses on a brown-skinned face, with a long jaw and somber expression, his long dark hair gathered in a ponytail. He wore a leather flying jacket with no insignia.

He handed a paper to the colonel. "The latest weather report, sir."

"This is Jean-Paul Mann," Rice said by way of introduction. "We call him Paul. His native name is Kisecawchuck, which means 'Daystar' in his native Cree language. He is Canadian, a civilian, since he has chosen to not join the military."

"Why'd you not want to join up?" Napier asked.

The Cree looked the sergeant up and down, as if evaluating if he were worthy of an answer. "My father died in the last war and my mother made me promise to not sign up. So I honor her in this way. Though she does think that I am in Newfoundland, working for the government as a radioman, not over here. She would not be happy to know that I'm over here."

"You speak with an American accent," Carter observed.

"I went to university for two years in Buffalo. I already knew English, but at home we mostly spoke Cree or French."

Minutes later, the aircraft took off, with the two rangers settled down in the passenger cabin with the Jewish refugee. The Canadian closeted himself in his small radio room just behind the cockpit. Other than two practice parachute jumps to qualify as a Ranger, Carter had never been on an airplane before. The sensation intrigued him, and made him nervous, his fingers tight on the arms of his seat.

"Is today the first of May?" Rosenberg asked.

Carter thought for a moment. "Yes, it is."

"May Day," Rosenberg said wistfully. "Back home this was the big holiday, especially if you were a Socialist. I was not a Socialist, but my wife was, so we marched with the workers and helped the labor unions. May Day was a happy day. She looked forward to it all year."

"Where's she now?" Napier asked.

Carter looked at his sergeant. Perhaps he had made the wrong decision, taking Carson out of the hospital so soon. Napier seemed to have lost all tact and common sense today.

Rosenberg looked down at the floor of the airplane. "She's gone. We fought. We were at Warsaw during the uprising in '43. That was a real fight. She died there."

"We heard that there was some fighting," Carter said. "But we don't always know what was happening in the occupied countries."

"These stories need to be told," Rosenberg said. "If we don't tell these stories, then these people will be forgotten."

"Tell us your story," Carter said.

"After the Nazis conquered our country, they confined us to the ghettos and then city by city they cleaned us out. Most of the time we Jews just went onto the trains and into the ovens. In Warsaw we decided to fight. We built hundreds of bunkers in the basements of houses, apartment buildings, and stores. We started by killing the collaborators and then we killed the

Germans when they came into the ghetto.

"We fought with what we had, just rifles and revolvers, and even knives. We had only one machine gun. We made grenades, but they didn't always work. It's very frustrating to get close enough to the enemy to throw a grenade and have it only make a loud noise or maybe just some smoke. They would actually laugh at us.

"I didn't do it, but a couple of friends of mine actually destroyed a German tank with Molotov cocktails. Only one of them survived that attack.

"In a way, none of us expected to live; we just wanted to hurt the Germans. To make them pay a little bit for how many of us had died...and would die.

"We lasted for almost a month. Then it all ended. Everyone was rounded up and sent to the camps. Some of the fighters managed to slip out through the sewers, or so I heard. I ended up in the camps."

Rosenberg's story was interrupted when Mann came back from his radio room. "Just came over commercial radio. The Germans have announced that Hitler died in the Battle of Berlin."

CHAPTER TWENTY-ONE

Krohn cried. When his father died, he hadn't shed a tear, stoically bearing the coffin, proud of his self-control. When his mother died, it had been more difficult and he had cried, but only in private—never where someone else could see him. Now the Führer was dead and Krohn's control failed him. The tears came in front of his two soldiers, the radioman, and the girl.

How could it have come to this? Rarely does a man arise from the masses who can, by an act of his will, change everything, who stands outside of the flow of history, who defines what it means to be great. Adolf Hitler, born in humble circumstances in Austria, had been such a man—forged in the First World War, showing his bravery, and seeing with clarity the subtle way in which the Jews sapped the strength of the Aryan people. Through his will he had shaped a Third Reich, conquered Europe, and now had fallen as the warrior that he was.

Krohn had seen the great man in person four times. At the three Nuremberg rallies that he attended, grand spectacles that showed Germany and the world that the Aryans had returned to power. The last rally in September 1938 had half a million people attend, and among that throng, Krohn had not felt lost, a solitary individual, but a part of a greater whole, a cell within that Aryan organism. The fourth time was at an awards ceremony for SS officers, in 1941, when Krohn had the honor of personally shaking the great man's hand. He was surprised at how soft the skin felt, but the grip was firm, and Hitler had paused long enough to look into Krohn's eyes and connect with him on a deep racial level.

As the war turned against Germany, Krohn had harbored his doubts. He wondered if Hitler was loyal enough to his Aryan roots; wondered if the former corporal was a true enough believer. Now that the great man was dead, Krohn felt only shame. How could he have doubted?

Brushing away his tears, Krohn saw that the twins were crying also, as was the radioman who had come back from the cockpit to tell them what he had heard on the radio. Krohn felt a surge of pride. Germans everywhere must be in sorrow, realizing the gravity of what had happened. Only the Irish bitch was not crying; her eyes were clear, so green, as she watched the heartbroken men warily.

Krohn hated her at that moment. He wanted to let the twins have their way with her right then and there. He wanted to watch her debasement.

The idea shocked him. Not the idea of the act itself, but that he would so quickly give in to his baser emotions. The death of Hitler did not mean the death of the dream. There was still hope and she was part of that hope.

All would be made right at the North Pole.

CHAPTER TWENTY-TWO

The commander of all the SS troops in Norway stood next to his command car in the early morning. The dew on the grass had turned his black boots shiny. The airfield north of Oslo had only a few aircraft left, and all but one of them were grounded due to the lack of parts. In the five years that he had lived in Norway, he had come to love the weather—so much more vigorous than his native Westphalia. This morning was calm and beautiful, with a few high clouds and a dawn that renewed his optimism about the war.

Albert Rediess was a bureaucrat before he became a believer. His father had worked for a state bureau in Westphalia, and Rediess had excelled in clerical and accounting classes at the gymnasium. The army rejected him in the first war because of his bad eyes and pronounced limp from when a horse had stepped on his foot when he was only four years old. The army physician had not known about his stomach problems, which caused him to become a vegetarian, since milk and meat played havoc with his bowels.

One might have looked on Rediess with pity, but that would have been foolish. During the war, he worked hard at the ministry responsible for rationing food. Others took extra ration cards for themselves or sold them on the black market, but not Rediess. That would be acting like a Jew.

After the war ended in ignominious defeat, he joined the Nazi Party because they advocated a strong future for the nation. He became a member of the SS in 1930 and following his father's

advice, did all that was expected of him with the utmost efficiency. He always tried to go beyond the assignment in some
way that would demonstrate his enthusiasm. Promotion came
quickly. Two years after Hitler came to power, Rediess became
a SS-Gruppenführer, equivalent to a Lieutenant General, even
though the SS rank of Senior Group Leader was only one rank
below that of Himmler. After the war started, Rediess received
his assignment to deport all the Jews from East Prussia. The
Jews were shipped to ghettos in the newly conquered Poland,
but the mentally defective were handled separately.

The gas vans took care of them.

His reward for such efficiency was the coveted posting in
Norway as the top SS leader in the entire occupied nation. He
had watched from afar as the Nazi plans for the Jews reaped
their harvest, with his own small contribution of 767 Jews from
Norway. Seeking achievement, Rediess looked elsewhere. The
Führer had always been worried that the Allies would invade
Norway, so he had stationed four hundred thousand troops there,
one for every ten Norwegians. That many troops, with too much
time on their hands, led to the inevitable, and soon Norwegian
girls were having German babies. Rediess stepped in and
expanded the Lebensborn program that had been so successful
in Germany. Eight thousand babies were certified as of pure
Aryan stock and special care devoted to their upbringing.

The sound of incoming aircraft carried far in the clear air.
Rediess stepped away from the car and began to pace back
and forth. The war had reached the final crisis. Troops had
been assigned to the Bavarian Redoubt, guerrillas were being
seeded behind enemy lines to strike like werewolves, and plans
for Festung Norwegen were coming along nicely. Though
Norwegians were of obvious Aryan stock, they were not enthusiastic in their racial allegiance. Only 5,000 had volunteered to
fight on the Eastern Front. Regardless of the reluctance of the
population, the Germans could hold out in their Nordic fortress
for months.

All the Nazis had to do was hold out long enough for the

American and British to fall out with their Soviet allies. Such an alliance between democracies and the communists was unnatural and could not last. When they fell to blows, the Nazis would be there to join the anti-Bolshevik crusade. With the economic might of America behind them, the Russians would be crushed and the Third Reich would rise like the mythical phoenix from the ashes of defeat.

The Ju-52 descended, circled the field once, and landed, spewing gravel as its wheels touched down. The pilot taxied the airplane over to the hangar near Rediess and shut down the engines.

Rediess greeted Colonel Krohn as the side door opened. "Welcome to Norway, Hans."

The colonel saluted. "Thank you, sir. We were delayed in Denmark by a fool, but I think that we can maintain our timetable if we leave here within two hours."

Rediess smiled. Krohn was such a serious man, much like himself, always ready to perform, ever formal, even though they knew each other well from numerous meetings and informal gatherings. At times, he envied the work that Krohn did, working on the edge of the supernatural, but Rediess knew that his faith was insufficient to do more than admire from afar.

"We have fuel for your plane and food for everyone," Rediess said. "A mechanic will go over the engines, add oil, and do what mechanics do."

When an SS soldier led a redhaired girl out of the aircraft, Rediess kept his eyes on her, memorizing every detail of her. With a German girl he would have been embarrassed at such a social gaffe, but he knew that she was no German girl. She was much more interesting than that.

As the aircrew and others went into the hangar to find breakfast, Rediess and Krohn hung back for some privacy. "Is she the one that you will use?" Rediess asked.

"Yes," Krohn said. "She is the only one that I was able to get hold of. The Dachau camp fell too quickly for me to get more. Even so, she is probably the one that I would have chosen. She is Irish, wonderful bloodline, though there is a bit of mystery to it."

"Mystery?" Rediess asked. "No tainted blood, I trust."

"No, nothing like that. No Jewish stain there. Her grandmother's line goes directly back to deep Celtic roots. Maybe even a sacred line."

"What does that mean?"

"Guido von List taught that there are certain bloodlines with special powers. The gods have touched these bloodlines, though not everyone with the correct ancestors has the gifts. For reasons that I have not been able to discern, sometimes the gifts are manifested, sometimes not."

"Is she gifted?" Rediess asked.

"I don't know. I have watched carefully, but so far I haven't been able to figure her out."

"Will her having gifts matter?"

"Only that Odin will be even more pleased if she has a gift."

"We are getting ready to hold out here, according to the Fortress Norway plans," Rediess said. "But I think that we are only waiting for what you can do. You are our last great hope."

"Operation North Pole has finally found success," Krohn said. "And none too soon. You read the message from Professor Adler?"

"Yes, the World Tree actually works," Rediess said. "It's too incredible to believe."

"Incredible, but not too incredible." Krohn placed his hand on Rediess's arm, stopping him. "Do you have any more news about the Führer's death?"

"Yes, we got a message from Admiral Dönitz. He was appointed the successor to the Führer in his will and has formed a new government in the town of Flensburg. He also gave us secret details that were not part of the radio broadcast. The Führer was trapped in his bunker and refused to leave. To prevent his capture, he shot himself, and his body was burned, as per his orders."

"Suicide?"

"The only choice really," Rediess explained. "He could have picked up a rifle and died in the fighting, but what if he had only been wounded? And what if his body had been recovered intact? I can't bear the thought of our Führer laid out for the film cameras. Think of the indignities that the Bolsheviks could have thought up, then filmed and tricked the world into believing?"

"I don't want to think about that," Krohn said. "He was in so much pain. I heard that his wounds from the assassination attempt last summer caused him unrelenting agony."

"I heard that also. It takes a brave man to continue to lead when he hurt so much."

"His death is such a great loss, but at least he is no longer hurting now."

Rediess nodded. "Yes, I agree, but I think that the failure of the German people to win this war hurt him even more."

"Just so."

As promised, two hours later, Rediess watched as the airplane took off, flying north. The skies over Norway were safe enough during the day, being too far from England for fighters to come and loiter, looking for prey.

Rediess called for his driver, his faith in victory having returned.

CHAPTER TWENTY-THREE

Carter and Napier stood on a hilltop overlooking Scapa Flow, where the Orkney Islands formed one of the world's finest anchorages. Ships of the British Home Fleet rested at anchor, hazy outlines in the mist—dark masses of battleships, the lean greyhounds of destroyers, merchant ships that looked fat on the bottom, with deck cranes pointing out like gigantic matchsticks. Occasionally the shrill tweeting of a boatswain's whistle came across the water, or the low rumble of a launch motor, a sound carried by the damp air much farther than one expected.

Just weeks into the war, a U-boat had sneaked into this water fortress and torpedoed a battleship, the *Royal Oak*. Even more annoying, the Germans escaped. Eight hundred bodies still remained trapped in the cold water in a coffin of steel. Rice had pointed out where the ship now rested, marked by an oil slick as its full tanks slowly leaked, but the mist was too dense to see any details.

The point of coming to this place was not the ships, but what was behind him. Carter had visited Stonehenge just a year ago, when his Ranger company had been stationed in the south of England, preparing for D-Day. Those stones, standing vertically on the Salisbury Plain, had been erected at different times, from five thousand to three thousand years ago. The place was impressive when combined with an historical imagination. True, it was nothing compared to a modern steel span bridge, or a ship, or even a decent-sized building, but for the people of that time, limited by technology and social organization, Stonehenge was more impressive than the Empire State Building and had certainly taken much longer to build.

Stonehenge was only the most well known of the megalithic circles and other sites in England. Rice had showed Carter a map and the stones seemed to be everywhere. The one furthest north was here on this island. Eight standing stones, with another toppled over, each the height of a man, arranged in a circle. In the middle of the circle, off-center, was a large boulder, its round top chiseled flat thousands of years ago. All the stones were pitted and worn from thousands of years of rain and snow, combined with the temperature changes that came with summer and winter. Grey lichen, with small patches of green, covered parts of the stones.

Carter and Napier found a spot just outside one of the upright stones and watched. Colonel Edgar Rice had donned a white robe over his uniform and placed a conical hat on his head. For some schoolchildren, it looked like the dunce hat that their school teacher might have placed on their head when they were forced to stay in the corner as punishment. Perhaps an image out of a Norman Rockwell painting on the cover of *The Saturday Evening Post*. For Carter, the costume looked much more ominous. His grandfather had such an outfit, that he wore with pride when he went to a rally of the Ku Klux Klan. All the upright men in the town belonged to the Klan. That had been a part of Carter's life until he went to Yale and learned to be ashamed of his family heritage.

Of course, the costume that Rice wore had nothing to do with the Klan. The robe and hat had been reported thousands of years ago in ancient Roman writings as the regalia of druid priests. Rice waited in the center of the circle. There were no pockets in the robe, but a convenient slit in the side allowed him to occasionally reach into his trousers for his pocket watch.

When high noon came, the sun invisible because of the clouds, Rice picked up an actual ram's horn and pressed it to his lips. The low mournful cry carried well across the moor. The spring equinox, roughly midway between the shortest day of the year and the longest day of the year, when the sun is directly above the equator, had been in March. The summer solstice, the time of midsummer, when the sun reached its highest point in the sky, would not happen until June. This day was not special, but Rice had assured Carter that it did not matter. This particular set of stones had apparently not been set up to align with those solar events, though perhaps there was some lunar pattern that no one had yet been able to divine.

The mist turned into a drizzling rain as a procession of white-robed people came up the hill. Carter pulled his rain slicker more tightly about his shoulders. He remembered the time he had sneaked out of his bedroom to spy on a Klan rally. Even at that age, he could feel the hate that radiated from faces made shiny by the torches as they listened to a speaker harangue them about the evils of darkies, immigrants, and miscegenation. He had no idea what that last word meant, but it had seemed nasty.

This ceremony felt different, more sacred, not filled with the darker emotions. Each member of the procession stopped to press their lips to the tallest stone before they entered into the round sacred space created by the megaliths. The dozen druids circled around within the stones three times, like moons orbiting Rice and the central stone.

The rain came down harder and the white robes turned grey, sticking to the bodies of the druids. The circle stopped turning. Rice raised his arms, saying something in Gaelic that Carter couldn't catch because the rain muted the sound. As Rice lowered his arms, the druids removed their robes and cast them outwards from the circle.

They were all naked. Six men and six women. Details were not visible because the rain had a tendency to make everything look washed out, like a bad Impressionist painting. The circle began to rotate once again, but this time, the druids waved their arms and skipped a bit, not in sync with each other, but as if celebrating life.

Carter and Napier glanced at each other, both with wide eyes. "This guy isn't playing with a full deck, sir," Napier whispered.

"I think, Sergeant, that Colonel Rice has a deck of cards that doesn't look like our deck of cards."

A half hour or so after it started, the ceremony wound down. The druids picked up their soggy robes, struggled to put them on bodies ruddy from heat loss, and filed away. Rice left the stone circle and came over to where the two soldiers waited.

"Let's go back to the house," Rice said, his teeth chattering.

Several hundred yards away, at the base of the hill, Mann sat waiting in the car, a 1939 Packard touring sedan—a fine luxury car with a long hood, hard top, and leather seats. He hurried out when the three men approached and opened the doors for them. Napier sat in the front, while Carter and Rice took the back seat. Before getting in, the two Rangers took off their raincoats, and Rice peeled off his robe.

"Mr. Mann, why didn't you come watch?" Carter asked.

"It's not my tradition, sir," the Indian said. "So I wait here."

"Where did you get the ceremony, Colonel?" Carter asked. "I thought that the druids refused to have their ceremonies written down, so we don't have any real information."

"We made it up." Rice laughed as he rubbed his hair with a towel. The druid robe had not prevented his uniform from getting wet; his seat was slick with moisture. "We don't have direct information from the druids, but we have writings of the ancient Romans, which should be treated with care because the druids were their enemies. We have archaeological evidence. We have writings from the early Middle Ages, mostly by monks and churchmen who were horrified by the pagan practices. And we have myths and stories that have been handed down. In some places, we even have practices that persisted for hundreds of years. On an island off Scotland called Inis Maree, the locals used to sacrifice a bull to Saint Maelrubha, their local saint, every August up until the late 1700s. The church didn't care for such a pagan act and finally got them to stop. This sacrifice was written about and became a source for me to use. A reverend in 1812 recorded that in Wales, the local farmers would throw a bullock over a cliff whenever they had plagues of sickness in the cattle."

"If you make a mistake in the ceremony, how can you be sure that it will work?" Carter asked

"I can't be sure that it works, but we have to try," Rice said. "I am not the only occult science officer. We have similar ceremonies being performed in Ireland, Wales, Cornwall, and Iceland. Across the water, we have ceremonies being performed by various Indian peoples. That's how I met Paul here. He is a Cree shaman who follows his ancestors. There is also a similar effort in the Pacific, with Maori, Australian aboriginals, Inuit, Melanesians, and Polynesians all doing their part."

"I thought that you were Catholic," Carter said to the Indian, who was driving them slowly through the rain, his head gently rocking in rhythm to the windshield wipers.

"I am Catholic, sir," Mann said. "Most of my tribe is. But we still have our own traditions that we nurse along when the priest is not looking."

"Who are the people who participated in the ceremony?" Carter asked Rice.

"Locals who try to maintain their ancient traditions," Rice said. "They have a local antiquities society here and I ran across them during my studies. They are patriotic and quite willing to perform their ceremonies in support of the war effort."

"How can any of this be true?" Carter asked. "I mean, actually work. I can understand a person believing that it will work, but I don't see how it would actually work."

"Do you believe in God?" Rice asked.

"I do," Carter said.

"The Christian god, I suppose."

"Yes."

"He's a powerful god, but a god of peace and love," Rice said. "He is not useful in helping people win wars, so we pray to him, but don't expect him to give us victory."

"But these Celtic gods, so ancient that no one has worshiped them for hundreds, even thousands of years, will make a difference?" Carter asked.

Rice pursed his lips for a moment before replying. "My studies have led me to believe that in the center of the Earth there is a presence, a machine if you will, incredibly powerful and full of energy. It is called Gaia. Human beliefs, ideas and faith, especially if held by many people, can cause a resonance with Gaia. This resonance can be used. Faith healers use it, ancient shamans used it, even people with their prayers might access it. Rituals are like keys to access the power of Gaia, and we have used them to win this war."

Colonel Rice lived outside of a village that overlooked Scapa Flow. The two-story house was made of stone, with grey lichen growing over parts of the exposed stone. A barn out back had been converted into a two-car garage, though the Packard was the only resident. Mann also lived in the house, while a nearby cottage had been rented for Wright. Rice's home reminded Carter of the SS Colonel's home near the temple of Odin, with its large library of full bookcases, exposed beams that made for sturdy ceilings, the feeling that a bachelor lived there, and the sense that both had plenty of funding.

Wright and Rosenberg had started dinner. Carter watched them move around the kitchen for a few minutes. She seemed to know where everything was and how to organize the cooking of the stew. Rosenberg obeyed her instructions quickly. Carter noted with approval that she had a tone of command in her voice, not affected, but something that came naturally. His mother had the same trait, though she only exercised it on the children and servants, and the women of her local United Daughters of the Confederacy group.

Having changed his clothes, Rice came down the stairs and asked Carter to follow him into the library. Napier was already there lighting a fire in the iron-bellied stove. He had removed his bandage, and the ugly bruise on the back of his head was quite visible because the doctor or nurse had shaved away so much of his hair.

Rice drew a metal tube from the luggage in the center of the room. He carefully removed a rolled-up piece of brown paper and spread it out across a table. Carter recognized that it was a medieval map, centered on Europe, with Asia not as big as it should be, with Africa oddly shaped, and the Americas as only coastlines. Bears, lions, and camels were drawn in areas that the cartographer obviously knew little about, like the interior of Asia and Africa. A dragon in China and unicorn in India showed that exotic animals lived in those places. It was odd, though, in that Africa was not shown as a continent, with ocean around its southern part, indicating that the cartographer lacked the knowledge that Portuguese sailors had obtained when they rounded the Cape of Good Hope and sailed into the Indian Ocean. Yet the Americas were drawn, although not in the right shape, and they had been discovered at about the same time that Africa had been circumnavigated.

"This map was drawn in 1433, by an anonymous scholar in Amsterdam," Rice said.

"That's not possible," Carter said. "The Americas weren't discovered until—

'In fourteen hundred ninety-two
Columbus sailed the ocean blue.'"

The quote came from a song he had learned in grade school and rolled off his lips like an old friend.

"Some scholars have argued that the Vikings even went as far as North America," Rice said. "We haven't found conclusive evidence of that, though."

"Are you saying that this map has information that was known to some other people, but not to Columbus?"

"Obviously. See the date in the corner? This map is from 1433. But this map also has other secrets." Rice pointed at the top of the map. "See here, far north of Norway, there is something there. Here's a magnifying glass."

Carter leaned closer and peered through the glass. There was a large circle, with strange shapes inside: a inner circle, a large tree, and many boxes. Between the outer and inner circles were drawn many smaller trees. Among the trees was a tall obelisk with an eye on the top of it. The faintest lines of ink radiated out from the eye. Outside of this odd circle and trees was only blank space, with the occasional drawing of a polar bear or the word ice written in fine Latin calligraphy.

"Odd," Carter said. "What is it?"

"I believe that is where our Colonel Krohn is going."

"Some odd place on an old map?"

"Yes," Rice said. "I have always been fascinated by our polar regions and have collected information for years. In 1926, when he flew to the North Pole, Admiral Byrd reported seeing mountains where no map showed mountains. He also reported that he had seen a green valley amid the white snow, which everyone discounted as hallucination from flying too long. A multinational expedition led by Amundsen flew over the North Pole at the same time, using an Italian semi-rigid airship, going all the way from Spitsbergen to Nome, Alaska. The Italians tried again in 1928, but their airship crashed. There have been a few other efforts, mostly flying out of Spitsbergen, and no one has found that green valley."

"Perhaps because it doesn't make sense for a green valley to exist in a place that is so cold," Carter said.

Rice smiled, as if tolerating an unbeliever. "That may be true, but there are still places on our planet that have not been explored. The polar regions are some of those places. Yes, we have been to the North Pole, but that was just a dash in and out. And there is also some more information. Read this. It was found just last week among some papers in Osnabrück that the Nazis were trying to burn when a British patrol stopped them."

Carter took the paper. The bottom half had been burned away, and the typewritten words were so faint and fuzzy that obviously this was a carbon copy and not the first copy; possibly the third or fourth. He could well imagine a secretary with a tight wad of papers in her typewriter, hitting the keys firmly in an attempt to get the force of the key strike through all those carbons and sheets.

Report of Captain Trott, 28 August 1944
Classification: Most Secret

SS Arctic Expedition

As required, our mission was conducted in the utmost secrecy. As you may recall, the last two Zeppelins were dismantled in 1940, their duralumin melted down to make fighters. When I received instructions to build a new airship in 1942, it took two years to gather enough duralumin to build the ship in our hangar at Friedrichshafen, even though the airship is only half the size of the *Graf Zeppelin II*. I considered this to be too small, but the considerable obstacles that continuously delayed us, detailed in earlier reports, prevented us building a larger airship.

We finished construction on 17 June 1944. Our maiden flight was two days later, flying at night to avoid detection by enemy aircraft. Because of the danger of detection, we only flew two more trials before heading for Bear Island on 24 June. The flight took 39 hours. At that location fuel and supplies had already been stockpiled. On 5 August, we launched our first exploration journey, taking an initial heading of 340°, returning five days later. Our equipment held up well, but the heaters are inadequate to keep the crew warm. The temperature in the cabin, even with the heaters going, was minus six degrees centigrade. Food was a problem. Our hard-boiled eggs were hard as rocks and bread made an odd crackling sound, like paper being crumpled, when we ate it. At least we could eat the bread.

The crew found the cold exhausting, so we rested for three days before going out again on an initial heading of 320°. The news from Germany was discouraging and we knew that we must succeed. Professor Alder kept our spirits up. Our second expedition lasted five days and we failed to find the valley. Four days of rest, and on August 22, we left again, on an initial heading of 300°.

On August 25, north of Greenland, at 83° 13' 54" N, 6° 54' 41" W, we found the green valley. Asgard. Professor Alder was very pleased. On approach, a wind caught our airship and we crashed....

CHAPTER TWENTY-FOUR

Aoife huddled against the inside bulkhead of the plane, feeling the vibrations of the engines come through her skin. She remembered a cat that they had on the farm who used to like to sit on her lap and purr. The old tom had not even needed to be petted; just sitting on her was good enough. She had liked that old cat, who was so good at hunting mice and making the lady cats pregnant. She wondered if he was still alive and if he missed her lap. He had been pretty old, but she hoped that he would still be there when she went home.

The last four years of captivity had taught her to be realistic. Her chances of seeing the cat again were slim, even if the old tom was still alive.

Outside a small window the country of Norway flowed beneath her. These mountains were unlike those at home, so ragged and sharp, still tipped with snow in the distance. Dark evergreens covered parts of their slopes like patches of fur and other places were just bare grey rock. Since she was on the right side of the plane, she only occasionally saw the sea as they passed over a fiord that cut deep into the country. Little fishing villages looked like colorful models, with red and brown roofs most apparent from her vantage point.

The Ju-52 landed in an airfield near Trondheim for fuel, and she was only allowed to leave long enough to relieve herself in an outhouse near the field. When she got back in the plane, she sat on the left side, and was pleased when Colonel Krohn came back aboard and looked exasperated at her changed position.

Then he shrugged.

Such small victories, where she made her own decision, rather than having the decisions of others imposed on her, made her feel better.

They took off and she nibbled on the bread and sausage that one of the twins gave her. From this side of the plane she could watch the sea, stretching all the way to the horizon, and she looked down as they crossed fiord after fiord. It was gorgeous; sheer mountainsides plunged straight down and into the water, as if the ocean were insignificant. She assumed that the color of the water, different shades of blue and green, told her how deep the fiords were. A cliff with dark blue water beside it indicated a truly deep fiord.

One of the pilots came back. "We just passed the Arctic Circle."

Sorting through her memories of school lessons and textbooks, she was proud of herself to remember what that meant. They were so far north that at least one day of the year the sun did not set. At the North Pole, the sun didn't set for a whole six months.

She dozed, head resting in her arms.

When she woke, she found one the twins sitting next to her, his breath reeking of bratwurst, leaning so close to her that she recoiled. He smiled and she shuddered.

"Please stay away," she said, annoyed with herself when the words squeaked as they came out.

"You need to learn to be a little more friendly, girl," he said.

He reached out to touch her and she glanced over at their officer. Krohn was just waking up.

"Private Steinhauer," Krohn said in a conversational voice. "Let me explain something to you and your brother. I recognize the right of a conqueror to do whatever to the woman he wishes. And you are certainly a conqueror; but for my purposes, you must not molest her. She must remain a virgin, because that is where her power comes from. Union with a man dissipates that power. I charge you and your brother with the sacred responsibility to make sure that she does not lose that power."

The soldier dipped his head. "Yes, sir."

CHAPTER TWENTY-FIVE

After a dinner of stew, bread baked just that morning and bought from the village bakery, and a bottle of prewar French wine shared among the five of them, they gathered in the parlor, where Rice crumpled some newspapers in a large stone fireplace, added kindling, and soon had merry fire going. Not nearly as warm as the stove in the study, but the dancing flames created a much nicer atmosphere.

"Tell me, Colonel," Carter said, feeling the warm glow of good food in his belly and the taste of good Virginia tobacco in his cigarette. "Where did you come from?"

"Oh, everywhere. I know that sounds like a silly answer, but I grew up traveling the world and have continued ever since." Rice picked up the remainder of the newspaper and returned to the sofa.

"You're an American, aren't you?" Napier asked. The sergeant looked exhausted as he slumped in his overstuffed chair.

"At present I hold American citizenship, but I consider myself to be a citizen of the world," Rice said, spreading his hands wide. "This has been my home for the past three years. Before that my home wandered with me."

Carter turned to Wright. "And how about you, Captain? Where are you from?"

She laughed. "I'm afraid that I am just the opposite of the colonel. I grew up in Kansas City. Both my parents were doctors and we didn't go anywhere. One parent or the other always had to work, so I didn't stray far."

"What about college?"

"I went to Western Reserve, in Cleveland," she said. "I got a degree in biology and trained as a nurse."

"And how did you come to be a pilot?"

"I always wanted to fly. After the war started, I considered signing up as a nurse, but when they opened up the WASP program, I signed up. We were sent to Avenger Field in Sweetwater, Texas. It was dusty, hot, and dry. We actually took showers with our clothes on just to cool off. The barracks were built for men, with urinals in the bathrooms, so we just stuck a sock down them and used them to wash our delicates. The uniforms were also made for men and many of the girls were too small for them, so we had to cut and sew them into smaller sizes. One girl was actually bitten by a rattlesnake; it didn't kill her, just made her sick. We worked hard to learn to fly. Out of 1,830 women, over a thousand made it through training. And we did a good job. We had a better flying record than the men. Even so, over thirty of us have died in crashes."

"You speak with pride," Carter said. "And justly so."

Napier made some sort of inaudible grumble and Wright looked away, making her act of ignoring him plain to all.

Rice had been reading the newspaper while Wright talked. "See here, there is an editorial calling for an immediate general election in England as soon as Germany is defeated."

"I have not been following British politics," Carter said. "What's the story there? I thought that Churchill was popular."

"Oh, Churchill is very popular," Rice said. "The man who won the war. A recent survey found eighty percent of the population approving of him. During the war, the parties agreed to a coalition government, and suspended elections. But while Churchill is popular, the Tories are not. Labour wants to take power and create a welfare state."

"Sounds like socialism."

"Oh, it is. They commissioned a report a couple of years ago that calls for full employment. If everyone can have a job during the war, why can't everyone have a job after the war? Or so the argument goes. They also want to create a national health care system and nationalize key industries."

"The people are all for this?" Carter asked.

"I think so. While Churchill ran the war, the Labour leader, a man by the name of Attlee, has run the rest of the show. He's not a charismatic leader, or a great speaker; he's a modest man, really, but people like him. And they like the Labour agenda."

"Churchill might just lose," Carter said, drawing the words out as if he was tasting the surprising idea behind them.

"How can Churchill lose if he is so popular?" Napier asked. He struggled to keep his eyes open and his words were slurred.

"In England, the prime minister is selected by Parliament," Carter said. "So whoever party has the most seats is usually prime minister. A man can be very popular, but he only wins his own seat in Parliament."

Then ensued a long discussion on the merits of the parliamentary form of government over the American form of government. The English had the advantage of being able to quickly change the prime minister and his cabinet if they weren't up to the job, while the Americans had to suffer through the remainder of the term of a president. The Americans also had the advantage or disadvantage, based on your point of view, of having a strong separation of powers, making it difficult for one man or group of men to accumulate too much authority, while the English system made Parliament the ruler of all. Only the figurehead monarch, His Majesty King George the VI, the hobbled House of Lords, and tradition, kept Parliament in check.

"Look at how hard it was for FDR to persuade the American people that the Nazis were a mortal threat," Rice said. "Only Pearl Harbor hastened that."

"Have you heard the nasty rumor that FDR knew that the Japs would attack us and let it happen so that we would go to war?" Angela asked.

"That's just pure rubbish," Carter exclaimed. "Where did you hear it?"

"I agree with you," she said. "I overheard some ground crew

talking about it back in the States when we were there three months ago."

"That's makes no sense at all," Carter said. "FDR wanted to go to war with Germany, not with Japan. War with one of the Axis powers did not mean war with all three. Look at Japan, an ally of Germany at war with us, but not at war with the Soviets. Besides, if I recall correctly, and I am sure that I do, Germany declared war on us, four days after Pearl Harbor. I think that Germany could have kept us out of the European War for many months, or even years, if Hitler had not been so rash."

"All you said is true." Rice packed his pipe with tobacco. "But conspiracy theories don't die, especially when they help us think badly about someone. FDR may have been popular, but plenty of people can't help themselves; they believe anything that makes him look bad."

"So true," Carter said. "We often believe what makes us comfortable, rather than what makes rational sense. Another thought occurs to me. Hitler declaring war on the US may have been his worst blunder of the war, even worse than invading Russia."

Rice lit his pipe and puffed for a few moments. "So true, my dear Carter. Everyone makes mistakes. The key is to make fewer mistakes than your foe and to take advantage of their mistakes. FDR was a great man, who made good decisions. I will miss him."

"You knew FDR?" Rosenberg asked. The refugee nibbled on a plate of leftovers from the dinner, even after a full meal.

"Not in terms of being his friend," Rice said. "But I knew him as a person who supported us. He created the Occult Science Service by secret executive order in 1940. He supported us strongly and never questioned our budget, or our contribution to the war effort."

"Is Truman as supportive?" Carter asked.

Rice took the pipe from his mouth. "Harry S. Truman is a fine man, but not at all prepared to abruptly become president. There were many secrets that he was not privy too, and all those secrets are gradually being revealed to him as events dictate. I don't know if we have been revealed yet. Or, I should say, I have not heard that we have been talked about, and I would certainly know if that happened."

The conversation continued for another hour. The fire burned down, and after the sun set, people excused themselves. Napier went first, his stalwart constitution obviously still recovering from the blow to the head. Soon only Rice and Carter were left.

It had been a long time since Carter had listened to intellectual conversation, and he rediscovered the deep satisfaction that it gave him. To have new ideas bandied about, examined and dissected, reminded him that the war was an aberration, not his entire life. He was also delighted to find that Captain Wright was well informed and not shy about voicing her views, unlike so many women he had known in college.

The colonel looked at his watch. "It's eleven o'clock already and, as pleasant as our conversation has been, I still have some work to do."

Carter took the hint. "I guess I should go to my room, sir. Since I'm not particularly tired, could I borrow a book from your collection?"

"Oh, yes, certainly." Rice stood up and went to one of the bookcases. "In fact, I would recommend this book to you. We might find it relevant in our search."

Carter had been assigned one of the bedrooms upstairs, barely large enough to hold the bed and a nightstand. Part of the ceiling formed the slope of the roof, but that was not a obstacle because it was over the head of the bed. Who wanted to stand up there? He normally slept in his clothes, and the sheets looked so clean that he put on a clean set of clothes before settling down, with the lamp turned on and the book on his knees.

The book was *Norse Mythology* and the author was Edgar B. Rice. Carter smiled. It had been so long since he had read a scholarly book—he was like a starving man presented with a feast. He consumed the pages with abandon. Much of the book was review, a refresher from college, with some new twists that he hadn't learned of before. Within an hour he closed the book.

Digging through his duffel bag, he found a novel that another officer had passed along to him three weeks ago. The Army printed cheap paperbacks and gave them to the troops; no doubt the initiative of some general's wife concerned with the cultural standards of the troops. The Army also printed and gave away comic books, where superheroes helped fight the Nazis, and no doubt that general's wife was appalled.

Lost Horizon, by the British writer James Hilton. His years of college had taught him to turn to the copyright page first. Published in 1933. He sat down and immersed himself in the story of a man crashing in an airplane in the high Himalayas and finding a magical valley of peace called Shangri-La. Carter remembered seeing the movie before the war, but the details were fuzzy in his memory, other than his date, an intense young brunette from Sarah Lawrence college who spent most of her time talking about the wonderful men of the International Brigades who had gone to fight Franco's fascists in Spain. In the end he had not passed her political litmus test—not radical enough and too confused when she talked about the importance of the dialectic. If she had just wanted to talk about Homer, Cicero, or Thucydides, he could have wooed her.

Two hours later he finished the short book. He mostly agreed with the oft-repeated theme of moderation in all things, whether it be food and drink, the passions, or lust for life. Such a Buddhist sentiment. But such an idea only worked in a world of mundane things. This war had taught him that in the face of evil, no extreme was too strong, and moderation just didn't make sense.

He looked at his watch—two o'clock in the morning, but he was not tired in the least. He had slept on the airplane ride up to Scapa Flow, plus his body was used to sleep deprivation. Another book was required.

Rice was hunched over the table in the middle of his study. In front of him was a silver globe the size of a man's fist. The light from a table lamp cast a circle of light that illuminated the globe and his hands, but kept his face in shadow. His fingers gently caressed the surface of the globe; Carter thought that he heard the colonel murmuring softly.

Carter stopped and watched, not wanting to intrude. The sound of bells from the anchorage, sounding the change of the watch, came faintly and Carter was surprised at how far sound carried at night in that remote location. After several more minutes of rubbing the globe, Rice ceased his whispering and leaned forward to kiss the globe, like a father with a child.

"What brought you downstairs?" Rice asked without turning around. He reached for a small wooden box and placed the globe inside.

Carter started and pushed aside his embarrassment. Getting embarrassed meant surrendering his self-control, giving control over him to another person, and he had tried for years to avoid feeling that emotion. "I just came down to find another book."

"You found the book I gave you boring?"

"No, I read quite quickly and I finished it, plus a novel I happened to have. I'd like to borrow another book, if I may."

Rice stood and went to the light switch. "Please come in. Which novel did you read?"

"*Lost Horizon*, sir."

"Ah, yes, the story of Shangri-La in Tibet. I was there before the war. In Tibet, I mean—not Shangri-La, since that's just a myth. The SS had sent an expedition to Lhasa in 1938. They fancied themselves to be scientists, taking measurements of Tibetan heads and their physique, trying to prove their twisted ideas about race. They thought that the Tibetans were a branch of Aryans, which is at least better than assuming that they were subhuman.

"They had another, more sinister purpose. They sought any Buddhist relics that might be useful in the coming war. I flew into Lhasa and did my best to thwart them, working behind the scenes so that they would not realize that we knew what they were up to. It got hairy there for a while, but they went home empty-handed.

"The Tibet expedition was only one of many sent around the world by the Nazis, seeking objects of power. They sent them to Egypt, South America, India, Persia, Yemen, the Maldives, South Africa, Afghanistan, China, even Canada. I've probably forgotten some of the places and we may not have even been aware of all of them. The Nazis even sought the Ark of the Covenant, but we sent an American archaeologist by the name of Jones to take care of that. He was also useful later in stopping them from getting the Holy Grail. We had missed finding out about that effort, so we were lucky there. We even thought of recruiting him into the Occult Science Service, but he was too independent to become a good soldier."

"The Holy Grail?" Carter couldn't keep the skepticism out of his voice.

Rice smiled. "I know that you find my words incredible, but if you stay around me long enough you will find that the world is a much stranger place than our science and rationalism have led us to believe. So, you came down for another book. Do you want to browse or shall I recommend another one?"

"Why don't we do both."

Rice selected the third volume from Sir James George Frazer's *The Golden Bough: A Study in Magic and Religion*, of which he said, "Not always reliable, but always interesting." Carter selected a volume of Plutarch's *Parallel Lives*, the volume that included the lives of the Greek Epaminondas and the Roman Scipio Africanus, all written, of course, in the original Greek.

Carter tucked the two thick volumes under his arm. "May I ask what you were doing when I came down here, sir?"

After a moment's hesitation, Rice said, "You saw me using what I have come to call my Guide. It's a most extraordinary device. Very ancient, I do believe. It answers questions and shows me the way to places."

"Where did you get it?"

"In Yemen, many years ago. An old woman gave it to me and refused any offer of payment."

"What does your Guide tell you?" Carter asked.

"That we must stop Krohn at all costs."

CHAPTER TWENTY-SIX

Karl Steinhauer was frustrated. It was easier to put women out of his mind if he was not around them. Now, for three days he had been in close proximity to that red-haired girl—eating next to her, sleeping near her, even watching over her during her private activities. Other than his mother, he had never been this close to a woman. It was almost like living with a wife. He could barely stand it anymore.

He could tell that his brother was feeling the same frustration. When they landed at Narvik, the colonel decided that they had to stay during the short night so that the aircrew could get some sleep. All three of them were looking pretty ragged, with dark bags under their eyes and the slow shuffle that Karl recognized from men who had been in battle too long.

As the aircrew left to find bunks in the airfield barracks, the pilot had explained that night was only four hours long at this latitude in early May. Krohn agreed that they could have eight hours to sleep.

"I need to send a radio message," Krohn told his soldiers. "You stay here and guard the girl. If one of you has to leave, the other must stay."

The colonel disappeared and Karl sat across from the girl, staring at her, imagining what her body would look like without her dress on. That just drove his craving to new heights.

"How many reichsmarks to do you have?" Karl asked his brother. "I'm going to go find a woman that we can use."

They pooled their cash and found that they had almost

seventy reichsmarks. That should be enough. Karl pulled on his overcoat, climbed down from the plane, and looked around the airfield.

The mountains thrust up near the end of the runway, which explained why the plane had made an unusual turn just before landing. A damp air coming in off the fiord caused him to pull his overcoat tight around his body.

Though the sun had about gone down, and the lighting was poor, he saw a stream of smoke coming from a stovepipe on the roof of a nearby hangar. He walked over and opened the door. Inside it was much warmer. Three Luftwaffe ground crewmen worked on an airplane with a long, narrow fuselage, twin tails, and two engines. Its bulb-like cockpit bristled with the barrels of a machine guns pointing forward. Two more machine guns pointed aft, one above and one below.

"Good evening," Karl greeted them. "We just flew in. What kind of plane is this?"

"A Dornier," one the men said, putting down his wrench and wiping his greasy hands on a cloth. The other two men turned away from the open engine cowling to take a good look at the newcomer.

"I'm just a soldier," Karl said, laughing. "What's a Dornier for?"

"Attacking ships."

"Got any ships lately?"

The mechanic shook his head. "No. We haven't flown for a month now. Not enough fuel. Besides, the war is almost over. You heard that the Führer died?"

"Yes, I did." Karl looked down at the hard-packed dirt of the hangar floor, confused about how he felt.

"Why are you here?" the mechanic asked.

Karl shrugged. "I don't know. Secret mission, I guess. We have some time before we leave."

"Your plane is the one that we are using our last fuel reserves for?" one of the other men asked.

"I guess so."

"No idea what your mission is?"

"Not the least," Karl said. "But I don't feel good about it, so I want some comfort. Could you direct me to where I might find a loving woman? I have a bit of money."

All three Luftwaffe men laughed. "Bad luck, soldier," the mechanic said. "They have all quit their work."

"What?"

"A week ago all the bitches got together and told us that they wouldn't service Germans anymore. They said it was their patriotic duty. Only Norwegians get them now."

"This is outrageous," Karl exclaimed. "You have a brothel, don't you? What about the women there?"

"We had a brothel," the mechanic said. "A good one too, with lots of pretty women, but they all quit. The war is ending and everything has changed."

Karl thanked them for the information and left, finding that night had completely descended on the airfield. He breathed in the freezing air and walked down the runway. The world had turned upside down. The Fatherland was falling, Hitler was dead, and now prostitutes had developed opinions.

A sense of foreboding had been building in him ever since they left Germany. He was not a man given to introspection, but he could trace the sense of dread back to four months ago. That is when Father and Mother had died in Munich, from bombs meant for a railroad yard that fell two miles short. At least that is what the graves officer said. Fritz had never cared for Father, a man quick with the belt, but Mother still lived in his heart.

He hadn't thought about his parents since then, but now the memories marched forward and demanded attention. Father was a stonecutter, a staunch member of a Nazi labor union, and so proud when his twins joined the Hitler Youth. It had been fun, learning to shoot, camping, flying in airplanes, even training to jump out of the airplanes. That first jump, flying high over fields recently harvested, was better than being with a woman. As soon as they were old enough, both volunteered for the Luftwaffe to be paratroopers. They fought in Norway, near Oslo, only firing their rifles once; they fought in France, much more fighting; and then dropped onto Crete in 1941. That was hell, a bitter fight that teetered on the edge of defeat, with so many of their friends lying dead, killed by the British or by the treacherous Cretans. Fritz enjoyed burning the villages in revenge. After Crete, Hitler decreed that paratroopers could not be used in their natural role ever again, and so they fought as infantry in Sicily and Italy. Mother was ailing and Father, who had become an important union leader in Munich, arranged for his sons to be transferred to the SS and billeted near their home. Only seven months ago, early last winter, they had joined the platoon assigned to Colonel Krohn. Easy duty.

And then his parents had died. Karl scuffed his foot against the hard surface of the runway, wishing that he had something to kick. He wanted to kick someone, pour his frustration into his fists and feet, break skin and bones, cause his hurt to go into them.

He thought about leaving the airbase and finding someone to hurt. There must be people on the streets of Narvik. Maybe he could find a woman and satisfy his craving. He had done it before. Except he didn't have a pass and the guards at the gate would surely stop him.

That left only the redhaired girl.

CHAPTER TWENTY-SEVEN

Jean-Paul Mann, Kisecawchuck to his people, woke early, as was his custom. The sun had not yet made its appearance. Mann pulled on his clothes, knelt on the cold floor, pulled out the rosary that his mother had made for him, and recited his morning prayers.

When the first rays skimmed across the water of Scapa Flow and touched his window, he went outside. The air still felt damp from the night's dew. He knelt again, picked up a pinch of dirt, pressed it to his lips, and greeted the Sun Father and the Earth Mother.

Having satisfied his spiritual needs, Mann went into the colonel's house. He lit the kitchen stove and started breakfast. Toast and porridge, as usual. Because they had guests, he had used some of the ration coupons to buy six eggs—one for everyone.

"Good morning, Paul," Angela said as she opened the door, carrying a large wrapped bundle. "A courier just brought a package for Edgar."

Rice appeared at the other door, already dressed and ready for the day. The three made a good team, beyond being an aircrew together. Each liked to rise early and Rice made their work pleasant enough. He was not career military, wedded to protocol and formal relations. When they were alone, they even used their first names, though neither Mann or Wright could bring themselves to call the colonel Edgar.

"Ah, Angela," Rice said. "The package is here, thank you."

"What is it, sir?" Mann asked.

Rice laughed. "A secret for the moment. You will know soon enough."

"I don't know half the time what you are up to, sir," Mann said. "But if I might inquire...we usually work as a small team and you keep our activities secret. Why have you brought those two Rangers and the refugee along?"

"The Guide told me that we needed to bring them."

Angela took out the bread and cut it into slices to make into toast. "The Guide is not always right."

"I know that our adventure in Madrid did not work out as planned," Rice said. "I have been thinking about it, though, and have concluded that perhaps I just interpreted the instructions from the Guide wrong."

Angela put down the knife and turned to the colonel. "That may be an answer that comforts you, but it doesn't comfort me."

Rice smiled, shrugged, and left the kitchen.

An hour later, just as everyone was finishing a leisurely breakfast, the colonel returned to the kitchen. "Would everyone please come into the study."

The five followed him and found large, glossy, black-and-white photographs spread across the central table. Rice went to the head of the table, and looked at each of their faces in turn as they ringed the table, his fingers pressed down on the wood.

"I received intelligence about two weeks ago that the Nazis were up to something on Bear Island, and I believe that it is the next step in our plans."

"Where's Bear Island?" Carter asked. Having stayed up so late reading, the major looked bleary-eyed.

"The Norwegians call it Bjørnøya, which means Bear Island, and it is located here in the western Barents Sea, about halfway between the northernmost tip of Norway and the Svalbard archipelago." Rice rolled out a map and pointed. "I contacted the Norwegian government in exile in London and asked for as much information as they could give me. They sent a packet of somewhat useful papers."

"Does anyone live there?" Wright asked.

"Apparently not. Occasionally there have been temporary settlements, whalers and fishermen mostly. There was a coal mine at one point, but it was abandoned in the early thirties. A casualty of the Depression, I think. The island is too far north for much vegetation or anything else of value, other than minerals."

"Are there bears on the island?" Carter asked.

"Sometimes. Polar bears come across the ice during the winters and sometimes they are trapped there for the summer when the sea ice melts. It is much warmer than one would expect for being that far north of the Arctic Circle. A sea current from the south brings up warmer water."

"Why are you interested in it, sir?" Napier asked.

"Two days ago a long-range PBY Catalina flew over the island and took pictures. Quite a long flight, really at the limit of its range, but it got good photos. British and Norwegian intelligence thought that the island was abandoned, but as you can see from that photo, there is an airfield there now."

"What's this here?" Carter pointed at a shadow that seemed to be a sharp point near the airfield.

Rice looked at his notes. "According to the photo analysts, that's a radio tower. It's probably needed because they are so far north."

"So we have an airfield and a few smudges that may be buildings," Wright said as she looked closer at the photograph with a magnifying glass that she had retrieved from a drawer at the desk. Carter noticed that she knew exactly where to find the glass. "I don't see any airplanes, a hangar, or even any sign of people. How do we know that it isn't abandoned?"

Rice shrugged. "I agree that we don't know much. It may be abandoned, but I don't think so."

"So what's your plan?" Carter asked.

"A two-pronged attack," Rice said. "Three days ago the destroyer *HMS Lydd*, with sixty commandos aboard her, left Scapa Flow. It will reach Bear Island tomorrow morning. They have two cutters aboard that should be able to land the troops.

And tomorrow we will fly up there along with two other aircraft, each carrying sixteen fully laden commando paratroopers. If the landing troops need help to take the airfield, then the paratroops will be there to help them."

"We will land on an airfield that has just been secured?" Wright asked. "How far away is this island?"

"1,232 miles."

She swallowed and looked at the map. "We will have maybe two hours of flying time left once we get there. We won't have enough fuel to go anywhere else."

"That is true," Rice said.

"'Audacious' is a kind description of this plan, sir," Carter said, keeping his expression neutral.

"You made a plan for attack before you even got these photographs?" Napier asked.

"Yes, I did," Rice said. "Your concerns have merit, gentlemen and lady, but time is too pressing for us to be overcautious."

"When do we leave?" Wright asked, the tone of her voice indicating that she found the need for further discussion unnecessary.

"Tomorrow morning at 0700."

Napier had replaced his bandage with a black stocking cap, pulled down snugly on his head. The cap pulled on his stitches and rubbed his tender skin if he was careless and jarred his cap. Pressing his fingers into his ears, he called out, "You may fire."

The Jewish refugee fired thirty rounds from his carbine, one round at a time, emptying the magazine. The target had only a few holes in it afterwards.

Napier grunted. Perhaps Rosenberg could provide covering fire when they needed it. The bright sunlight felt pleasantly warm to the sergeant, but not so much that he had doffed his jacket. Surrounded by earthen berms to protect the surrounding naval base from stray rounds, the firing range gave them a feeling of isolation from the busy activities of a navy at war.

"Change your magazine as quick as you can," the sergeant

instructed.

The refugee ejected the magazine, stuck it in his pocket, pulled out his next magazine from his ammunition belt, and fumbled as he tried to slip it back into his carbine. The magazine fell to the ground.

"I'm used to bolt-action rifles," Rosenberg said as he knelt. Napier saw the flash of blue numbers tattooed into the Jew's wrist as his sleeve rode up his arm. Rosenberg picked up the magazine, blew on it to make sure that no sand had gotten inside, and managed to get the magazine into his weapon.

"No problem," Napier said. "I'm trying to teach you in a couple of hours what we normally would take a week to teach. Now fire slowly and get as many hits as you can."

Fingers went back into the ears. Several hundred brass shells already littered the ground. Rosenberg had said that he had some training from the Polish army before the war, and after escaping from the ghetto, he had gotten some more training with the Polish Home Army, a group of partisans who had lived in the woods, waiting for their opportunity to rise up and strike back at the Germans. Then he had gone back into the Warsaw Ghetto to fight with his kinsmen.

This time there were more holes in the paper. The target was a good three feet wide and set up forty feet away. Napier figured that the refugee had hit the target about a third of the time.

"Let's take a break," Napier said.

"I have never been a great shot," Rosenberg said.

Napier nodded his acknowledgment of this apparent fact. "Chewing gum?" Napier offered the pack to Rosenberg after pulling out a piece for himself.

"You Americans and your chewing gum," the refugee said with a smile as he took the offered pack. "I really missed that after I came home from New York. Such an odd custom."

"The Army gives it to us for free," Napier said. "The children like it. We are always giving it away to the young 'uns in France and Belgium. They also like the chocolate."

The two men sat on a bench and chewed their gum. For the

first time since he had been hit in the head, Napier felt more like himself; he was calm instead of being on edge. Beyond the barren berm he could see circling sea birds and faintly hear their cries. It reminded him of back home, when a farmer plowed a field and the seagulls descended on the harvest of worms and bugs that had been exposed. Oddly enough, Utah had seagulls—the California Seagull, to be precise—and it was even the state bird. He suspected these gulls were circling a refuse dump or maybe one of the ships had just dumped its garbage overboard.

"I've got something more interesting than chewing gum," Rosenberg said, reaching into his pack and pulling out a bottle of Scotch whiskey.

"Where'd you get that?"

Rosenberg looked down at the ground. "A man learns to acquire things during a war."

"You're not in the camps anymore," Napier said. "I imagine that *acquiring things* was a matter of survival then, but now it would be stealing. I assume that this came from the colonel's liquor cabinet?"

"Yes."

"Why don't we just return it and not tell anyone," Napier suggested, and reached into his own pack. "Besides, I was saving this for the end of our day, but why not right now." He pulled two bottles of beer out of his own pack.

Rosenberg laughed. "And where did those come from?"

"Bought them at the pub in town," Napier said. "As medicine, you know."

Napier took out his combat knife and popped the caps. He was only half-joking about the beer being medicine. He was not given to drinking; he broke a promise to his mother every time he touched a drop, but occasionally he craved a brew. Past experience had also taught him that a bit of alcohol would distract him from dwelling on the dream. Aoife had been there once again last night, so sad and needing him to find her.

"Ah, that's bitter stuff," Rosenberg said after taking a long swallow. "The English know how to make good beer."

Napier grunted in agreement.

"Have you ever known a Jew?" Rosenberg asked.

"There was a family back home in Utah. They owned a grocery store. Not a company store, owned by the mine owners, but one they owned themselves. They gave a fair deal. Their youngest daughter was a few years older than me. Very pretty, and I fancied her, but only from a distance, never to her face."

"Any in the army?"

Napier felt a pleasant buzz coming over himself. Two beers and he would be face down, examining the dirt from an inch away. Embarrassing that a child of Scottish parents couldn't hold his liquor.

"There were a couple of Jews in boot camp," Napier said, feeling his tongue loosen up. "I found out that they were Jews in the mess one day. It was really crowded and there were some empty seats next to these three guys. I was heading over to sit down when some Joe with a New York accent told me not to sit there because those were Jews. I stopped and asked him what was wrong with Jews. I was pretty naive then. He told me that they had killed Jesus Christ. I looked over at them and said that they looked too young to have killed Christ; I mean, that happened nineteen hundred years ago. The Joe asked me if I was a smartass. I told him to go play with himself and went and sat with the Jews."

"What happened?" Rosenberg asked.

"Chatted with them for a while. They were in a different company and I didn't see them much. The Joe met me outside and tried to teach me a lesson."

"And?"

Napier looked at the refugee, noticing how the clothes fit oddly on the emaciated frame, and the stubble on his chin. Needed to get that man a razor. "I'm sorry, what was the question?"

"What happened with the Joe? Did he beat you up?"

"No," Napier answered. "I've never lost a fight in my life. I'm like Superman, in the comics, muscles of steel. It also helped that I used to box in an amateur league. Thirteen wins, eleven by KO, no losses, no draws."

Napier flexed his right arm, though only the forearm was visible below his rolled up sleeve. Muscles bulged there. He had never lifted weights or done any of the other exercises that other kids did for sports; he had been born husky and strong. Perhaps God had given him this strength in exchange for not having any ability to hold his alcohol. Like Samson in the Bible.

Napier pushed out his arms as far as they would go and said, "I won even though I have these short arms. Took a lot of punches in the face getting close enough to do damage to the other guy."

Rosenberg laughed. "I would like to say that I've never lost a fight."

The American swallowed more of his beer. The headache that had tormented him ever since being hit on the head was gone, replaced by a pleasant buzz.

"I was called a Christ-killer once, on the street in New York," Rosenberg said. "I was so astonished to find the same prejudice in America that I thought that I had left behind in Poland that I just stood there gawking like some rube just off the boat."

"At least we don't kill our Jews," Napier said.

"Sometimes Jews were killed in America, but it's true that the hatred didn't run as deep as in Europe. Besides, the Jews didn't kill Jesus, the Romans did."

"That's true."

"All this anti-Semitism neglects to recognize the Jewish contribution to world history. We gave the world the Bible, a great work of scripture. We gave the world the idea of monotheism. We gave the world Christianity and Islam, which evolved from Judaism. People always seem to forget that Jesus was a Jew. Christianity was a fulfillment of certain ideas of Judaism, though it eventually abandoned most of what made a Jew a Jew.

"Look at all the scientists in the past century and today. See how many of them are Jewish. Much higher percentage than you would expect. That's because we Jews emphasize education, teach our boys to think, and want to make our contribution, even if we are despised."

His tirade wound down, as if Rosenberg was exhausted, so he just sipped some more of his beer.

"Bad things happen," Napier said, emptying the last of his beer. It was a strong brew, leaving a slight taste of sawdust in his mouth. He felt so melancholy that tears trickled from the edges of his eyes. "I did a bad thing a while ago." He coughed to clear his throat, took a deep breath and continued. "I haven't told anyone else. I couldn't tell the major or any of my buddies. I just couldn't face them. It happened just a month ago, when we were near the Rhine. I shot a woman. No one saw me do it...I didn't do it on purpose. We were in the middle of a fight in a village and she came through a door and surprised me. I thought that she was a German soldier. Her dress was grey, the same color as their uniforms, and I only saw her out of the edge of my vision. Pure instinct and then she was dead. I think that she was a grandma, though this war is hard on people and she may have just been a mother. Doesn't really matter."

Tears fell from his face to the dirt of the shooting range.

"We have all done things in this war that we are ashamed of," Rosenberg said, setting down his own empty bottle, and absently patting the American on the shoulder. "A war can make you choose the wrong choices, even if they seemed right at the time. War makes you less of a man. At least, it did that to me."

CHAPTER TWENTY-EIGHT

They called it Bear Island and Aoife found it to be a cold and desolate place. As they flew in, she looked down at the island, shaped like a triangle with the southernmost point bumpy with mountains and sheer cliffs that reached down into the green water of the ocean. The northern part of the island was flatter, with patches of snow and small lakes and ponds. Not far from a cove with a rocky beach, near a large hill, was a graveled airfield. Other than a metal tower some twenty meters high, there were several small buildings all covered with dirt, whether to disguise them or provide insulation, she couldn't tell. No hangar, no vehicles, no other obvious signs of life.

There were some small tufts of grass, and moss grew on some of the rocks, but that was it, except for the birds. They sat on the tower and she saw a flock of dark spots over near the ocean.

After they landed, everyone disembarked, and she gasped at the bitter cold that swept up her legs.

Krohn offered her a grey army coat, which she wrapped around herself. It came down to her ankles and the sleeves were much too long. That was better, but still the breeze ran up her legs.

"Can I change into some pants, sir?" she asked the colonel.

He turned from where he was waiting to greet the uniformed men that had emerged from some of the huts and were approaching. "Of course not," he said. "Women wear dresses, not pants."

"May I stay in the airplane?" she asked, hating every word, because they showed that she had no control over even the most basic acts in her life.

Krohn shrugged.

Aoife climbed back into the plane, went back to her seat and pulled her legs and feet up inside the coat, wrapping the bottom of the coat up like swaddling an infant. She watched out the window as the colonel talked with the Germans already on the island.

She had felt grateful when Krohn returned before the solider. The feeling of gratitude, a sense of obligation to the Nazi colonel, repelled her. But the threat from the twins was more immediate. She had listened to their conversation about wanting a prostitute, and when the twin had returned, he did not act like he had found a woman for money.

She knew that there was only one reason that they wanted to keep her a virgin. The same thing that had happened to her friends at the camp.

Human sacrifice.

CHAPTER TWENTY-NINE

Angela Wright pushed the engine throttles forward, released the brakes, and *Jenny* rolled down the runway. She called her aircraft *Jenny* after her best pal back in Kansas City, a tomboy with more guts than common sense. They didn't go to the same schools because Jenny was a Negress, the daughter of the family that lived in a cottage behind the family home. Her mother was the maid and her father served as the chauffeur and gardener. With both her parents always at either the office or the hospital, Wright admitted to herself that Jenny and her parents were more of a family to her than her own parents.

While most pilots of multi-engine aircraft had a mascot or other image painted on the sides of their cockpits, Wright chose a different location. She had painted a picture of Jenny on the nose of the Skytrain herself, taking care to get the tightly curled hair just right and bring out that mischievous sparkle in Jenny's eyes. Jenny had the white wings of an angel that swept back on either side of the cockpit. Polio took Jenny when she was sixteen, happening fast, paralyzing her body so that she couldn't breathe. Though Wright had prayed for her friend, she was grateful that the girl had died. For Jenny to be a cripple never seemed right.

The British called the C-47 the Dakota, though it was exactly the same plane as the Skytrain, made in the same factories. The two Dakotas loaded with commandos had taken off before the *Jenny* and were circling the airfield. As she joined them, they turned northwards, with Wright trailing. Even though she was relying on the pilots in the lead plane to guide them, she kept her own navigation track.

Ocean navigation was always a challenge; she had gotten spoiled by checking her position by looking down to find a river, coastline, city, or road. When they passed over the northern-most of the Orkney Islands, she marked the time, her heading, airspeed, and the prevailing winds with a pencil on her chart.

Rice looked over at his pilot, her brow creased with concentration as she scribbled notes onto the folded chart attached to a clipboard. Angela was a beautiful woman, with a sharp nose, high cheekbones, and a full mouth. The keen mind and tongue ready with pointed words also made her interesting.

While he enjoyed her company, the fact that she was a woman meant nothing to him. Rice was celibate—not by choice, but by nature. In the three centuries that he could remember, he had never once had an erection. He understood sexual attraction only as an intellectual abstraction, information obtained by reading, listening, and observing the tension between the sexes.

His observations of human behavior had also taught him that people responded to self-confidence, seeking out the certainty that they saw in another person that they did not feel in themselves. Rice assiduously projected his self-confidence. In most cases, he felt it was justified, but he admitted that this adventure did not inspire the same feelings in himself. By nature he was a cautious man, and this was the most audacious venture that he had ever taken. At least that he could remember.

He was trusting his Guide. The silver globe had never failed him and of all the strange things that he had seen in the world, it was the most magical.

Carter, Napier, and Rosenberg sat on the floor of the aircraft between the seats, the pieces of their carbines spread out on blankets before them. The air smelled of gun oil. Napier occasionally pointed out a part to the refugee and told him how to handle it.

The men chatted absently among themselves, telling silly jokes and stories from home, anything to keep their minds occupied and off of the fight before them. Carter knew that Rice's plan didn't have the three men doing anything more than providing security for themselves, since all of the fighting would be over by the time that they landed. No plan, though, survived contact with the enemy, and this plan relied on an enemy being surprised and acting in a certain way. In Carter's experience, the enemy never cooperated.

"Will Aoife be on Bear Island?" Napier asked.

"I don't know," Carter said. "The colonel thinks that is where Krohn has gone. And if he kept the girl with him and he actually went there, they should be there. Lots of if's, but we don't have anything else to go on."

"She is there," Napier said, with a certainty in his voice that Carter found chilling. "I know because I had a dream."

Carter raised his eyebrows. "I assume that it was an unusual dream?"

"Yes, three nights in a row with similar dreams."

"In what way?" Carter asked.

"In every dream I see Aoife," Napier said. "In the first two dreams she was in an airplane, with handcuffs. In the last dream she was in a dark room and it is cold. In all the dreams she wants me to come quickly and rescue her."

"That's a very interesting dream, Sergeant," Rosenberg said. "Do you often have such dreams?"

"Never."

"She's a pretty woman. It makes sense that you should dream about her," Carter said.

Napier looked indignant. "It's not one of those kind of dreams, sir."

Mann had come back to join them, part of a regular break from radio duty. "You say that you have had this dream three times?"

"Yes."

"A dream seen three times is a powerful vision from your

spirit helper," Mann pronounced solemnly

"I don't have a spirit helper," Napier said.

"We all have spirit helpers, it's just that some of us are more aware of them and know how to talk to them."

"Do you have a spirit helper, Paul?" Carter asked.

After some hesitation, Mann said, "Yes."

"May I know more?"

"I am a Woods Cree and my spirit helper comes from the forest. It is a robin. Not a real robin, but the essence of what makes a robin. I came in contact with my spirit helper during my vision quest and he has been with me ever since. He brings visions to guide my life. We Cree believe that the sacred can come from many directions and the Cree have always been open to religious ideas from others. That is how I can follow my spirit helper and still worship Christ and believe in the Catholic tradition."

"What do my dreams mean?" Napier asked.

"Only you can find that answer," Mann said. "Not me or anyone else."

Mann returned to his radio duty and the conversation among the three men lapsed, each forced into their own minds for company. Carter finished the ritual of assembling his rifle, wiped his hands as clean as he could get them without hot water and soap, and climbed back into his seat. He pulled out the other weapon that he carried.

Carter disliked the Colt .45 that the Army had wanted to issue him. He was always afraid that the slide on the semi-automatic would jam and he would die trying to get his pistol to work. So he favored a revolver that his father had given him. It was forty years old, made of the finest Bethlehem steel, six shots, and had never jammed in firing thousands of rounds. His father had carried the pistol in the Great War, shooting Germans in the trenches, and now it served to kill more of the master race.

Of course, his real killing weapon was the carbine that he carried, thirty rounds in each magazine. He looked over at Napier and Rosenberg. The two men were dozing, their carbines lying on seats near them. Winter gear, packs, boxes of food, and everything else that they could think of was strapped down as well as they could manage in a airplane interior that was designed for comfort, not utility.

Carter slipped the revolver back into his holster, buttoned the flap securely and settled down to sleep.

Wright marked her chart with the time at their approximate location. She estimated that they were making 157 miles per hour, and at this rate had another four hours of flying. Putting the clipboard aside, she brushed away the sandwich crumbs that littered her jacket.

"Sir, we have a headwind," she reported to Rice. "It's increasing our fuel consumption."

"Will we make it?" Rice asked from his copilot's seat.

"Yes, but our margin of error is getting smaller."

Nothing more to be said on that account. She peered out the window, making sure that she could see the other two aircraft in front of them. Every ten seconds or so, no matter what else she was doing, other than going to the head, she made sure that she was in position.

Scattered clouds appeared ahead, several thousand feet below their path. They were flying over three miles above the ocean surface, at 17,000 feet, above the predicted cloud cover. Of course, meteorologists didn't know everything, and had failed to predict the headwind. That's why they called weather predication an art and not a perfect science.

She had never flown into combat. Had never expected to. In her own way she appreciated the War Department rules that had kept her out of way of flak and fighters.

She picked up her clipboard again. Concentrating on navigation kept her mind off of how scared she was.

CHAPTER THIRTY

Louis Batten, Lieutenant Commander in His Majesty's Royal Navy, captain of the *HMS Lydd*, stood on the starboard flying bridge of his destroyer. The flying bridge was a sort of open balcony off to the side of the enclosed bridge. He wore a blue sea coat, buttoned up tightly. The sky was mostly clear, with a light breeze coming off the forward bow, enough to flick up whitecaps. Occasional sea ice had been sighted and Batten was concerned that his destroyer not turn into another *Titanic*.

The ship was making a steady fifteen knots, conserving fuel, in what promised to be the last mission of the war. His crew of one hundred and fifty-eight officers and sailors was sharing quarters with sixty commandos and it was a pretty tight fit. The *Lydd* had been assigned this task because she had ferried commandoes on two earlier raids on Norway. Those had been quick night dashes, where the soldiers mostly stayed on deck, out of the way. He admired the commandoes, brave men who dared go into the occupied countries of Europe even though Hitler decreed that every one caught be executed. The policy violated the Geneva Convention, which the Germans usually followed with regard to the British, but the success of the audacious commando raids had driven the madman of Europe into a tantrum.

Batten put the binoculars to his eyes and scanned the horizon. He didn't expect to see much. Most of the German fleet had been sunk, and the U-boat threat had mostly disappeared, confined to port by the lack of fuel. Batten was not regular Navy, just a

Merchant Marine officer brought in from the reserve who had proved himself. It sounded childish, almost unmanly, but all he wanted was to get back to Liverpool and see his mother. She was ailing and needed her only child to care for her. His father had been ill for years, and she had nursed him without complaint, before he died in '42; now she needed her last kin. That responsibility drew him more strongly than the call of the sea.

Again he put the binoculars up to his eyes. There, a patch on the horizon. It had to be Bear Island. It was in the right spot and there was no other land for hundreds of miles. In just a couple of hours, he would be landing the commandos.

"Periscope!" The lookout shouted from above. "Directly to port. Six hundred yards."

Batten looked up to see the crewman pointing to the left. He moved with experience as he hurtled through the bridge to get to the port flying bridge. "Flank speed," he said in a calm voice as he passed the helmsman. "Hard to starboard."

As he pulled the outside hatch open, he told the officer of the watch, "Sound general quarters."

The claxon began to make its grating sound as he reached the port flying bridge and flung himself up against the bulwark. He didn't need his binoculars to see the two white tracks in the water.

Torpedoes.

The ship was already turning away, following his order. The first fish missed the bow by a good twenty yards, but the turn was too slow to avoid the second. The bow of his ship exploded in a burst of spray and fragments of metal. He felt a sting on his cheek and a burning sensation that brought tears to his eyes.

Batten stumbled into the bridge, moving by instinct. "All stop."

His greatest concern was that continuing forward motion would just drive more water into the ship, possibly breaking through watertight bulkheads. He heard the jiggles of the message being sent to the engine room.

"Sir," the helmsman said, a lad from Norwich. "You're

bleeding."

Batten felt a cloth being pressed against his cheek. "What's our situation?" he mumbled through the pain and the blood in his mouth. The shrapnel must have cut a hole through his cheek.

"Sir, the bow's torn all to hell and we are settling down forward." He recognized the voice of the officer of the watch, Ensign Marsh, only nineteen years old and his most inexperienced officer. That's why Batten had been on duty with him.

He spat the blood in his mouth out onto the deck. "Where's the sub?"

"Can't see her periscope, sir," March called out from the flying bridge. "I'll bet she dived after firing the torpedoes."

Batten wiped his eyes with his sleeve and found his blurry vision improved. He spat out blood again. Two priorities presented themselves, stopping the ship from sinking and being prepared to kill that sub when it resurfaced.

The ship lurched abruptly to one side, leaning heavily to the port. Batten grabbed hold of the frame of the hatch and slid out onto the flying bridge. He looked forward and was dismayed to see that the destroyer had settled down forward far enough that the tip of the bow was underwater. The list must have been at least twenty degrees and now water was making its inevitable way further aft.

A captain hates to think the thoughts, but he had no choice. His ship was sinking.

"Abandon ship," he said quietly, as if the sea gods wouldn't hear him. He spat again, then shouted, "All hands, abandon ship!"

The bell sounded its frightening wail and Batten observed his crew running back and forth. The commandos, already dressed in their combat gear, were doing their best to help. The two extra cutters on the deck were being slid directly into the water, along with the two longboats. Other men were inflating life rafts.

Batten knew these waters from escorting conveys on the run to Murmansk and Archangel, delivering vital supplies to the

Soviets. A man in the water lasted for no more than a half hour, and a man in an open boat might last a day, unless he had good gear to keep him warm.

"Mr. March," Batten called. "Make sure that a mayday is sent out. In the clear, damn the encryption. Our position is twenty miles south of Bear Island."

"Aye aye, sir." The young man rushed back to the radio room.

"You men down there," Batten called. "Make sure that you have weather gear. It's going to get cold out there."

What an awful way to end a war. He had no idea how many had been lost below to the torpedo, dozens certainly, and he had no idea if anyone was still trapped below. He just needed to get as many off the ship that he could.

The two cutters managed to pull away, men at their oars, riding low in the water from the number of commandos and sailors jammed aboard. The commandos had thrown away their weapons and packs to make more room. Already six life rafts had launched. He had a good crew and he was proud of them.

The ship made an odd slipping movement and Batten clung to the bulwark. The list increased to thirty percent; water from forward had reached the superstructure. Not too much longer now.

The two longboats were launched and two more life rafts joined them. Batten estimated that one hundred and twenty men had gotten away, not quite half, but the best that could be managed.

"Signal sent and the radioman is maintaining his post," Ensign Marsh said from behind him. "He thinks the signal is going out, but he's not sure."

"Thank you, Mr. Marsh," Batten said. "Damned bad luck to run into what must be one of the last U-boats."

"Quite so, sir." The words bubbled out of a quivering throat. "Perhaps Bear Island means something to them."

"Hard to believe."

"Look, sir. The U-boat."

Batten looked. The U-boat was actually surfacing, just three hundred yards away. Most odd behavior. Of course, the ship was listing so badly that the rear guns could not be brought to bear, and the forward gun turret was mostly underwater.

"Perhaps they will save some of our men," Marsh said, his voice full of hope.

"Perhaps," Batten said. "Not much extra room on a sub. But it may be the only hope for any of our men. It will take days for anyone else to get here."

"Oh, my God," said March. "They are uncovering the deck gun."

"And mounting their machine guns. The bastards."

The *HMS Lydd* slid beneath waves, the bridge disappearing last, as if the ship was struggling to breathe its last breath. Her captain wept, distraught to see his helpless sailors and the commandos dying under a hail of shells and bullets.

Had the Nazis no honor?

CHAPTER THIRTY-ONE

The airfield was on the northern shore of the island near a large hill. The photographs had shown a few smaller hills nearby, as well as some mounds that, according to the Norwegian documents, were piles of tailings from a failed coal mine.

Because sound could carry so far and clearly in the Arctic air, depending on the winds, the commandos had decided on a clever tactic. Each aircraft circled around to the north and as it descended, the pilot shut down the engines. Ninety-five feet of wingspan gave the aircraft an excellent glide ratio so that they traveled fourteen feet for every foot that they dropped. The aircraft used the large hill to shield them from the view of anyone watching from the airfield.

Carter came forward to watch, crouching in the middle of the cockpit behind the two pilots. The nap had refreshed him and he felt a sense of eagerness, quite the opposite of how he had always approached battle before. Perhaps expecting the commandos to have all the fighting over before they landed had put him in an optimistic mood. He hoped not, since he didn't like the idea of other men doing his fighting for him.

Wright looked back at him. "You can stay there until we're about to land. Then I want you strapped in."

"Aye aye, captain," Carter responded. "How much fuel do we have left?"

"Forty-five minutes."

Wright reached forward and cut the engine power. The sudden quiet was unnerving, but as Carter's ears adjusted he heard the sound of air rushing past. The sky was wonderfully blue against the green ocean. The hilltop was marked with rills of snow, with patches of green struggling to assert themselves against the grey rock of the island. The two lead airplanes were coming in high enough, at about two thousand feet, high enough that the people in the third airplane could still see them across the top of the hilltop.

"Sir, our radios are being jammed." Mann's voice came over the loudspeaker.

Carter saw Rice thumb his intercom switch to talk. "Are you sure?"

"Positive." The Canadian was shouting so loudly that Carter could hear him directly through the open door back to the radio room, a strange pre-echo of the words coming over the loudspeaker. "Static over all the main bands. Too strong and constant to be sunspots."

"Does that take a lot of power?" Rice asked.

"Yes, sir."

"Shit, that means that they know we're coming."

"They're under fire!" Wright called out, her voice cracking. Carter and Rice leaned forward. A black splotch appeared next to one of the commando aircraft. Small forms started to tumble out of both planes at regular intervals, with what looked like flimsy filaments trailing behind them as the ripcords attached to the aircraft pulled their parachutes from their packs. The first blossomed out into a fully expanded canopy.

"Going to power," Wright said, pushing the starter button for one of the engines, then for the next one. "No reason to be quiet now."

As the engines sputtered to life, one of the aircraft in front of them exploded in a ball of flame. Carter felt sick, counting the falling men to see how many commandos had gotten out. Maybe half.

The other plane continued to drop its paratroopers.

Hans von Krohn shouted with glee, unable to maintain his cool demeanor when the first airplane blew up. He danced about for a moment before pawing for his holster, wanting to use his pistol to join the others in firing at the paratroopers.

When the U-boat that guarded the island caught the British destroyer unawares that morning, Krohn had been astonished. What was a destroyer doing here? When the captain of the submarine reported that some of the floating bodies had been clad in camouflage, Krohn knew the answer. Commandos, the scourge that had tried to hurt the Reich with dozens of pinpricks, had been on the ship. The only answer was that the Allies wanted to take Bear Island. The island itself meant nothing, which meant that they were really after Krohn.

The very idea shocked him. He knew that what he was doing might turn the tide of the war, but he had no reason to suppose that anyone else knew about it. There must be a spy in the SS, someone very well placed to know about his plans. Only a few dozen men who knew all the details.

Krohn had immediately demanded that the island be prepared for a full defense. A pretty weak request considering that there were only thirty-six other Germans on the island, and most of them were technicians. They possessed small arms only, except for the contents of two of the smaller huts.

Inside the huts, protected from the weather, were two old Flak 30 anti-aircraft guns, mounted on skids, with a single 20-millimeter cannon on each. More powerful equipment had replaced these prewar flak guns back in Germany, and the cannon could only send its shells up to 2200 meters, so it was no good against high-flying bombers, but it sowed fear in the hearts of low-flying pilots. Krohn took charge and had the huts ripped apart to expose the weapons. Everyone else mustered out on the airfield with whatever arms they could find, waiting in their parkas, sipping hot water to keep warm.

Krohn also ordered the generators run at full capacity, generating electricity for the radio antennas on the mooring mast to spit out as much radio noise as they could manage.

When the two transport aircraft came around the hill, everyone leaped into action. Four men manned each flak unit, one man continuously feeding twenty-round magazines into it, exhausting each magazine in less than a second. One man rotated the gun while the crew leader adjusted the elevation, tracking the target through his iron sights. The sound of the cannon firing sounded like large pieces of paper being brutally ripped to shreds.

The commandos descending below brown parachutes made wonderful targets. The Germans ran around, shooting up with rifles, pistols, even a flare gun. The flare arched up and veered away, spewing red sparks.

Krohn called out to his soldiers. "Karl and Fritz, I'm not even sure that our bullets are making it up that far. Take care, make your shots count, and leave no survivors."

The twins nodded and parted ways, hunting with their assault rifles.

Many of the commandos were armed with Thompson submachine guns. They struggled to get the guns out, aimed down between their feet, and fired back at the ground. A couple managed to toss down grenades as makeshift bombs.

Krohn felt it prudent to get closer to one of the buildings, really little more than a shed made of cast-off lumber. It made him feel safer. He fired up with his Luger pistol, excited to be part of the action, frustrated that his bullets would hit no one. Gravity arced them too much.

The second airplane seemed to have dropped all its troops. As it passed over the airfield, it abruptly swerved to the side. Its right engine trailed flames and it gracefully nosed forward and dove into the ground, about two miles beyond the airfield.

Krohn searched for his two warriors. He found one calmly shooting up at men still dangling in the sky. The other was making sure that the crumpled forms that had landed were dead, single shots to the head.

Wright pulled back on the control yoke, gunning the engines for more power, turning as quickly as she could to the right. They didn't want to fly into that kill zone. The airplane groaned as if being asked to stretch too much, but it performed as requested. They quickly gained altitude as they flew north out to sea. She rolled the aircraft as she did, so that she could look back and see what had happened.

The other plane had disappeared also.

Their path took them over the beach near the hill. From this height, the rocks forming the beach looked like gravel, which meant that they must have been the size of boulders.

"There's no ship down there," Rice said.

"What does that mean?" she asked.

"I don't know. The HMS *Lydd* should be standing off that beach near the airfield."

All three heads competed to see out Wright's side window. Nothing there. "Sunk," Rice said, all his discouragement weighing down that single word.

"We've got half an hour of fuel and are heading out to sea," Wright said, her voice surprisingly calm considering the tight white skin of her pursed lips.

"Obviously, we have to land on the island somehow or become fish," Carter said.

"Landing on the airfield would be suicide," Rice said, unbuckling his seatbelt. "We need to land somewhere else. Major, get the aerial photographs and find a place to land. I'm going to send a message to London."

Carter rushed back to the luggage secured at the back of the plane. He pawed through it, seeking the large bundle. He found it, cut the twine holding it with his knife, and pulled out the glossy photographs, spilling the rest of the papers to the floor.

"What's going on, sir?" Napier asked. "We saw an explosion."

"We're in the crapper, Sergeant."

Hunched over because the fuselage of this metal tube that

they were stuck in was too small, Carter begin to skim through the black and white images. Most of the southern part of the island was too rugged to even contemplate landing on. Carter's mind clicked through their options. They could crash land as far from the airfield as possible and hide from the Germans until a rescue party came. Would a rescue party come? Only if Rice got through to London and if they weren't forgotten during the chaotic celebration of the end of the war. Carter had heard too many stories of soldiers left behind on exercises or forgotten by higher command; sometimes the generals even deliberately forgot about someone because rescue was not convenient or feasible.

They could crash as close as possible to the airfield and launch their own assault. He looked over at Napier and Rosenberg; not much chance of success in that, even if there were still survivors among the commandos who were fighting. As distressing as the idea was, he realized that surrender might be the best option. The war was about almost over; it would just be a matter of waiting it out. Unless, of course, the Germans just shot them out of hand.

Carter found the three best photographs of the area near the airfield, left the rest in a mess on the deck, and pushed his way back up to the cockpit. As he passed the radio room, he met the grim-faced Rice.

"Any luck?" Carter asked.

"No, the jamming is still strong enough to stop us. Paul will keep trying."

"Will there be a rescue attempt, or at least a recon flight to see what happened to us?"

Rice shrugged. "I just don't know. All the Occult Service operations are pretty secret and we might be considered lost at sea."

"Perhaps surrender is our best option." The words felt nasty in his mouth.

"That may be our destiny," Rice said as he shook his head.

Carter shook his head in bewilderment. Destiny? That was

an idea for fools and the uneducated. Destiny implied that we all walked paths already laid for us, that we had no free will to make choices. Carter felt the urge to chew the colonel out, but the man outranked him; besides, this was hardly the time or place.

Rice returned to his copilot's seat. Carter crowded into the cockpit and shoved the three photographs forward.

"Looks to me like our best bet is to land there." He jabbed his finger at a place that looked bland enough from 14,000 feet in the air. "It's behind one of the smaller hills near the airfield. If we come in from the west, we'll keep the hill between us and those AA guns. I figure it's two miles or so from the Germans."

Wright tapped her fuel gauges, making sure that the needles weren't sticking and lying to her. "I figure we've got twenty minutes of flying left," she said. "That should be enough for me to fly over the site once and get a better look before we belly flop in."

"No landing gear?" Carter asked.

"Too great of a chance of one of the gears hitting a mushy spot and going in," she said. "That would ground loop us and send us ass over heels. Better get back to your seat and buckle up. Make sure that everything is secure back there."

"Aye aye, captain," he said, astonished that he had heard her swear. Hearing a woman curse was just so rare in his experience.

Back in the passenger cabin, Carter instructed the two others to unload the carbines and secure themselves. He checked the luggage and tugged on the loading straps. He decided that the paper and photographs that he had scattered about did not constitute a hazard and returned to his seat.

Pulling his seat belt tight, he relayed the plan to the others. He looked out his window and saw that they had come back over land again and were flying low enough to see that it was harsh ground, with scraps of grass here and there and far too many menacing rocks.

Carter prayed to his god, the divine man of power that his

mother had taught him to worship, his Lord Jesus. At Yale he had become a deist, and no longer believed that Jesus was there ready to intervene after a word of prayer, but Jesus was part of the Father, a clockmaker who created the universe and then stepped back. That didn't stop him from praying, because he found comfort in the act of supplication, but it did mean that he didn't expect to have his prayers answered.

CHAPTER THIRTY-TWO

What looked good on the photograph didn't look so nice from close up. Wright kept glancing quickly out of the window as she flew over the proposed landing spot at only five hundred feet. She would have preferred a nice meadow, with soggy mud, where the grass and shrubs covered up any hazards and made her feel better. With the sun low in the south, the shadow of every obstacle stood out strong and dark, perhaps making rocks and humps in the ground look larger than they really were.

No real choice in the matter. The lights signaling low fuel had started blinking ten minutes ago and were now solid red.

She tilted the control yoke to the right to sweep around in a great loop, feeling the familiar rush that came from the giant aircraft being completely under her control. Rice sat next to her, his hands light on his control yoke, following her lead, his face solemn in a way that she had never seen.

Perhaps she should say something, profound words that would comfort the others, or at least herself. Nothing came to mind, and besides, she had no time for words.

Three times she had seen aircraft come in on their bellies. Twice it had worked fine: a bomber coming back from Germany, shot up and trailing parts from a wing, had kissed the ground as sweetly as it could, sliding to a stop. Another time was in training when a new pilot forgot to drop his wheels. That was embarrassing, a total loss of the plane, but he had walked away from it alive enough to wash out of training. The last time was one of the other women pilots, back in Texas. One of her wheel supports had collapsed as she landed and skidded down the runway, spilling fuel that the sparks from the dragging wing ignited. By the time that they got to her, she was dead. Not really a belly landing, but close enough. The important point of all these memories that marched through her consciousness like the episodes that she could learn from was that they had all come down on runways, not an open field of menacing shadows.

Flaps down to kill speed and increase lift at low speeds, fuel lines turned off, electrical master switch off to reduce the chances of sparks, eyes fixed on the ground rushing by at over sixty miles per hour. She had hoped to avoid hitting any boulders, but the ground was just a blur. She had little control now; the aircraft was really just a dead weight with some aero-dynamic characteristics, a paper airplane made of lead. The engines sputtered as they died from the lack of fuel.

They were perhaps ten feet off the ground. She eased the control yoke back, ever so gently, as if she was afraid of the consequences.

The ground hit them. Like a luge sled out of control they slid across the rocks and dirt, the entire airplane vibrating and jumping. Metal against rock made an awful sound. The C-47 that had been her home for a year, always reliable, was dying.

Wright wrestled with the control yoke, moving them left and right, wanting to know if she had any influence. Even the smallest affect would make her feel better. Nothing. Perhaps the control wires running back had been cut by rocks punching through the belly. Did the wires for the tail run through the bottom of the plane? She couldn't remember and felt silly wondering about such a useless detail right then. Of course, the control surfaces were designed to move air, not ground, so it didn't really matter. Such silly, random thoughts at such a time.

"Save us, Jenny," she said under her breath, irrationally hoping that her friend in heaven could influence the airplane named after her.

The skidding airplane crested a rise and for a moment hung in the air, a microcosm of sanity, with the sound of scraping gone, a sense of flight, and then a hard jolt as they hit the ground again. Their skid had visibly slowed; Wright looked at their air speed indicator. The needle flopped back and forth, all over the range of numbers, from 0 to 400. Of course, the instrument that fed the information back to the dial had been ripped from the plane.

They slowed even more, perhaps down to as little as twenty miles an hour, and Wright breathed out in relief. They were going to survive.

The windshield in front was quite clear, though the side windows were covered with dust. A boulder as big as a house appeared in front of them. She hauled at the control yokes, trying desperately to turn the aircraft.

Completely futile.

The nose hit the boulder directly, crumpling the image of the Negress angel, shattering the cockpit windows, and pushing the front of the airplane into the cockpit.

Wright cried out as she felt her arms bend too far, then snap.

CHAPTER THIRTY-THREE

Carter blinked, taking a moment to collect his thoughts. The crash had been a wild ride, with dust covering the windows so that he couldn't look out, only feel the vibrating chaos of a plane breaking up. The airplane now lay canted to the left and pieces of wood and splinters covered everything. The decorative paneling that made the aircraft feel so cozy failed to be useful in a crash. Cracks were also visible in the grey metal of the fuselage, with tufts of yellow insulation spilling out like blood. Many of the side windows had cracked and some were completely gone. The curtains on the windows remained intact, hanging limply with the new side angle of the floor.

During the long seconds of the crash, his thinking had become clarified. He was not going to surrender, at least not yet. They could head inland, keep going for a couple of days, see if a rescue mission was coming. If that failed, they could always surrender to the Germans.

What about Aoife? If she really was there in the German camp, they weren't going to be rescuing her as prisoners, and the end of the war served as her best hope. Damn, all this had really clustered up.

"Everyone still alive?" Carter asked.

"Yeah!" Napier shouted from his seat. Rosenberg's words were just as happy, if not quite as enthusiastic.

"Get your carbines loaded," Carter ordered. "Sergeant, I want you to reconnoiter and stand lookout. I figure that we have at most fifteen or twenty minutes before the Germans get here.

Rosenberg, find our weather gear and our food and water and get it outside. We are heading for the hills."

Carter worked his way forward, stepping on the broken wood, pushing aside some wiring that had broken free from the ceiling. As he passed the radio room, he found Mann sitting in his seat, holding his forehead with both hands, stanching the flow of blood. A small electronic box lay on the small table before him, having obviously bounced off his head on the way down from the rack above him. The Indian's glasses poked out of his shirt pocket, no doubt put there to protect them during the crash.

"Paul, are you okay?" Carter asked.

"Yeah, I'll be okay," the Cree Indian said. "How are the colonel and Angela?

The door to the cockpit was slightly ajar. Carter pulled on the handle. The door would not budge. He slid his fingers around the side of the door and pulled. Still no luck.

"Colonel, Captain," he called through the small opening. "Are you okay?"

There was no answer.

"Rosenberg!" Carter called back. "I need Carson in here now."

Turning to the radioman, Carter undid the flying scarf around Mann's neck and wrapped it around his forehead as a bandage. He got a good look at the wound. Shallow, no bone showing, but wide and oozing blood. It really needed stitches.

"What do you need, sir?" Napier asked from behind him.

"I need you to open this door," Carter said, taking Mann by the arm and guiding the radioman back into the passenger cabin to give the sergeant room to work.

Napier left his carbine on one of the passenger seats, came forward, knelt down, grabbed the edges of the door, and experimented with different places for his feet. He finally settled on putting both feet against the side of the doorway to the radio room. This left him on his hip, arms stretched out fully and his legs bent at the knee. He breathed in deeply twice, then raised himself up off the floor as he pulled with the muscles in his arms, shoulders, and legs.

With a screech of metal scraping along metal, the door bent as it slid backwards. The veins and cords of muscle on Napier's neck stood out on red skin. His entire body shook from the effort as the door came back even further.

The bottom hinge broke and the door popped up, slumping Napier to the deck. The sergeant stood up and pulled the door aside, leaving it on the upper hinge with the lower part of the bent door poking out into the passageway.

"Excellent work, Carson," Carter said as he squeezed past and into the cockpit.

The whole deck felt odd, pushed up against a giant boulder, the top of which was visible through the shattered windows. Green and brown lichen grew on it. Rice sat in his seat, not moving. Carter quickly checked him; at least the colonel was breathing. Angela sat in her seat, her arms folded, face drained of blood and blanched white, a low moan coming from her trembling lips.

It was obvious that she was in shock and they needed to get her lying down, covered up and with her feet elevated, to drive blood back up into her head. "Angela," Carter said softly. "We're here. Where does it hurt?"

"Arms," she moaned, so quietly that he barely heard her.

Carter looked at her arms. Dark bruises were already forming on her forearms. One of her arms was bent just wrong. Down below, her legs were pinned between the collapsed instrument panel and her seat.

"Can you feel your legs, Angela?" Carter asked.

"Yes." Again so faintly.

"Do they hurt?"

"No."

A good sign, Carter thought, though he admitted that his medical knowledge mostly came from novels and the innards of men on the battlefield. "We're going to get you out of here," he assured her, patting her gently on the shoulder.

Carter bent down to look at the bottom of the seat. Bolts fastened it to the floor.

"Here you are, sir." Napier thrust a wrench into Carter's hand.

"Where'd this come from?" the major asked, pleased to find that it was the right size. He began to twist one of the bolts free.

"Paul found the toolbox for me," Napier said. "He's still kind of groggy. He's sitting down."

"What about a lookout?"

"I sent Abe."

The bolt came free and Carter started on the next one. "Abe?"

"Rosenberg has a first name, sir."

Carter grunted as another bolt came free. "So he must."

The final bolt for the support came free. Carter reached up under the seat to the front two supports and found that they had been ripped free of the floor by the impact of the crash. That left one more support. He worked on the bolts, barely noticing that Napier was leaning over him, reassuring the pilot in quiet tones.

Three of the bolts came off easily, but the fourth had bent and no amount of twisting at it was going to make it yield. Of course, they didn't need it to yield; they could rotate the seat with the bolt as the pivot.

"Let's move her," Carter said, standing up. The sergeant moved back further.

The seat came around easily before being blocked by the center controls. No matter, she had her legs free enough. He reached around and worked the buckle to release her harness.

Carter placed his hands under her arms and pulled her from the seat. He was surprised how light she was; she loomed large in his imagination, as if her personality and willpower had greater bulk than mere flesh. She cried out and he stopped with her half out of the seat.

"I'm sorry, Angela," he said in her ear. "We've got to get you out of here."

She didn't speak and he assumed that she was too listless from shock. There was no room in the cockpit to pick her up, so he dragged her out of the room, her feet flopping to the deck as they came up and over the seat. Carter winced in sympathy.

Back to the center of the passenger cabin.

"Get her feet up," Carter ordered, as he laid her down on a winter coat already arranged by the radioman. Paul knelt down and placed her feet in his lap. A trickle of blood had escaped from his bandage, running down the side of his face. He swiped at it, rubbing a red streak across his cheek. Tears welled up in his eyes as he looked at the pilot.

Carter gently moved his hands up and down her legs, feeling for any breaks or tenderness. Didn't seem to be any breaks and there was no wetness from any wounds, though he suspected that the legs would show horrible bruises in just a couple of hours.

Napier brought a blanket to cover her, tucking in the corners to make her snug, while Carter headed back to the cockpit. To his astonishment, he found the colonel awake and experimenting with pushing against the instrument panel that pinned him in a manner to the way that Angela had been pinned.

"How you feeling, sir?" Carter asked.

"Annoyed." The voice was strong and free of pain. "Where's Angela?"

"In back," Carter said. "She's broken her arms and is in shock."

"We need a doctor," Rice said.

"I agree."

"I have some medical training, but I seem to be quite trapped here."

"Give me a few minutes," Carter said, kneeling down and going to work with his wrench. Remarkably, considering how well Rice seemed to be doing, the damage underneath was even worse than under the pilot's seat. The front two seat supports were broken clean through and the back two supports were bent. Two bolts on one of the back supports came off, as did three of the bolts on the other support. The remaining bolts did not want to budge and Carter banged his knuckles when the wrench slipped off and his right hand pounded into the edge of the support.

Carter called to Napier, feeling like he was summoning Doc Savage from the pages of a pulp magazine to save the day with his superhuman strength. The major withdrew to the radio room, murmuring a few instructions to the sergeant.

Napier pulled on Rice's seat and it gave way easily. The colonel climbed out of the seat on his own, waving away the offer of help. His pants were torn, but no blood; all and all, he seemed completely hale.

Back in the passenger cabin, Paul had placed two more coats on the pilot. He was pulling a sweater on himself, while he kept her feet elevated. Rice knelt over the woman. Her face was still pale.

Rice reached under the coats and blanket. "Her pulse is racing, very thready. Did she have any wounds? Any bleeding?"

"No," Carter said. "I checked."

"That's good. We don't have blood loss. I'm going to loosen her belt to help her circulation. Could you find me some warm water and salt pills?"

Napier found the five-gallon water can first, while Carter came across the medical kit. Inside were salt tablets.

"The water's a bit chilled, sir," Napier said, as he poured some of it into a canteen.

"It will have to do," Rice said. "I want to make sure that she is hydrated and get that salt in her."

Angela allowed her head to be tilted and swallowed when told to drink from the canteen. For the first time since finding her in such a poor state, Carter allowed himself to feel optimistic and let his thinking go beyond the immediate concern for her. Such a focus for a single person was uncharacteristic for him, drilled out of him in officer's training. In the battlefield, an officer should be concerned with the entire situation, not just a single man, even if she was a woman.

He looked around with searching eyes, assessing the larger situation. All four men had fallen into the same trap, clustering around the prone woman like worker bees around their hurt queen. No food and water had been sorted out, weapons were neglected, and the packs with the weather gear were opened like presents on Christmas morning, all chaos and without order.

"The Nazis are coming," the refugee called from the open door. "Be here in just a couple of minutes."

"How many?" Carter asked.

"About twenty, I think, all carrying guns."

"Dammit, my plan's not going to work," Carter said.

"What plan?" Rice asked.

"I thought that we ought to hide in the hills instead of surrendering. But we spent so much time getting you two out of those seats that we don't have time to get ready. And we can't leave Angela behind."

It was a moment that required no further words.

With the pilot bundled up, the five men assembled outside the airplane, holding white cloths in their hands, waiting to see if the Nazis on this island took prisoners. Hopefully they had glutted themselves on killing the paratroopers.

CHAPTER THIRTY-FOUR

The five naked men stood shivering in the cold as Krohn inspected them carefully. He recognized the young American soldier that Karl had struck on the back of the head with the butt of his Sturmgewehr, just a few days ago back in Germany. A fine specimen, with thick shoulders and meaty hands. Krohn was not as good at phrenology and physiognomy as some of his fellow SS intellectuals, but he suspected that this American possessed considerable Slav ancestry. Good physique for a slave.

The Jew was also obvious, with his circumcised organ and the stenciled numbers on his arm. The two officers looked like any other men, now that their insignia lay in the piled clothes before them. The younger man had hard, wiry muscles, and a lean look to him. The other man, the colonel, with his white hair and young features, had bruises all over his legs and chest.

The Indian intrigued him. Like so many of his fellow Germans, including Hitler, the saga of the American West resonated with him. A time of sturdy pioneers, whores with hearts of gold, and stalwart cavalry, all menaced by the noble savages.

"What is your name?" Krohn asked the Indian. His command of English was poor: two classes at the university, some books, and regularly listening to the BBC broadcasts to learn more accurate information about the progress of the war.

"Jean-Paul Mann, sir."

"Sounds French, yet the accent is wrong. Where are you from?"

"Canada."

"Why are you wearing civilian clothes?"

"I'm a civilian, sir."

Krohn nodded, walking back and forth in front of them across the uneven ground. As soon as he had seen the airplane return and heard the crash, he had collected enough troops to overwhelm a plane that he suspected was full of more paratroops, and had run to this place. The sweat still drying under his clothes chilled him, but nothing like the men turning pink before him.

"What brought you here?" Krohn demanded.

There was no answer for a long moment, then the colonel spoke. "I am Colonel Rice of the Royal Commandos. We were instructed to take this island. We didn't know what we would find."

"And the destroyer came with you?"

The prisoner looked startled for a moment. "Yes, sir. May I ask what happened to them?"

"They are dead, all dead."

The colonel nodded his acknowledgment.

"Come now, Colonel. I am a colonel also. Hans von Krohn of the SS. You must know more about why you were sent here. Tell me."

"I was not the ranking officer. Colonel Smith on the destroyer was in overall charge. We did not receive our orders until yesterday. I don't know why we are here."

"You are lying," Krohn said cheerfully. "But no matter. You will talk soon enough."

"Sir, there is a woman in the airplane. Our pilot. She needs medical attention right away."

Soldiers searching the plane had already informed Krohn of this. "A woman pilot is most unusual. Why did you have her aboard?"

"Our regular pilot took ill and she was the only qualified pilot available."

"Women do not belong on the battlefield," Krohn declared.

"Nevertheless, she is here, and she is hurt. Will you help

her?"

"Of course. We are not monsters."

The clothes had already been searched and stripped of anything that might be used as a weapon. While the Americans, the Jew, and the Canadian put their clothes back on, Krohn supervised the construction of a stretcher from two poles, a blanket and some twine.

The day had been exhilarating, bringing the thrill of successful combat and a victory when all looked bleak. Truly the gods did smile on his endeavor. Despite that, they needed to get off the island as quickly as possible. The destroyer and three transport aircraft were certainly only the first attempt to stop him. More would be on the way. But he couldn't leave the island for another day. He had to wait. Not that Krohn expected his enemies to make the same mistakes again, but the U-boat still patrolled the waters off the island, while the garrison was alert and ready beside their two anti-aircraft guns.

The prisoners took up the woman on the stretcher and walked away, accompanied by all of the German soldiers, leaving von Krohn behind, with only Fritz to serve as his bodyguard.

Carter and the three others carried the stretcher across a bleak landscape. Their breath came out in clouds of steam and frost crunched under their feet. Mann trailed behind them, still woozy from his head wound. Every five minutes or so, they stopped, traded sides and resumed their walk. Easier on the arms that way. The soldiers walked along them, rifles and sub-machine guns held casually, as if this island had always been their turf.

They rounded the hill and moved towards the airfield. Carter was amazed how far he could see in the crisp air, like standing on the top of one of the Blue Ridge Mountains back home. The ground sloped down towards the sea, giving them a panoramic view, extending far out to sea to a distant horizon. The airfield looked like a grey pencil stretched across the ground. A German airplane sat at one end of the runway. Lacking any competition, the radio tower dominated the landscape like the Eiffel Tower, a latticed needle of metal.

Two columns of smoke from the downed British transports marred the scenic vista. One was near the airfield and the other was further inland, maybe two miles away.

The Germans still at the airfield were already picking up the bodies of the dead British paratroopers, laying them in a row near the runway, next to where other soldiers worked at digging a trench with shovels and picks. The sight of so much wasted life, of men that he had met, if only briefly, the day before when they visited the naval base, drove a sharp point of anger into Carter.

"This attack plan was a dumb idea," he hissed at Rice. "I knew that it was tactically unsound and did not voice my objections strongly enough."

Rice looked over at him, his eyes sad. "You're right. I'm a scholar, not a soldier, and now hundreds of men have had their lives cut short because of me. Most of them have mothers, wives, and girlfriends, even children who will miss them for the rest of their lives."

The major kept his eyes locked on the green eyes of the white-haired man who looked too young. He wanted to nurse his anger, vent it like a poison that threatened to overwhelm him, but he saw that nothing he could say would add to the pain that the colonel felt, and always would.

Carter had made mistakes, and men had died, always one or two at a time. The only way that he kept their ghosts from haunting him was by promising himself that he would learn from the mistakes and preserve other men's lives by making better decisions.

The soldiers led the prisoners past the airfield and the small buildings made of rock, turf, and lumber salvaged from packing crates, past the two anti-aircraft guns and their smug crews, and towards a large hill beyond. The ground here was different, made of a thick layer of scattered rocks, all obviously taken from the dark hole in the hill ahead. Carter remembered that there had been an unsuccessful coal mine. He had expected it to be an open pit, but apparently the miners had burrowed into the ground.

All but two of the soldiers left the group to take up positions at the airfield, their eyes glancing skyward often. Carter felt a perverse sense of satisfaction that even though the Germans had bested the commandos, they still feared a new assault. He hoped that their fears were justified. The war was almost over, and perhaps when the radio announced the end the Germans here would release their prisoners and offer their own surrender. A happy scenario and not at all too unrealistic.

One of the guards led the way, while the other trailed behind, his hand on his submachine gun. The Germans had built a wall of stone with a large wooden door set in the middle, just inside the mine entrance, completely blocking the tunnel. Inside the door, bare electric bulbs struggled to light the long tunnel. A hallway ran down the center, with side rooms created with slats from packing crates and hanging blankets. The air smelled of too many men crowded together too long; a faint breeze against their faces, along with the throbbing in the air, indicated that fans were circulating the air.

The men with the stretcher shifted to work their way down the narrow hallway, brushing against the blankets and trying to avoid other walls that looked too flimsy to withstand being touched. Within a minute, Carter had unbuttoned his coat. The temperature in the mine was much nicer, perhaps fifty or sixty degrees Fahrenheit. He recalled that caves maintained constant temperatures regardless of the outside temperature. Smart place to live, especially during the long frigid night of winter, when sea ice rimmed the island.

What in the hell were the Germans doing here? He had seen nothing that showed that the location had military value. Flying missions against convoys running supplies to the Russians made no sense, since the missions could fly from Norway, and everything else had to be flown in to the island, like fuel and spare parts.

"You leave the woman here," the soldier in front said, speaking in German.

This room obviously served as an infirmary, with two cots, a medicine cabinet, and an orderly dressed in white. The room faintly stank of medicine. No other patients stood in the way of her care. Not one German had been wounded and not one British paratrooper had survived to need care.

They laid Angela on one of the cots. She looked like she was asleep and her face was flushed from the heat. Carter removed the coat that covered her, finding that she had started to sweat in the warmth.

"Are you a doctor?" Carter asked in German.

"No, I am a medic."

"Do you have a doctor?"

"No. I know how to set bones though."

"The rest of you come outside," the guard said. "You will help bury the dead."

Carter stood up, alarmed at the prospect of leaving Angela behind. He looked at the guard and saw hate in the man's eyes. Best to approach the problem from an angle, not argue straight ahead.

"One of our men has a head wound." Carter pointed at Mann. "Could we please leave him here?"

The guard nodded his assent and the other four men followed him back outside. The German soldiers had already scraped a section of ground clear, and white marks in the frozen dirt showed where picks had tried to break through. The officer in charge was pleased to have the four prisoners show up and ordered them to lay the bodies on the cleared ground and use tailings stones to make a cairn.

"Do a good job," the officer declared, his smile unfriendly and smug. "These are your allies and the polar bears will come in the winter. They will think these men are tasty snacks."

Twenty-nine dead commandos. Three short of the total, who must have died in the airplane before they could jump. All of their pockets had been turned out and everything else of value stripped.

The four set about their grim work.

"I thought that I had left this kind of thing behind," Rosenberg said, carrying the legs of a corpse while Carter carried the arms.

"How's that?" Carter asked.

"In the camps we had to clean up the dead, take them to the ovens. It was hard at first, then you stop thinking of them as men or woman, or little children. They are just bags to be carried. Empty husks to be discarded."

"I think that they are still men to me," Carter said, not wanting to know any more about the camps.

"I think that they will be men to me again also...someday."

Carter arranged to share his work with Rice instead of Rosenberg, leaving the refugee to work with Napier. The two men seemed to have bonded, like one enlisted man with another, reminding Carter of the gulf that separated the grunts from the officers.

They collected rocks, carefully laying them on each body. It wasn't that hard, until it came time to put a rock on a man's face. Carter built up the rocks around the head, and laid a larger flat rock over the face, creating a small chamber. He noticed that the others did the same.

The hard work involved much stooping and walking, forcing them to set aside their coats. It felt to Carter as if his muscles had been jarred loose from their moorings by the crash and they ached as he worked. He kept an eye on the others to see that they were up to this duty. Strictly speaking, under the Geneva Convention, officers could not be compelled to work. Carter decided to not have a legal discussion with the hard-eyed guard who stood far enough away that they couldn't surprise him with a quick rush.

"I'm surprised by your remarkable recovery," Carter said to the colonel. "I initially thought that you were in much worse shape than Angela."

"I guess not," Rice said. "Just some bruising. I guess I was knocked out. I'm lucky when it comes to not getting hurt."

"Pretty remarkable recuperative powers for a scholar."

Rice smiled. "It comes from lifting all those books."

Carter's body told him that it should be night, but the sun still remained, even after they finished making their oblong cairn. The four exhausted men gathered in a group and observed their handiwork.

"There should be a prayer," Napier said.

"Of course," Rice said.

The colonel recited the Catholic Rite of Committal in Latin. He ended by quoting a scripture from the book of John:

> Amen, amen, I say to you, whoever hears my word and believes in the one who sent me has eternal life and will not come to condemnation, but has passed from death to life.
>
> Amen, amen, I say to you, the hour is coming and is now here when the dead will hear the voice of the Son of God, and those who hear will live.
>
> *For just as the Father has life in himself, so also he gave to his Son the possession of life in himself.*

Rosenberg added some words in Hebrew, singing the haunting phrases, and then the men stood silent.

CHAPTER THIRTY-FIVE

Krohn thought of the time as late evening, 2300 by his watch, though the sun had not disappeared. Yesterday, the second day of May, was the first day on Bear Island when the sun did not set, remaining in the sky until mid-August. Even so, the sun was deep enough down on the horizon to cast long shadows. Despite having placed two lanterns inside the crashed airplane, Krohn also used a flashlight to poke about in the piles of gear that the Americans had brought with them. He had made the right decision to search the airplane on his own, not trusting the twins to recognize the value of what they might run across.

He had known that the American colonel was lying to him, but the truth was even more remarkable. The aerial photographs of Bear Island were expected, but the documents from his safe were not. When he had fled his house, he expected that everything would have been destroyed—and here were his journals. What a twist of fate, a real blessing, to recover what he had thought was lost.

The report on the SS Arctic Expedition, even if mostly burned, showed that the enemy had learned much about what was happening. Krohn had assumed that the SS occult activities were so secret that he had only to worry about random events and the opposition of disloyal Germans. That was obviously not true.

The old map, rolled up in its tube, fascinated him. In the far north a tree grew, an ancient memory of Yggdrasil.

His instinct was to execute the whole lot of them, but he realized that would be an act of fear, a futile attempt to pretend that the Allies would remain ignorant if these men died. An alternative was to interrogate them, force them to tell him all that they knew; while tempting, he just didn't have the time. In the end, it would not matter. He would succeed in the north or he would fail.

The central question: what would Odin want? The sacrifice of the virgin was obvious and necessary. What about the sacrifice of enemies? Yes, the fates had contrived to deliver into his hands exactly what was needed. Three soldiers, a Jew, and an Indian. What a perfect slate for the knife, combined with the virgin. What about the other woman? The pilot? She was older, but was it possible that she was also a virgin? Unlikely, given that she was an American who acted like a man, but he would check, just to make sure.

"Fritz, go and get twenty soldiers," Krohn said. "I want to carry everything back to the base."

After the twin left, in one of the packs, surrounded by clothing, Krohn found a small wooden box. Opening it revealed a silver globe.

He gasped, instinctively aware that he was in the presence of a sacred and powerful object. The SS had scoured the world for such things, even before the war began. The Spear of Odin had been found in the backroom of a museum of Prague, but proved to be a bejeweled toy made at the request of the Holy Roman Emperors, not made of ancient wood that Odin himself had blessed. In Tibet they had been thwarted, as well as in their search for the Holy Grail. In Persia they had found Zulfiqar, the sword of Ali, son of Mohammad, but no one could figure out how to take advantage of the weapon.

SS officers had even sought out Jewish artifacts and schemed to find the Ark of the Covenant in an ancient Egyptian tomb. That ended badly on an island in the Mediterranean. Lost everyone. It had been a bad idea from the start, thinking that they could find power that they could control in a Jewish artifact.

All in all, not much in the way of any successes in finding

useful artifacts.

Krohn held the globe up in the light from one of the lanterns. Its surface was covered with fine etchings. He tried to identify the language, but some looked like the fine curves of Arabic, others reminded him of the straight lines of Phoenician, and some looked like Chinese ideographs. How odd to see so many influences in one place. None were Norse runes.

Taking out a knife, he pressed it tight against the silver surface and tried to scratch it. He peered at the result and hummed with satisfaction. That knife was good Krupp steel and it had not left a mark. He wished he had a diamond to try. He suspected that even it would not mar the surface of the artifact. Such a test would be absolute proof that this was no hoax, but the real thing.

One of the prisoners, the owner of this artifact, knew much more than he was telling.

CHAPTER THIRTY-SIX

"You came," Aoife cried, standing up and throwing her arms around the sergeant. With her handcuffs still on, her arms came down around him like a trap. Fortunately he was about her height and the maneuver came off easily enough.

She buried her face into his shoulder, inhaling dried sweat, dirt, and a musky scent that reminded her of her father and brothers. The fears that she had held at bay for the last four days flowed out of her, like poison from a wound. She felt safe with him there. Squeezing him as tightly as she could, trying to merge into him, she felt tears come to her eyes. She was no foolish girl, love struck and blind. The last time that he had tried to protect her, her last sight of him had been of him lying on the ground, blood coming from his head. Now he had come and he was obviously a prisoner also, with a bandage still wrapped around his head. Curiously, none of that mattered to her. She still felt safer.

"Are you okay?" he asked.

"I am now."

The room where she had been confined for the last day had three walls of wood, an inner wall made from the wall of the tunnel, and a floor of rough stone and dirt. A single lightbulb of low wattage dimly lit the room. With no furniture and only a single blanket, she had huddled in the corner most of the time. A bucket had been provided for her personal needs, but so far she had refused to submit to that indignity.

She looked at the other men who entered the room. She

already knew Major Carter, so the sergeant introduced the other two men. The man with the white hair looked tired and sad. The Jewish refugee looked hungry to her—not just for food, but for a reason to live.

"I don't even know your name," she said to the man trapped by her arms and handcuffs.

He laughed, a weary chuckle combined with a smile that made her feel warm inside. "After spending so much time in my dreams, I would have expected that you to have learned it somehow. It's Carson Napier."

"You dreamed about me?"

"Every night."

"What did you dream?"

"That you were a prisoner and needed me," he said. "You were flying up here and in danger. There were three men, that colonel and the two soldiers that look the same."

"They are twins. Truly evil men. Only the colonel kept my virtue intact."

The anger that darkened his face at hearing this pleased her. "I won't let that happen," he growled.

"I know that you wouldn't," she said, snuggling closer. "Not that you will need to be called upon. The colonel wants me to remain a virgin. He plans to sacrifice me, just like my friends back at the camp."

"Are you serious?" Carter asked from the other side of the room. "Of course you are. That's what that bastard does. How could I forget?"

No one answered that question.

A few minutes later, two others joined them in their cell, making the room feel crowded. Everyone was elated to see the woman, whose face looked drawn, with dark bags under her eyes. The cast on her left arm reached up to her shoulder, while the cast on her right arm only went to just below the elbow. The man was an Indian with a bandage around his head.

Aoife was the only one not exhausted. The major arranged for everyone to donate their coats and make a bed in the middle of the room for the pilot. For a moment she looked ready to object to this special treatment, then she gave in and lay down. Within minutes everyone else found a place by one of the walls to lean their heads against. One man even began to snore.

Aoife took the sergeant to her corner and they sat there, holding hands, as he struggled to keep his eyes open. She rubbed his hands gently, enjoying the feel of his calluses and the thick muscles in his fingers.

"Why would I have dreams about you?" Carson asked.

"Because I'm pretty?" she asked, dipping her head into his shoulder playfully, watching his eyes.

The mixed look of embarrassment and happiness on his face made her giggle. She had never teased the boys back home and felt only annoyance when they teased her, but this teasing was much more fun, and much more complex. Not since Ireland had she felt any measure of power or control, with herself in charge, and this new sense of control felt provocative and intoxicating.

Aoife rubbed his wrist, as if she was taking off a bracelet. Napier thought that he saw something, but maybe it was just a trick of the light. She mimed putting the invisible bracelet on her own wrist. "You don't need this anymore," she said.

"What?"

"It's what made you dream about me."

"You're just confusing me," he said

"I don't want the others to hear me." She pressed her lips against his ear. "The women in my family remember who we are. I know that this will sound strange, but we were the priestesses of the old religion, before Christianity came and saved our souls. We worshiped in the trees, acted as soothsayers, used the power that came from our mothers. Some people would call us witches. We cast spells, made magic things, told the sacred stories."

"Can you do these things?" Napier asked. He wondered if she had gone daft.

"I know that it all sounds incredible. Maybe it's just stories that the women in my family told me. But I have seen curious things, incredible things, that make me believe that the stories are true. You had your dreams; were they not extraordinary?"

"Yes."

"So you see. Let me tell you one of the stories. One of my grandmothers, hundreds of years ago, was named Báirinn. The chronicles say that she was the fairy lover of Cormac Mac Airt, but that is a lie. She was his wife, married in a sacred ceremony in the trees, and his most trusted advisor. She made him the greatest high king in Irish history, not only as a warrior, but as a wise and just ruler. Báirinn is only one of many of my grand-mothers who were queens and powerful priestesses."

"So you're an Irish princess?" he asked.

"I thought I was your princess," she said, squeezing his hand. "And you are my prince."

He kissed her on the cheek.

One of the twins came in. He held up a handful of short lengths of rope. "Put on your coats and gloves and cross your wrists behind you."

Aoife didn't like this development at all. She watched each of the other prisoners submit to having their hands bound behind themselves. The tension in the room, the thwarted desire to fight back, was apparent. She held Carson's gaze, trying to commu-nicate that he should not fight back. Not at this moment.

Even Angela's hands were bound, though in front of her, since the casts prohibited any other choice.

"It's time to leave," the German soldier announced.

CHAPTER THIRTY-SEVEN

When he emerged from the dim lighting of the mine, Carter stumbled, then stood for moment blinking to adjust his eyes. The exclamations of the others encouraged him to look about.

What an extraordinary sight, as impressive as visiting Westminster Abbey or St. Paul's Cathedral in London. Monuments to what the descendants of apes could do.

A dirigible airship floated before them, moored to the radio mast. No, not just a radio mast, but a high mast. Carter had thought that airships had disappeared after the fiery crash of the *Hindenburg* in New Jersey, just a couple of years before the war broke out. The Germans had been the best in the world at building the dirigibles. The American and British built numerous blimps that Carter had seen floating over London and over the invasion fleet on D-Day—big balloons to scare away enemy airplanes.

He had read enough about dirigibles in magazines as a youth to know that they differed from blimps in that they had skeletons made of lightweight metal with huge bags filled of hydrogen or helium attached inside the skeleton. Despite being a prisoner, the awe he felt overwhelmed him with aesthetic bliss. The dirigible was so large, bigger than the largest whale, yet seemed so light and graceful. Its silver skin shimmered in the harsh glare of the sun, creating delicate shades of color.

This dirigible looked wrong, since two of its bags in the middle hung limp, giving the airship the look of a great beast mortally wounded. The grey cigar was at least two hundred yards long, with a long cabin slung underneath, and both vertical and horizontal tailing. Two engine cars forward of the cabin, and two more aft, held propellers taller than a man. Numerous mooring lines hung from the dirigible, from both the airframe and the four engine cars and the control cabin, like a hag's stringy hair. Stenciled onto the rudder was the name *Himmler*.

Germans swarmed around the airship, making fast the mooring lines to small concrete blocks on the grounds. Others hauled boxes and assorted other gear out of the surrounding huts and carried them towards the *Himmler*.

"Move," the guard urged.

The prisoners left the mine entrance. Rice and Carter walked on either side of Angela, like mother hens anxious for their young. She walked well enough, which was fortunate, since with their hands bound behind them they could do little to help her. Aoife and Napier managed to keep holding hands, fingers clinging to each other, only possible because her handcuffs kept her arms in front of her. Rosenberg and Mann brought up the rear.

Carter tried to see everything, intrigued by such a novel sight. Men used hand cranks to pump fuel into the engine compartments from barrels that they moved on wheel barrows. With remarkable speed, the Germans piled supplies and gear onto nets made of thick hawsers that hung from the sides of the cabin. Carter recognized some of the suitcases and bags as their own, coming from the crashed airplane. Why would they take everything? Surely the airship had limited capacity.

"That's not right," Wright said.

Carter looked at the pilot.

"That airship is too small for what it's carrying," she said. "It shouldn't be able to carry that much gear."

"Do you have much experience with dirigibles, Angela?" Carter asked.

"No, but I have an instinct for aircraft, and with the loss of lift from those collapsed air bags, they should only be able to fly if they dumped absolutely everything that they don't need. Look at that, they're even putting metal girders on her."

The girders were not I-beams, but were designed with a lattice shape, and curved. Carter looked up at the exposed skeleton of the dirigible where the air bags had torn. He noticed that the shape of the airship behind the cabin was wrong, with bent girders. The girders that they were loading must be replacements for the damaged girders, but why were they loading them up instead of using them to repair the airship?

"I do believe that you're right, Angela," Carter said. "They're putting a lot of stuff in there."

When had he started to call her Angela, instead of Captain? At the crash landing? It felt more natural to him than calling her Captain or by her last name.

"They want to leave as soon as they can," Rice said in a low voice. He had been mostly quiet since their capture, keeping to himself. "I think they are afraid that there will be another attack."

"I hope their fear is justified," Carter said, almost in a whisper. He knew that the SS colonel could speak English, and who knew which of the other Germans might be able to eavesdrop.

The cabin of the airship stretched for about sixty feet, with of row of bubble windows on each side, convex shaped to let the people inside look down at the ground more easily. The metal was painted a pale gray, with rivets and bolts plainly visible.

The SS officer, Krohn, stood near the open door to the cabin, shaking hands with the pilot and another SS officer, whom Carter had not seen before—a pudgy man with a fleshy face red from the cold.

The guard led them over to Colonel Krohn. They entered the large area of shade created by the vast bulk of the airship blocking the sun.

"Ah, welcome, gentlemen and ladies," Krohn said in English, then switched to German. "You are about to embark on a most extraordinary journey and see things that few have ever seen. Consider yourself my guests."

"Where are we going?" Rice asked in German.

"That will be a surprise." The SS officer seemed almost gleeful.

"How far away is it?" Carter asked.

"Allow me to introduce Captain Erich Trott, who designed this impressive dirigible and is our pilot."

Trott stood six inches taller than any of the other men, in a rumpled uniform of trousers, a worn sweater, and a wool coat. Tufts of blond hair stuck out from the sides of the only indication of his rank, a battered officer's cap with an insignia of a winged zeppelin above a swastika. Scraggly blond whiskers covered his face; like an adolescent, he obviously couldn't grow a full beard. Blue eyes, narrow shoulders, and oversized hands completed the picture of an odd man. Such disdain for German trim in his appearance bespoke a man assured of his own competence and self-worth.

His voice was soft and gentle, surprising coming from such a large man. "We are traveling one thousand, four hundred, and ninety kilometers. We should be able to make it there in two days, even with this headwind."

Krohn looked at the prisoners. "You will all be held in the crew's quarters while on this voyage. I expect proper behavior. Escape is a foolish thought this far from anywhere, and any attempt to interfere with the operation of the dirigible or any of its officers or crew will be severely punished. Quick frankly, I think that I would be forced to execute one or more of you as punishment."

After what amounted to his legalistic diatribe, Krohn motioned for the prisoners to enter the cabin. One of the soldiers led the way, while the other followed. They carried only pistols, not the impressive assault rifles that Carter had seen them with earlier. Aoife had told the others about her fears and the way that the twins looked at her and already Carter despised them.

Three lightweight metal steps led up to the open door set near the front of the cabin. Beyond the door was the bridge, which occupied the entire front of the cabin, with windows set all around in a semi-circle. Two tables at the back held large charts and navigation almanacs. On the rear bulkhead were clocks, weather instruments, and a row of telephones, each with a hand crank to apply an electrical charge, with small lettering on each handle indicating that the phone connected to the Crews Quarters, Engine 1, or the Rigger's Station. Dials and levers covered the rest of the wall, though Carter didn't have the chance to identify them.

In the center of the room was a small object, about a foot square. It didn't look like metal, but had the sheen of rock, perhaps obsidian. Strong steel bands crisscrossed the object and bolted it into the floor, as if they were afraid that it might escape. The oddly placed object was obviously a recent addition, considering the lack of paint and the fittings that didn't match the rest of the room.

A spoked steering wheel resembling that of a ship was in front. Two chains in front of the wheel extended upwards into the ship; Carter surmised that they controlled the rudder. Another spoked steering wheel on the far side of the bridge faced directly out to the side of the airship. Carter looked back and saw that Captain Trott had followed them in.

"Excuse me, Captain," Carter said in German. "Why do you have a steering wheel over there?"

The German smiled, not arrogantly, but in a tolerant way. "That is the Elevator Helm, the position that I once held—a most important one. The helmsman there controls the aileron that directs the dirigible's elevation. The helmsman is positioned so that he can sense any change of angle immediately. He also watches that inclinometer in front of him, so that a machine backs up what his inner ear is telling him. A moment's inattention, especially close to the ground, and the airship will begin to descend or perhaps even climb in an uncontrolled fashion, like a rearing horse. Such mistakes can be fatal."

"Indeed. And what is that?" Carter pointed at a panel near the Elevator Helm, where a series of tubes came down from the ceiling. Each one was labeled with letters and numbers and had a dial and round handle at the bottom.

"That is our gas board," Trott said. "It is used to release gas from each gas bag, allowing us to descend properly."

"I think that you have answered enough questions, Captain," Krohn said as he climbed the steps to the bridge. "Fritz, take the prisoners to their quarters and remove their bonds." He looked Carter in the eye. "Try nothing, or you will be shot."

A small hallway led towards the stern. On the right side was a radio room and a closed door labeled Machine Room. On the left was the galley, with a stove, sinks, iceboxes, and a pantry. Beyond was a larger room that went from bulkhead to bulkhead, with tables and chairs, obviously the commons area and dining room. In every corner of the room was a yellow fire extinguisher.

The passageway resumed beyond the dining room. Here were the quarters, with the Captain's Cabin and Officers Cabins clearly labeled. Their new home was on the right side, a room about fifteen feet long and six feet wide. There were five sets of triple bunks, and to Carter's delight, two of the bubble windows. Carter learned later that at the stern were the heads: two toilets, a single washroom, and a shower stall.

One of the soldiers cut their bonds and closed the door, leaving them alone, rubbing their wrists.

"I think that this will be a grand adventure," Rice said.

Carter looked at the colonel, to see if he were joking. Had the man ever joked? "If we weren't prisoners, I would agree," Carter said.

Angela chose to lie down on one of the bunks, maneuvering her casts in the narrow eighteen inches between the mattress and the bunk above, as tight as a submarine. The others crowded around the two windows. Just below them the crew was finishing loading extra supplies into the external nets. How could the airship carry so much?

An hour later a klaxon sounded and Captain Trott's voice came on over the loudspeaker, a small wooden box with a speaker in the corner of the room. "Prepare to weigh off."

The prisoners watched the ground crew release the mooring lines from cleats stuck in cement. Some of the men on the ground waved. Carter found his own hand twitching with the normal urge to reciprocate.

"Start engines."

The four diesel engines growled, creating a jagged hum that made the air vibrate. Each of the mechanics in the engine compartments reported themselves over the loudspeaker ready for more.

Trott's firm voice again. "Up elevators."

The answer to the command did not come over the loudspeaker.

"Bring the engines up to fifteen hundred revs."

The airship lifted up, an effortless and graceful motion, a majestic monarch of the sky. The ground receded and moved under them as the engines drove them towards the beach. Carter estimated that they were over five hundred feet in the air when they left the island behind. Small whitecaps showed that nature had rewarded them with a brisk breeze.

"Leveling out at four hundred meters and seventy knots," Trott said. "Loudspeaker off."

"Why are we flying so low?" Napier wondered aloud. "Planes always fly higher."

"Planes fly so high because it is more efficient to fly through thinner air," Wright said, sounding tired. "An airship needs the lift that comes from flying in thicker air, closer to the ground. Or sea, as it is. They can go higher if they need to skip over some weather."

"How high?" Carter asked.

"I don't know," she said. "Weather has always been the biggest problem for airships. It mixes up the air and makes it hard to have lift. And they aren't that fast. And they get hit with lightning."

"Won't that blow us up?" Rosenberg asked. "This is filled with hydrogen, isn't it?"

"Yes," she said. "It is full of flammable gas, but they have some kind of lightning rod system. I read somewhere that most of the great dirigibles had been hit by lightning and survived it."

"That's a relief," Carter said. "Though is there much lightning in the Arctic?"

"I have no idea."

For hours they passed over ocean so blue that it hurt to look at it for too long. Once they saw small grey objects and decided that they must be whales, perhaps coming north for the summer. Quite quickly, ice rimmed the windows, narrowing the field of view. Though a vent in the ceiling blew in warm air, the room was still cold enough for everyone to keep their coats and gloves on. Carter stripped the blankets off one of the bunks and wrapped them around Angela as she lay on one of the other bunks. He waited for her doze off again before returning to the window.

One of the crew came in to feed them, his shoes covered in grey wrappers. Carter asked about the odd footwear and learned that the covers were to prevent static discharges, though the small man was taciturn in his responses. The crewman brought food from the galley to the mechanics in the engine cars and to the riggers, using the walkways inside the dirigible, between the gas bags.

The twin soldiers stayed in the hall, pistols at the ready. Carter gnawed at the sausage; the bread was so cold that it was crunchy. After the meal, the prisoners were allowed to go use the head one at a time. The toilet was in a separate closet from the washroom and was small enough to force the guard to remain outside. Afterwards, as Carter washed in his hands, he noted with some surprise that there was a second door in the washroom that exited the airship on the port side. A stenciled warning on the door advised against opening the door while in flight.

The crew fed them regularly and the meals served as the only way to measure the passage of time in the eternal day, since the Germans had even taken their watches. Carter examined each of the bunks and was pleased to see that one set was longer than the others, able to accommodate his six-foot frame. As he lay under a blanket, trying to encourage sleep to come, he reflected on the day. He felt so odd, not tense at all, just waiting for an opportunity to make his move. An intercom near the loud-speaker, with a send button near it, meant that the Germans could be listening in to them, so he had not talked to anyone else about hatching plans to escape. Of course, escape to where? Not a lot of choices on an airship.

He woke when the airship encountered a strong wind and joined the others at the windows. The sky was overcast, turning the eternal day into twilight. The airship lurched back and forth, like a swing breaking free from the bough of a tree. The noise of the engines occasionally rose to a higher pitch, as if the great beast were straining to keep its way. Snow falling out of the frigid sky looked like glitter.

They left the rough weather behind and the sun reasserted its authority, shining low on the horizon. Carter looked down and saw that they had left the ocean behind and were flying over an ice shelf. The sea ice looked like a mixed-up mosaic of white and blue watercolors, the blue coming from puddles and small pools of melted water. After an hour of this beauty, the ice firmed up, no longer melting, and they were flying over track-less wastes of white that stretched from horizon to horizon.

Many hours of watching the ice passed.

CHAPTER THIRTY-EIGHT

Angela Wright hurt. Every muscle in her body felt like it had been stretched to the limit, the connections to bone still barely attached, and her head just throbbed. The cold didn't help. She had her coat on, though the odd angle of the cast on her left arm forced her to leave that arm out of the coat, wrapped in a blanket instead. Major Carter stood near her, gazing out of the window. Even while she suffered from shock after the crash, she had been lucid enough to be aware of the care that he and the others offered her, a gentleness that she had not expected.

She had admitted to herself long ago that men frustrated and bewildered her. Her mother had always told her that her sense of social propriety was underdeveloped. No doubt about that, though Angela preferred to think of that complex tangle of perceptions as her social radar, trying to pick up signals from other people. Sometimes the radar failed.

Time to practice the art of conversation.

"Tell me about yourself, Major," she said.

Carter looked down at her, his face a bit perplexed. He shrugged and knelt next to her. "I wanted to thank you for a fine landing back on Bear Island."

She looked at him sharply, trying to detect whether he was mocking her. "Was it really that fine of a landing?"

"Everyone lived and that makes it a great landing," he said. "I know that we had some damage, especially you, but it was much better than we had any right to expect—especially considering how rough that terrain was."

"I was just lucky."

"Don't underrate yourself. Skilled people make their own luck."

The compliment embarrassed her and she reached for the next question on her memorized list. "Where did you grow up?"

"Richmond."

"I've never been to Virginia," she said. "What's it like there?"

"It's still part of the South and I learned to revere my Confederate ancestors. My great-grandfather lost his left arm at Chancellorsville. Over seventy years later, the family still maintains the grudge. Not just against the North. We know that the cannonball came from a cannon attached to the Indiana 6th Infantry Regiment, so the family is never friends with any Hoosiers."

"That's ridiculous," she said. "My father grew up on a farm near Bloomington."

Carter grinned slyly at her. "I'll have to forgive you that."

She smacked him in the arm, hard enough to make him wince. She winced herself from the impact. The cast on her right arm gave her enough freedom of movement, but those muscles were not ready for rough play. She felt embarrassed that she had just treated him like her brother, but he seemed to not notice and continued the conversation as if nothing was amiss.

"It's not really my fault," he said. "We were very provincial in my neighborhood. It's odd that we were so unsophisticated, yet we were part of the upper crust. I was named after my great-great-uncle; he was an officer that disappeared after the Civil War. There was an odd rumor that he went to Mars and married a princess there."

She looked at him as if he had just confessed to a naughty sin. "What?"

"Just an odd family story. We have a bunch of them."

"How would he get to Mars? And who says that there are princesses there?"

"It's just the family story. You do know that the surface color of Mars waxes and wanes with the seasons, and that astronomers have seen canals on Mars?"

"So I've heard, but not all astronomers believe that they were made by intelligent beings."

"The canals are straight. Nature doesn't make straight things."

"That makes sense, but you were telling me about your childhood, not Mars."

"True. As I was saying, we were very provincial, and we didn't care for the Negroes either. My grandmother couldn't understand why the slaves hadn't stayed slaves of their own free will. She figured that their skin color made them permanent slaves."

"Not very progressive of her."

"No, and I believed the same thing, until I went to Yale and a professor there opened my eyes. It was strange.... I had Negro friends when I was a kid. We played together all the time. They were mostly the children of domestic servants. I considered them my pals, but as time went by, I adopted the racist attitudes of my parents. Now I have repented and support full civil rights."

"Why don't you have a southern drawl?" she asked.

"I lost it at Yale. Too many people made fun of it, so I went to a voice coach in the drama department, who taught me to speak proper."

She smiled. "When did you join up?"

"Right after Pearl Harbor. Most of my friends at Yale joined up, too. They went into intelligence and logistics postings, but I wanted combat training and I wanted to be the best, so I joined the Rangers."

"Why combat training?"

"Didn't want to get too bored."

"Did that work?"

He looked at her with eyes older than his twenty-something years. "My ideas were clouded by too many adventure novels. A combat soldier spends a lot of time being bored...and a lot of time doing other things."

"You survived the war," she pointed out.

"No, I did not survive," he said. "I just lived. That's a different thing. The person I was died and I don't know who this new person is."

CHAPTER THIRTY-NINE

Krohn stood at the front of the gondola, pressed up so close to one of the windows that he had to keep wiping away the fog of his breath. Amid the white expanses of the north a spot of green had appeared. As they approached, it resolved itself into a great tree, reaching hundreds of meters into the air.

Yggdrasil.

He had been right, damn them all. Vindication. His faith in the Nordic myths finally confirmed. While others at the university had studied mathematics, philosophy, and literature, he had studied ariosophy—occult wisdom of the Aryans. There was no degree in that field, so he listened to his history professors and regurgitated their meandering exhalations long enough to stand for his degree.

The attitudes of the other students at the university frustrated him at times. Aside from the Jews, many of them were from good Aryan stock, but they insisted in only believing what scholarship or physical evidence showed them to be true, instead of believing in what must be true. It showed how far the German race had fallen from the Golden Age, when the Aryan races on the lost continents of Atlantis, Lemuria, and Mu had ruled in a sublime paradise. The new Germany had to be taught how to believe in the ancient truths, to find the ancestral soul in their blood, to hate what had to be hated, to purify the unclean, to worship the power of the individual will, and honor blood and soil.

Ancient prophecies had predicted the coming of Adolf Hitler, a wise leader who would unite the Aryan people and create a new order of purity and prosperity. Krohn had joined the party in 1930 and was gratified to see that after the party gained power in 1933, that a university position in Munich as a lecturer came as his due. He found teaching wearisome and after only a year returned to full-time studies and his duties in the SS.

The airship drew closer and wiping the window again, he saw the Green Valley more clearly. That name came from legend, sailors and pilots who had seen it from a distance, a story told around glasses of rum or whiskey, written about in breathless prose, published in lurid magazines with half-naked women on their covers. Krohn knew that its true name was Asgard.

Friedrich Adler came to stand behind him. "Even though I've spent months there, the sight still awes me."

Krohn had known Adler ever since they met in a history seminar at the university. Adler had gone on to obtain his second doctorate and earn the title of Professor. His name meant "eagle," which didn't fit the man at all, other than his intense eyes. His pudgy belly that jiggled when he walked, fingers thick as sausages, and cherub-like jowls, reminded Krohn of what Reichsmarschall Goering had become. Adler's saving grace was a sharp mind and stamina that put thinner men to shame. Like Krohn, he reported to the SS Race and Settlement Main Office, in the Occult Branch, though he remained a civilian rather than an SS officer.

"My dear Friedrich, I truly envy all the time that you have been able to spend there," Krohn said, clapping the man's shoulder.

"It has truly been the greatest period of my life. If I had died there, I would have felt my life complete." The professor's voice was gruff and gravelly. "After our dirigible crashed, I was certain that we would be there for all time. I had no thought for anything else other than my studies. By radio we heard of the Reich collapsing, but it meant nothing until Captain Trott volunteered to try the fruit."

"I am going to try the fruit also," Krohn said.

"You are a braver man than I," said Alder.

"It is the only hope left for our great nation."

The prisoners crowded around the two bubble windows, awed by the sight of the giant tree. Carter judged that it must reach at least two miles up into the air, and the branches spread out for thousands of feet, covered with green leaves. The branches themselves much be the size of redwoods or sequoias, trees that he had only read about. Oddly enough, the size of the tree distorted his sense of proportion, as if the tree had always been meant to be there and was not out of place.

The surrounding valley stretched for miles out from the tree, up to a rim wall of hills that thrust up sharply, protecting the lush plants of the valley from the freezing ice of the Arctic outside. Forests and meadows covered the valley floor, with streams of water trickling down from the rim wall. Carter thought he saw some buildings among the trees. People lived here.

"It's the world tree," Rice said. "It really exists. I thought it might, but the idea seemed too incredible. I never expected it to be so big."

"Tell us about it," Rosenberg said.

"Carter, you just read a book on it, perhaps you would recall better."

The major nodded his head, though he doubted that his recall trumped Rice in any way. Rice never seemed to forget anything.

"This is Yggdrasil, a tree that runs through the axis of Midgard, which is what the Norse called our world. The tree also leads to Hel and to Asgard, the home of the gods. In other words, the tree connects heaven, hell, and earth. It is said that at the base of Yggdrasil is the dragon Dreadbiter. One of the most curious stories is that Odin, king of the gods, wounded himself with his own spear and hung himself on Yggdrasil for nine nights. No one gave him food or drink. Odin was rewarded with the wisdom to rule the nine worlds and the knowledge of how to read and write runes."

"Nine worlds?" the sergeant asked.

"Not a clue to what that means." Carter shrugged. "Nine seemed to be a sacred number to the Norse."

Napier looked over at his officer. "And people think that those science fiction and adventure stories I like are weird."

CHAPTER FORTY

"That's where we crashed," Alder said, pointing at a clearing about a mile in from the rim wall. "We came in too low and the updraft of warm air tossed us up in the air and cracked two girders. That caused some of the bracing wires to snap, and they sliced though four of the gas bags like a knife—long cuts that quickly vented the hydrogen. Captain Trott was magnificent, totally calm, issuing orders to the helmsmen and the elevator man in a manner that calmed them down. As you can see, most of this area is forest, and coming down on trees would have been a real disaster."

"How long did it take to get to that clearing?" As they passed the clearing, Krohn saw tree stumps and rough sheds that the crew had built.

"It all happened in perhaps just a minute, though it felt much longer. We were losing lift so quickly and had to go for the closest spot that was clear. Even so, the captain brought it down so beautifully that we only cracked a few of the rivets on the undercarriage, and one of the engines got damaged."

"How did you repair everything?"

"We didn't. Oh, we tried, using wood for the girders, and trying to repair the gas bags. But the bags had been shredded as they came apart and were a loss. We would have been stranded here if the captain had not been willing to eat of the fruit and receive the Lifter as his reward."

Krohn nodded. He had heard that part of the story only the day before and its implications were very exciting.

The *Himmler* drew much closer to the giant tree, slowing down to a crawl so slow that a man walking on the ground moved faster. Trott was taking no chances with his airship this time. Near Yggdrasil, on a grassy field far from any trees, the Germans had built a mooring tower out of a single log driven vertically into the ground, with more logs laid in a square around its base to support it.

Krohn pointed at the upright log. "That must have been a challenge to move."

"You have no idea," Alder said in agreement.

As the airship came closer to the ground, crew members leaped down and ran to grab the mooring lines that always hung from the dirigible. The total crew of the airship numbered twenty-five, all technical people: eight mechanics, three riggers, an electrician, two wireless operators, a cook, six helmsmen, three officers, and Captain Trott. All of them had training with weapons and party membership was required to be part of the crew; still, the only real soldiers aboard were Fritz and Karl.

Normally a ground crew of dozens of men were required to berth an airship, a process akin to hooking a large fish and reeling it in. Lacking such a crew, even though all but seven of his men were on the ground, tying mooring lines to wooden stanchions that they had built into the ground, Trott resorted to carefully settling the airship down, issuing orders to the elevator helmsmen as he worked the gas release board himself.

Krohn admired the captain, as awkward looking as the man was, because such skill and competence could only come from a true Aryan. Other peoples could only imitate; an Aryan created.

The keel of the airship settled onto the ground. The crew outside untied and retied their mooring lines, making every-thing fast to the ground. The droning of the engines ended, bringing a silence that surprised Krohn.

"We are secure, and I turn over command of Operation North Pole to you, Colonel," Captain Trott said, removing his gloves. The valley floor was quite warm, like a brisk autumn evening in Germany, unlike the colder temperatures only a few hundred meters up in the air.

"I assume command, Captain," Krohn said. "Excellent work."

The colonel went to his cabin and retrieved the marvelous silver globe. Fritz was standing guard outside of the prisoner's quarters. "Open the door."

The soldier held his pistol at the ready, opening the door and entering first, prepared for any mischief by the prisoners. The prisoners turned from where the two groups clustered around the windows. They had already removed their coats and gloves, adapting to the new temperature.

Krohn held out the silver globe, trying to quickly gauge the reaction of each of them to the sight of it. The Jew, the Indian, and the stout American all looked puzzled, as did the Irish girl. The rest of them had seen it before.

"I don't know who owned this, but I am certain it must be one of the senior officers. Colonel Rice, Major Carter, you will come with me."

CHAPTER FORTY-ONE

Though it had only been two days, Carter felt relief wash over him when he stepped out of the airship door and felt firm ground beneath his feet. The valley smelled of pine and flowers, an eternal spring. Birds sang in the trees and Carter noticed a bug bustling across the ground, some sort of small beetle with streaks of yellow and white along its back.

"Where are we?" Carter asked.

"Asgard," Krohn replied.

Carter was about to retort with a "you must be joking," but held his tongue. The giant tree before him showed him that the Nazi officer was entirely correct.

Krohn led the way, accompanied by the pudgy professor and Captain Trott. Rice and Carter followed, with the twin soldiers bringing up the rear. They had traded in their pistols for assault rifles. Carter had not gotten a good chance to look at their weapons, but he wished that he had one. The Germans were all clean-shaven, except for Trott, and their uniforms looked crisp, unlike Carter and Rice's rumpled uniforms. Three days in the same clothes and he had began to notice his own stink; not a good sign, since a man is the last to smell his own odors. Three days' worth of stubble on his cheeks had reached the stage where the whiskers began to itch.

After walking for half an hour, they entered the zone of shade offered by Yggdrasil; the grass grew shorter here and was no longer as vibrant a green. As they approached the tree, Carter tried to judge how thick it was; eventually he decided on an estimate of perhaps a quarter of a mile. The lowest of the branches above them were perhaps five hundred yards in the air and were thick enough to hold complete villages on them. Such an idea might have seemed silly an hour ago, but he did not automatically discard it now. Like Alice in Wonderland, the rules of the normal world no longer applied. He would have to learn new rules.

The grass faded to be replaced by rocky dirt and large boulders. Mushrooms grew here in abundance. Or maybe they were toadstools—he could never tell the difference. He wondered why the flora had changed. This must be an area of permanent shade. The sun circled around the horizon during the course of the day, never setting during the summer, allowing partial sunlight in the areas where the sickly grass grew. Here was a zone of permanent shade created by the tree and its branches. The sun had not touched here since the tree had grown. If the Norse myths were correct, the world tree had never grown; it was the primary axis of the planet, the center of Genesis itself.

Coming closer to the tree, Carter saw that its light-grey bark was rough and scaly, reminding him of truly ancient trees. The trunk sprang directly out of the ground, without any widening at the base to indicate a root system, as if the tree had its roots much further below their feet. Smaller branches also grew near the base of the tree, their bark smooth, like a young ash tree. Some of the branches grew close enough to the ground for a person to reach up and touch. The long narrow leaves were normal-sized, about three inches from stem to tip. To his surprise small, grey, plum-sized fruit grew among the leaves.

"The Fruit of Life," Krohn said, his tone reverent, as if he were in a church.

"Yes, just as in the legend we found in Oslo," Alder said.

Krohn turned to the airship pilot. "Tell me, Captain, how did the fruit taste?"

"I did not notice any taste. It was like an explosion in my mind. I felt ransacked, dissected, understood, loved, and used, all at the same time. I realize that those are not compatible emotions, but that is still an accurate description of what I felt."

"To feel two irreconcilable emotions is ancient wisdom," Krohn said, bowing his head slightly. "You should feel honored to have experienced this."

"I am, Colonel."

"Tell me, how did you keep in mind the idea of your greatest desire? The text from Oslo was quite explicit that the Norns only award that which we wish for more than anything else."

Concentrating intensely on the conversation, Carter was surprised to hear of the Norns. He realized that he shouldn't be; everything here was a new world and required that he abandon old ways of thinking. The story of the Norns was integral to the story of Yggdrasil, three sisters who sat at the base of the tree, weaving the destinies of each person, like the Fates in Greek and Roman mythology. These women even had names: Urd, who wove the past; Verdandi, who wove the present; and Skuld, who wove the future.

"I did not try to concentrate," Trott said. "The *Himmler* is my life, and repairing the dirigible truly was my greatest wish."

"How quickly was your wish granted?" Krohn asked.

"I think to characterize it as a wish is inaccurate," said Professor Alder. "A wish is a surface thought, something that a child does on his birthday. The fruit grants the deepest desire of a person—something not on the surface, but truly down deep. Conscious thought is not required."

"You are entirely correct, my dear Friedrich," Krohn responded. "Terminology is always important. It is a desire, not a wish. Still, Captain, how quickly was your desire granted?"

"Immediately. The Lifter appeared at my feet."

"Just like magic," Krohn said.

"Not magic," Alder interrupted. "Magic is parlor tricks, designed to deceive the ignorant masses. This is a fundamental power. No, *the* fundamental power of the earth and the power of Odin himself."

"Yes, Odin's hand is certainly in this," Krohn said. "The faith that we have nurtured for all these years has been confirmed."

"Perhaps it's just a technology that we don't understand," Carter said, breaking his silence. Rice had not said a word since they landed; his eyes alive with wonder and confusion.

"Lo, the prisoner speaks," Krohn mocked. "You are obviously not a believer. 'Oh, ye of little faith,' to quote your misguided religion."

Carter dug through dusty memories of Bible lessons. "'Thou shalt have no other gods before me.'"

Krohn laughed, obviously in an excellent mood. "So, do you have any information for us? Perhaps something that the silver globe told you?"

"Not that I know of," Carter said, while Rice just shrugged. "May I ask, though, about this Oslo document that you referred to? What did it say?"

"We found it after we took Norway," Krohn explained. "Or, I should say, Professor Alder here found it. It was in the king's castle, hidden away for centuries, where no one had looked at it. Another set of sagas, even older than the Icelandic sagas. They told us that Asgard really existed and they told us about the wondrous fruit of Yggdrasil."

"And what is the Lifter?" Carter asked.

"An object that defies gravity," Krohn said. "You saw it bolted to the floor of the bridge. All that Captain Trott has to do is stroke it with his fingers and he has greater lift, he strokes it again and lift decreases. It is the only reason that the *Himmler* was able to recover from its accident and bring us here."

Since the colonel seemed to be a talkative mood, Carter pressed him. "And what do you plan to do with us, Colonel?"

Krohn smiled. "Wonderful things."

Carter recalled what Aoife had said to him and the awful evidence he had found at the temple outside Dachau. That had been only seven days ago.

As if to confirm Carter's suspicions, Krohn turned to his friend and said, "Friedrich, we must build an altar, as quickly as possible."

Further conversation dribbled away as the group of men

became aware of another party approaching them; two men and two women who wore tunics that came down to their knees, leaving their arms exposed. The air felt warm to Carter after two days of being too cold, but not that warm. They wore sandals, and the cloth of their simple clothes formed a riot of colors—red, green, and yellow swirls. Around each neck was a small golden torc, its metal twisted like strands of yarn.

The most arresting feature was how youthful they looked despite their solid white hair, cut short on the men, tumbling down to the shoulders of the women. Carter found the women attractive, like great paintings, but they were not women that roused sensations in him.

Carter looked sharply at Rice and his white hair.

The colonel just smiled and shrugged ruefully. "Don't ask me."

CHAPTER FORTY-TWO

"We welcome your return, Captain Trott and Professor Alder," the man in front said in fluent German. "And we see that you have brought others. May we be introduced?"

Alder introduced everyone, even the two soldiers. The valley residents bowed to each of the men as they were introduced. The Germans did not bow in return, but Carter and Rice did so.

"My name is Fotudeng and I am selected to lead this group for this day." The others introduced themselves. The women were named Jakucho and Ayya and the other man was Xuanzang. Carter had the overwhelming sense that he was in the presence of gentle people, monks and nuns, dedicated to loftier matters than the details of mere existence.

"Professor Alder has told me of you," Krohn said. "He says that you answer his questions only with riddles."

"We teach the only way that we can. While there are many methods of teaching, we find that direct answers, uncluttered by preconceived notions, are the best way."

"Where do you come from?" Krohn asked.

"We came from here." Fotudeng gestured with his hands, moving gracefully, as if he were shaping his words in the air as they flowed from his mouth, like a sculptor. "We live in the woods and on the grass, drink the water in the streams, and we think. We think all the time."

"What I mean is: where did you come from before you came to this place?" Krohn asked.

"We came from many places. I myself came from a small

island, a place of great fertility and abundant fruits, but also a place of arrogance and pain. We hurt each other and we hurt other people." He gestured toward the tree. "A root from the world tree thrust up into our island, reminding us of our follies, and the island was ripped asunder in fire and water. Blessed be the world tree."

"Blessed be the world tree," the other three newcomers said in unison.

"We call it Yggdrasil," Krohn said.

"That is one of its names. It is the Tree of Life. Most peoples of our world, with their limited understandings, have some sort of story about this tree. As we all should, since it gave us life."

"Do you worship it?"

Fotudeng looked blank. "We honor it. Only the Divine deserves worship. The tree is only the instrument of the Divine."

"Do you worship Odin?"

"No, we worship only the Divine."

"What do you call yourselves?" Krohn asked.

"We are the Seekers."

"Don't you have another name?"

"We have no other name for ourselves."

"Are you Aryan?" the German SS officer asked.

Fotudeng smiled indulgently. "Professor Alder told us about this idea of Aryans. It is an old idea. Some old ideas are wrong and some are right. It is the nature of ideas."

"But this place exists," Krohn said. "The stories of the Norse are true. For you to live here, you must have the purest blood and are surely of Aryan stock."

"These are the ideas of weak minds," Fotudeng said, laying out his hands open before his chest. "Not our ideas."

"Weak?" Krohn said, his face turning red. "We represent the greatest empire the world has ever known. We alone built the dirigible that brought us here. And we alone found this place. We alone found you."

Fotudeng was placid in the face of Krohn's anger. "We were not lost."

Krohn turned to Alder. "You are right, Friedrich. Very frustrating people." With a visible effort to calm himself, the colonel turned back to Fotudeng.

"Tell me, have you eaten any of the fruit of this tree?" Krohn asked.

"I am not ready to do so. One must prepare his inner soul. To do otherwise is just foolishness. The world is full of foolish people and we have learned from our observations."

"Have any of the other Seekers eaten any of this fruit?"

"Yes." Again, as placid as a pond in still air.

"I want to talk to some of those who have done so."

"They're no longer here."

"Why not?" Krohn burst out.

"They ate the fruit."

"You are a very petty, frustrating man," Krohn said through clenched teeth. "What happened when they ate the fruit?"

"You already know the answer. They obtained their deepest desires."

"And what was that desire?"

"To transcend."

Carter broke into the conversation. "You say that you are not ready to eat the fruit? Does that mean that your deepest desire is not yet to transcend?"

Fotudeng turned to the American. "Of course."

"What does it mean to transcend?" Carter asked.

"To become more than we are, to be something that we can't even imagine. To be with the gods."

Carter bowed. "Thank you for your answers."

"Fritz," Krohn said, his hands twitching and his tone so controlled that Carter expected the man to began cursing any moment. "I want this man to come back with us."

Alder placed his hand on Krohn's arm and spoke softly. "Not prudent. Remember what I told you about last time."

"Oh, yes. Completely passive and useless." Krohn motioned for his soldier to stay back.

"We have spoken to you and answered your questions,"

Fotudeng said. "Now we would like to talk to the Wanderer."

"Who?"

Fotudeng ignored the SS officer and turned his attention to Rice. "Welcome back, Wanderer."

"You know me?" Rice asked.

"You are one of the Seekers, who became the Wanderer. You have been gone for a long time."

"If I am one of you, why don't I remember this place?"

Fotudeng stepped back and offered his place in front of the group to one of the women. She stepped forward. "I am Ayya. You are the Wanderer. You are my blood brother; our mother was the same. Our mother has transcended since you left."

"Why don't I remember you?" Rice asked.

"You ate the fruit without the desire to transcend," Ayya said. "You wanted to leave the valley and explore. The world tree granted this wish."

"How long have I been gone?"

"Hundreds of years."

Rice did not visibly react to this statement. Carter made an intuitive leap as he looked at the man he had come to think of as a friend. Rice was not astonished, because he already knew that his life was much different from everyone else's.

"What is my name?" Rice asked.

"Alosa, son of Puela." She stepped forward and placed her hands on his cheeks. "Welcome back. This will start the remembering." She pulled his face to her and kissed him on the lips.

Rice smiled and touched her hair with a fond caress. "I remember nothing."

"Give it time." Ayya smiled at her brother. "You always were so impatient."

"That describes me," Rice laughed.

"I perceive that you are not here of your own free will," she said. "That you are prisoners of these other men. This man called John Carter is also a prisoner. He is your friend?"

Rice looked at the major. "Yes, he is my friend. Say hello to my sister, John."

Carter bowed. "You have a beautiful home here."

"Provided by the gods," Ayya said. "You are here during the summer, when the sun stays in the sky all the time. Our other seasons are much more interesting. The valley forms a perfect bowl that invites fog to settle in every morning, only burning off after the sun has risen high enough into the sky in the spring and autumn. On those long winter nights, when daylight comes for a few short hours from a sun just peeping over the horizon, the fog stays all the time."

Krohn found the reunion of brother and sister intellectually fascinating, but time was passing and his Reich was dying by the minute. "We must be on our way," he said. "Perhaps we will have time to talk in a few days. We are leaving."

The brother and sister did not want to part, but a gentle prod from Karl's assault rifle sent the white-haired prisoner on his way. Krohn led the way and he noticed that Trott fell behind a bit, walking closer to the prisoners than to the two German leaders. Krohn glanced back and looked closely at the dirigible captain. He looked miserable. Krohn's hackles rose as he perceived that the man's sympathies lay with the Seekers. Was that a result of eating the fruit? Not necessarily. The captain's SS personnel file contained evaluations that showed he was lukewarm as a Nazi. Normally he would never have been chosen for this important a mission, but his expertise was too vital.

The party skirted around the edge of Yggdrasil, as if they planned to circle the tree, though Krohn already knew that was impossible.

"The Seekers speak German like a native," Krohn said to his friend.

"Yes, they picked up our language in only a few days," Alder said. "All they did was listen to us. I asked them about it and they said that all human languages are children of our primal language, so they had to only learn the details of our dialect. They also seemed quite aware of what is happening in the world outside the valley. Though they live in huts, I suspect that they have some technology that lets them watch what others are doing around the world."

"Remarkable, if true," Krohn said. "We must find that technology after we save the Reich. What a boon for intelligence collection."

"The moment that I saw your prisoner back on Bear Island, I wondered if he was a Seeker," Alder said.

"I also wanted to see what the Seekers would think of him," Krohn said. "I was not disappointed."

As they continued around the tree, they left the mushrooms behind, passed through a short swath of yellowed grass, then came out into the sun. Ahead of them appeared a great valley, with a cliff face of weathered stone on the far side. A warm breeze blew against their faces and Krohn sniffed the air for clues. A faint tang of exotic foliage, perhaps.

They came to a stream, small enough to easily step over. Krohn bent down and cupped some of the water in his hands. Very cold, but refreshingly clear, like drinking from a glacier-fed stream in the Alps.

As they drew closer, it became apparent that it was not a valley before them, but a great hole a mile wide, completely ringed by grey cliffs. On its far side, streams that came from the rim wall found the lowest point in the valley and fell as three waterfalls, glistening water scattering into spray.

How suitable for Yggdrasil to have such a hole at its side. Krohn knew from Alder's report of his explorations of the valley that the trunk of the tree actually formed part of the wall of the hole. The breeze on their faces came from the hole. Like the tides, the hole exhaled a breeze twice a day, alternating with a breeze that blew the other direction as air flowed into the hole.

The Earth breathing in and out.

The ground abruptly sloped down towards the hole and Alder held up his hand. "We should stop here. The ground is not always stable, and if we slip there will be no stopping us."

"What a magnificent sight," Krohn said. "I would love to look straight down."

"I once secured a rope up here and descended all the way to the edge and looked down," Alder said. "It goes down as far as the eye can see, like a great tunnel. It is better lit than you would expect, since the sun's rays can only go so far."

"What about using the *Himmler* to hover over it?" Krohn looked at Trott. "After you have completed all your repairs, of course."

"I am concerned about the crosswinds we might find above the hole," Trott said. "But I too am curious."

Krohn turned to his two prisoners and gestured like a host showing his guests one of his most prized treasures. "There lies Pellucidar, the worlds inside our hollow Earth."

CHAPTER FORTY-THREE

Kneeling on the hard floor of the crew's quarters on the *Himmler*, Carter clenched his fists in tight balls while one of the twins tied his hands together behind his back. He had read about the trick in a Hardy Boys novel. Keep the fists tight and flex the muscles to make the forearms bulge, so when you relaxed your hands, the bonds were looser. It sounded good in theory and he now had a chance to test it in reality. The twins tied up every other man in the room, and even Angela had her hands bound before her, the casts holding her arms out at awkward angles.

Aoife was the exception, still in her manacles, which had never been removed. Carter suspected that this meant she was Krohn's most prized prisoner. He relaxed his fists. The Hardy Boys seemed to have gotten that one wrong. What's worse, the bonds were tighter this time and Carter worried that his hands were going to go numb, and he worried even more what the extra precautions for Aoife meant for her prospects.

The twins left the room and the prisoners were alone. "I turned off the intercom," Mann said. "They can't hear us."

"How'd you do that?" Carter asked.

"Used a dime to loosen the screws and I pulled out the right wire," the Canadian said. "Easy enough to do."

"So where did they take you?" Napier asked.

Carter told the story, even about the reunion of Rice with his sister. "Is it true that you have lived for hundreds of years?" Angela asked the colonel.

"I have lived for hundreds of years," Rice said, looking

down at the floor as if he were telling a shameful secret. "I can remember being in London in the early 1600s. I even went to a play in which Shakespeare acted. I don't remember which one, but I think it was *Richard the Third*. I have wandered the world ever since that time."

"Can you die?" Carter asked.

"I think so. I can get hurt, I just heal quickly, and I do feel pain. I may have been hurt worse than Angela in that plane crash, but my body healed me so quickly that it really didn't matter."

"Do you remember anything about this valley yet?" Carter asked.

"I can remember a little...just hazy outlines of a bigger story," Rice said. "We came here from many places, drawn by a desire to find spiritual food. My mother brought my sister and me here after our home island was destroyed by a volcano. We are Minoans, from an island called Thera in the Aegean sea. There isn't much there anymore. The remaining land forms a crescent around a deep harbor, which is where our volcanic mountain used to be. The layer of ash on the remaining land is so deep that no one realizes that Minoans used to live there. Archaeologists think that all of us were on Crete. They didn't even know we existed until about fifty years ago, and they have not realized our wonders. We were a great civilization, ruling the sea with our ships, trading all over the Mediterranean and even into the Atlantic Ocean and up to England. We had no walls around our cities because we feared no attacks. We actually had indoor plumbing, long before the Romans, and we cultivated the arts and knowledge of all things."

"So not everyone came from Thera?" Carter asked.

"Other people in the valley came from the ancient cities of the Indus. The world was warmer then, and it was possible to sail almost all the way to this valley."

"How long ago was that?" Carter asked.

"A very long time ago."

"Why did you leave the Seekers?"

"I came to believe that we were wrong. We only sought the inner peace necessary to transcend. We withdrew from the world and become only observers, never actors. I wanted to be an actor, a positive force for creating good."

"I wonder if you are the only one to have left?" Angela mused.

"I do remember one other person who left long before me. He went back to his homelands and shared our teachings, to seek spiritual attainment and not material things, to not be bound by desire, even the desire for relationships with your families, to seek transcendence with the divine. After teaching for a time, he returned to take the fruit and to transcend. His name was Siddhartha; he is known to his followers as the Buddha."

"I wonder if any other religious leaders came from this place?" Angela mused.

"I don't know," Rice said. "I don't remember. But we also saw something else, something as incredible as the great tree. Tell them, John."

Carter described the great hole in the ground. "Krohn said, if I recall the words correctly: 'There lies Pellucidar, the many worlds inside our hollow Earth'."

"That makes no scientific sense at all," Napier said. "I know that I'm not college-educated like some of you, but I have read a lot of articles on science and technology. Those magazines have more than stories in them. The idea of a hollow earth is impossible. The physics don't make any sense. Gravity comes from mass, so the Earth can't be hollow, because where would we get enough mass for the gravity that we feel?"

"I guess when theory meets reality, the theory has to be changed," Rice said.

"You don't understand," Napier said. "This is impossible."

"I think that we have seen many impossible things today," Rice said. "I am a skeptic by nature, but my skepticism goes farther than questioning received wisdom. I am an example of someone who breaks the rules, and so I have always known that there are other rules that we don't know about. I also think that some of these rules, or at least hints of them, are found in various legends and mythological stories. That is why I have studied religion, the occult, and the mystical for so long. Science did not tell us that this tree might exist. In fact, I think that botanists and physicists would tell us that it should collapse under its own weight. But there are legends that told us that the tree exists."

"I see what you mean, sir," Mann said. The Canadian Indian usually listened, rather than revealed his own thoughts to others. "We have a legend that only a few of my people know anymore. It is one of the stories of the creation. It is said that the earth in the beginning was bare, then the divine spirit came down and planted a seed. From this seed grew a giant tree, reaching all the way up to the stars. Then the divine spirit touched the tree and a fruit grew—and grew and grew and grew. It grew so large that it burst to become the sun. Other fruit also grew on the tree, and from these many fruit the animals and birds and fishes were born. The animals and birds and fishes spread out into their own places, the land, the air, and the sea. Finally, the first man and woman came out of a fruit. Instead of immediately walking the land, they ate another fruit, and that is why we people think of ourselves as godlike."

"Sounds similar to the story of Adam and Eve in the Bible," Carter said.

"Many important stories sound similar because they are speaking the same truths," Rice said.

"Is there more to the story?" Aoife asked.

"Yes. We remember the story when we make our medicine lodges. In the center of the circular lodge is a medicine pole. A tree is carefully chosen to represent the first tree and then is cut down, but we don't let it touch the ground. We trim it and carry it to the lodge, spiritually prepare a hole, and place it there. The roof to the lodge is not complete, so that the top of the medicine pole touches the sun. We play our drums, sing our songs, and ensure that the sun continues to come every day."

"Did your people have a story about a hollow earth?" Carter asked.

"Only vague stories, though stories about an inner world

where people live are common throughout the world."

Carter expressed his surprise. "Where people live?"

"Yes, why not?"

Carter just looked bewildered. This is how Alice must have felt when she fell down that rabbit hole.

"We have stories of trees also," Aoife said. Everyone turned to the young Irish woman. She still wore the blouse and skirt of a German country girl. "I read a book once on Irish mythology. It said that we Irish had lost all our creation stories and only have Christian stories left. The author should have asked the women in my family what the true stories were."

"What would they have told him?" Carter asked.

"He was a she. The author was a woman, Lady Ada Swift. My mum would have told her that the trees are where the men went to worship. They called them druids. That was for the men. The women of my family worshiped Danoā. Before Saint Patrick brought Christianity to Ireland, many people worshiped the mother goddess. From her came the bounty of the fields, fresh water in the rivers, and the fertility of women."

"You said that you were a Catholic," Napier said.

"Aye, I am a Catholic, but I can also worship Danoā. I am sure that Jesus doesn't mind."

"I think that your priest would mind," Carter said.

"He is a man who will never know a woman," Aoife said. "How can he ever understand Danoā?"

"But if God is the only god and his son Jesus Christ is our only Lord, where does Danoā fit in?"

Aoife shrugged. "I know that it might be confusing, but we just don't know. Some people believe that Danoā is the Heavenly Mother for our Heavenly Father. Someone must have birthed Jesus in the mind of God before he was born of Mary on this Earth."

"Her ability to reconcile what we find irreconcilable is not unique," Rice said. "Some archaeologists have found small soapstone molds for casting both Christian crosses and the hammer of Thor at the same time. Some graves had been excavated with both symbols in them. As the Nordic peoples abandoned the Nordic gods and embraced Christianity, individual people often covered both bases."

"As fascinating as this conversation is, we have more immediate concerns," Carter said. "Krohn is up to no good and we need a plan."

"I agree," Rice said. "We haven't been able to talk about it before now because of the intercom."

Aoife reached inside a pocket of her skirt and brought out a small penknife. She popped it open to reveal a three-inch-long blade. "Here's your plan," she said.

CHAPTER FORTY-FOUR

Napier twisted around and presented his bound hands to the young woman. Carter stood and came over to watch her. The knife was dull and she had to saw at the fibers, like a frustrated carpenter with flawed tools.

"After we are all free," Carter said, his mind racing in tactical mode, "we will burst out of the door—there is no lock—and overrun the airship. There must be an arms locker aboard."

Napier's hands came free and he turned around. Taking the knife from Aoife's hands, he surprised her by kissing her quickly on the lips. Her face turned red in embarrassment, but the big smile and pleased look on her face conveyed other emotions.

The sergeant began sawing at Carter's ropes. As he felt his hands come free, the door to the room started to open. Carter was in motion, coming around the bunks, before the door was completely open.

The German crewman held a platter with sausages and bread on it in one hand, his other hand still on the door handle. Carter flung his body against the astonished man, driving him across the hall and into the opposite wall. Food flew everywhere. Carter pounded both of his fists into the man's face. And again.

Out of the corner of his eye, he saw Napier come out of the room and lunge at the guard, like a linebacker hitting an unwary quarterback. The pistol in the guard's hand skittered away, down the hall towards the bow of the airship. Carter's eyes followed the pistol, which slid to a stop near some shoes clad in anti-static coverings. Carter focused upwards and saw the surprised face of a crewman standing in the commons room.

The crewman shouted, "Alarm! Alarm!"

"Dammit!" Everything had gone wrong. Not enough time to release the others and that crewman was a lot closer to the pistol than either of the Americans.

"Follow me, Sergeant," Carter yelled, startling himself with the unnecessary volume of his voice.

"We'll be back," Carter called as he turned towards the stern and ran to the washroom. Napier was right behind him.

Slamming the door to the washroom closed behind them, Carter opened the side door to the outside. Carter's toe caught the lip of the frame around the door and he tumbled outside, landing four feet below on the grass. The aroma of crushed grass in his nostrils reminded him of cutting grass back home, a momentary flash of memory quickly pushed away. He leaped up and looked around. A nearby group of three crewman, working on one of the girders recently brought back from Bear Island, stared at him in astonishment. The control cabin blocked Carter's view of whoever else might be around.

Napier dropped to the ground behind him, landing on his feet.

"Make for the trees," Carter said, starting to run. He felt a twinge in his ankle, perhaps from the fall, but he pushed through it, hoping that motion would work it out. Napier kept up with him until the twinge in Carter's ankle eased, then the longer legs of the major allowed him to pull away. He slowed down, seeing no reason to run too far ahead of his friend.

The trees were only several hundred yards away. Carter looked back, already a party of five crewman was chasing them and at least two had pistols in their hands. Good, no rifles. Carter did not relish being picked off like a deer. The twins and their deadly assault rifles must be elsewhere, perhaps back at Yggdrasil, building the altar.

It felt wrong to be running away. They were soldiers, they were supposed to fight, but fighting without weapons was folly. Running away and staying free preserved their options for later.

As they neared the trees, Carter decided that they should follow the tree line rather than go into the woods. Make it a foot race and see if German aircrew could keep up with American soldiers. If the race looked lost, they could dodge into the trees and make a stand there. After all, in training, they had regularly gone on twelve-mile runs with light packs.

Napier kept up with him, puffing like a panting bulldog, red in the face. Carter's lungs heaved and his muscles felt ragged. He could not pretend that they were in as good a shape as they had been two years ago while in training. Months of combat had worn down that edge. And having people chasing them made them run faster, burning more energy than the steady loping gait favored in training.

The land dipped down towards a stream, but it was only about four feet across. Carter leapt, falling to his hands and knees on landing. He gasped for breath. Napier crashed down behind him, one foot slipping back down the bank and into the water before he could yank it out.

Carter took a moment to reach down and grab a handful of water, splashing it into his mouth as he resumed running. The water was icy cold and painful on his lips and throat.

The land rose before them and the two men dug in, keeping up their speed as much as possible. Carter looked back. The aircrew were in even worse shape than the two Americans and were falling further back. They reached the stream and splashed through as if they didn't have the energy to jump over it.

The hill before them stretched from the edge of the valley down to Yggdrasil and the gateway to Pellucidar, like the spokes of a wagon wheel. A rise not more than two hundred feet in height, but for the panting men, it felt much bigger. The forest to their left dwindled into grass before reaching the crest of the hill. Carter didn't like moving away from the possible refuge that the trees provided.

As the two soldiers reached the top, Carter looked back and was surprised that the Germans had stopped chasing them.

He didn't feel good about that.

CHAPTER FORTY-FIVE

"I want every man issued weapons," Krohn ordered. "You do have enough weapons, don't you?"

Trott straightened his back. "Yes, sir, pistols or rifles for every man."

"Do it now." The captain scurried off.

Krohn had been on the way back from the altar when the escape of the two prisoners happened. The aircrew disgusted him, letting unarmed men get away.

Ordering two aircrewmen to stand with pistols ready, Krohn went into the prisoners' quarters, with his own pistol out. He saw the cut ropes on the floor and looked around at the remaining prisoners. The women avoided his eyes. The Jew looked at the floor, the Indian examined his fingernails, and the Seeker met his gaze.

Krohn struck the smug man with the barrel of his Luger, raking across the cheek of a man who had lived for hundreds of years. No longer so smug, the man cried out and stumbled back. The Indian stood from his bunk, quick and ready. Krohn pointed the pistol at him and swore at him in German, gesturing for him to sit back down.

He hit the Seeker again and again, driving him to the floor. Then he kicked him repeatedly, aiming for the crotch and the ribs and the head, as the man curled up like a scared child, unable to bring his bound hands over his face.

"I will have no more escapes," Krohn said in a quiet voice, using English.

No reaction among the prisoners. "Where did the knife come from?" he demanded.

"Major Carter had it," Aoife said, looking up from the bunk where she lay. "He took it with him."

Made sense. Krohn wondered briefly where the major had gotten hold of the knife. Was there treachery among the aircrew? No time to follow up.

He called for more ropes and personally tied up everyone's feet, binding them to bunk supports. No one else was getting away.

After binding the pilot's feet, he asked her, "Are you a virgin?"

She looked away,

"You will either answer or I will have the medic look and tell me what evidence he finds."

"I'm a virgin."

"Very good."

Two virgins to serve as brides of Odin. The Irish one had excellent ancestry, while this American bitch was undoubtedly of a mixed mongrel background, but she was a virgin. Plus the Jew, an Indian, and a Seeker to round out the offering to Odin. A nice variety, certainly the best that he had ever offered. Still, he had wanted to include the two soldiers. The idea of sacrificing enemy warriors, something that the ancient Norse and Aryans had done, excited him. He had always wanted to do it, but Himmler had always been afraid to ask Hitler for permission. Damn Hitler for his unbelief.

Angela Wright squirmed. The bonds cut deep and she felt her hands and feet going numb. This had become a nightmare. A plane crash, being a prisoner, and now trussed up and facing a limited future as a sacrifice.

Their only hope was the two American soldiers. If the major and sergeant had been caught, she was sure that they would have heard them being returned to the airship. If they had been slain, she was sure that Krohn would have told them, if only out of cruelty. The only other glimmer of hope came from the knife in Aoife's pocket. When Carson dropped the knife as he followed his commander out the door, Aoife had quickly recovered it. But it was such a small knife.

"Edgar? Edgar?" she called out, speaking softly. She had never called the colonel by his given name. "Are you okay?" Stupid question. "Can we help you?" Not much opportunity of that either, with everyone tied to a bunk. Rice had been tied to the one nearest to where he lay on the floor.

The Seeker stirred, but did not speak.

She had always admired the colonel, for his intellect and his warmth. He was also a handsome man in his own way. Normally such a combination would have led to attraction, but it had not. She had on occasion wondered why this was so; perhaps a part of her had sensed that he was fundamentally different. Certainly Seekers were different. Had it been feminine intuition? She normally didn't credit that supposed trait as being anything more than paying close attention to social and personal cues.

"Edgar," she whispered. "Are you healing?"

"I am and it hurts like hell," he said, his voice coming in gasps. "I just need to rest."

Hours passed with no conversation. It was remarkable how much one could hear if one remained still and silent. She heard the occasional shouts or laughs from working men outside, and then the noise of men eating their evening meals in the dining room. No one brought them any food. Then, little by little, the sounds quieted. The men of the aircrew were sleeping.

"Angela, you still awake?" Aoife asked from the next bunk.

The pilot twisted her head around to look at the younger woman. "I can't sleep. My hands and feet hurt too much to settle down."

"I dreamed about one of my friends back at the camp last night," Aoife said. "She took one of the pills that they offered us at night."

"What were the pills for?" Angela asked.

"They gave us the pills to keep us calm, so that we wouldn't make a fuss. I threw mine away. I like to see life as it really is, even if it is ugly."

"So where is your friend?"

"Gone." Aoife looked down at her hands. Her lips trembled as she struggled to not cry, but the tears came anyway. "She was sacrificed, just as we are going to be."

CHAPTER FORTY-SIX

Carter and Napier walked across the crest of the hill and found themselves looking down into a small valley. Instead of the green of grasses and trees, they saw only grey. Withered grey grass covered the valley floor, and the gnarled trees that crouched like hunched-over men had no leaves on them. Thin layers of crusty snow covered large patches of the ground. Perhaps half a mile away, a single building stood, made of timbers thrust up vertically, with a peaked roof made of large round shingles, and carved ornaments at each end of the main beam that formed the apex of the roof.

In front of the building men were fighting, swinging swords and axes at each other, using shields to block the blows. The sound of curses and clang of steel on steel came to the two Americans across the valley.

"What should we do?" Napier asked.

"Normally I would say that we skirt around and try to avoid those folks," Carter said. "But we need to find out everything that we can about this valley and that means taking risks."

"Taking risks is fine until you're dead," Napier said. "We won't be able to help the others if we're dead."

Carter grunted his approval. He was glad that Napier was with him.

As they walked down into the valley, the air grew chillier and Carter regretted that he no longer had his coat. His physical discomfort became a secondary concern as they drew closer to the building and fighting men; a suspicion began to grow in Carter. It was now obvious that the roof of the building was made up of large, round wooden shields, some with a blunt metal point in the middle, others banded by iron, and many painted in garish colors.

He remembered the description from the book that Rice had given him. This was Odin's Hall.

The men stopped fighting as they saw the two Americans approach. They wore the clothes of Vikings—wool tunics over trousers, leather boots—and many had cloaks draped around their shoulders in a manner that allowed them free movement of their arms. Some of them wore coats of mail; others had only leather jerkins over their tunics.

Not a single Viking helmet had horns, he was disappointed to see, though he knew that such flourishes existed only in fiction. Most of the helmets were completely metal, though a few seemed to be made of wood with metal rims. Some of the helmets had nose guards, or nose guards combined with fixed visors with two holes for the eyes, covering the upper half of the face.

These men had been fighting for a long time. All the armor was dented, scuffed, or scratched.

One of the men, carrying a large battle-axe with both blades marked with blood, came forward. He carried a spear in his other hand. Watching the man gave one the sense of great brawn, worthy of a linebacker. "I am Ragnar. Who are you?" he demanded in Norse.

Carter struggled with the words, dredging up the sounds of words spoken in a classroom at Yale on a warm spring afternoon, the windows open to let some air into the stuffy room.

"Greetings. We are strangers to your valley," Carter said, hoping that he was picking the right words and getting the pronunciation right. "I am John Carter and this is Carson Napier."

"You know that this is our place and that you are supposed to stay on the other side of the hill," the big man said.

"We are fleeing our enemies."

The Viking looked disgusted. "What kind of man runs from a fight?"

"We do not shun the fight," Carter said, standing up taller and breathing in deeply in an unconscious effort to make his chest seem larger. "They have weapons and we do not. We need weapons to go back and fight them."

The big man laughed. "Then pick up weapons and learn to fight."

"We have no quarrel with you and come in peace," Carter said.

The big man bent down and pried a sword from the hand of one of the dead and tossed it at Carter. Carter twisted and caught the sword by the hilt, like a shortstop fielding a short hop.

"We have no quarrel with you either," Ragnar said. "Every man who enters this valley must fight. No exceptions."

"Carson, pick up a weapon," Carter said. "This may get nasty."

The sergeant kept a wary eye on the Vikings as he walked over to two men who looked as if they had slain each other and lay intertwined in death. Next to the limp hand of the man on top lay an axe, single-bladed, with a handle sheathed in metal. Napier picked it up and hefted it in his hand. It reminded him of the family axe back home that had he used to chop firewood. As a teenager, swinging at the cut logs, trying to split them with one blow, he had imagined that he was Conan or Kull or whoever he had just read about in *Weird Tales*, smiting his foes. Now it was real and he was beyond nervous, certain that he was about to die. Death by blade seemed much worse than dying by a bullet.

Napier returned to the side of his officer, glad that he would be dying with a friend, the man he respected more than any other man in the world. Despite his fear, he was not going to let down the major.

Holding the axe lightly in his hands, he settled into a boxing stance, taking comfort from the familiar feel of having his feet aligned just right.

Carter hefted his sword. Having been sent to a military academy as a youth, he had been compelled to take fencing classes. At Yale he had been on the fencing team and fancied himself to quite good with a rapier. The three trophies back at his mother's home in Virginia showed that his confidence had some basis in reality.

This sword was straight from a museum, with a three-inch-wide blade and a metal handle. Much heavier than a rapier, requiring entirely different tactics. He swung it back and forth and noticed that the heavy pommel, like a large cap on the top of the handle, acted as a counterweight and made the blade much handier than he expected.

Ragnar came at them first, swinging his battle-axe like a farmer scything his grain. Carter stepped back. The Viking laughed and lunged forward, swinging again, as if only brute force were necessary.

Carter avoided the swing and quickly stepped in, slashing with the sword. With a rapier, the maneuver would have looked elegant, but the heavy sword caught the chest of the Viking, ripping sideways, tearing his fur jacket and scraping across the coat of mail underneath.

No damage done, but when Ragnar came at the American again, he did so with more respect, moving warily and using short swings. Carter saw no reason to kill the Viking; it might just bring bad consequences. Out of the corner of his eye, Carter saw that the rest of the Vikings had also resumed their fighting. Occasionally he saw Napier, who seemed to be holding his own, but Carter didn't dare look too closely, lest Ragnar take advantage of his inattention.

Like two dancers, the men moved around the battlefield, with Carter yielding ground most of the time. Occasionally he launched an attack, thrusting and swinging, trying to give Ragnar pause. The Viking deflected these attacks easily by swinging his axe or by stepping aside.

Carter realized that the big man was toying with him, like a cat with a hapless mouse. What happened when he got bored?

When another man fell against him, Carter twisted out of the way quickly, barely avoiding the slice of Ragnar's axe. The Viking had taken advantage of the opportunity. The man on the ground had his skull cleaved open, grey matter spilling out. His killer went to find another opponent.

The clang of metal on metal and grunts of men had fallen in volume. Carter skipped back six or seven steps quickly, wanting to put enough distance between Ragnar and himself so that he could try to see what else was going on. He saw that most of the others were dead, added to the corpses. Only Napier and his foe, plus two other Vikings fighting each other, were alive besides Carter and Ragnar. Six men.

"This won't end until you kill me," Ragnar roared, rushing up with his axe swinging recklessly. Carter startled and stumbled back, falling to his knee. The axe came slicing through the air and the American ducked, feeling the wind in his hair as it passed by. Springing up, Carter thrust with both hands, aiming below the Viking's face.

The sword caught Ragnar's throat and cut through the side of his neck. The big man stopped, dropped to his knees, and pitched forward.

Cater looked around. He saw one of the other Vikings fall from a sword thrust into his chest. The victor stood over him, placed his foot on the still twitching man, and pulled his sword out with both hands. He was a smaller fellow, with wiry muscles, and a coat of mail covered with blood that came from an open wound on his face. He looked exhausted.

The Viking walked over to where Napier was still fighting his foe. Fearing for his friend, Carter started to run toward the three, dodging corpses.

He was too late. The smaller Viking thrust his sword into the base of the back of the Viking fighting Napier. The man fell; only one Viking remained with the two Americans.

Napier waited for the smaller Viking to make his move, but he ignored the sergeant, walking across the battlefield with his eyes on the ground. Carter joined Napier and they watched the

Viking until he found a spear and picked it up. It looked like the spear that Ragnar had been carrying, with carvings of runes up and down the length of its shaft and a long point with two sharp edges. Ragnar must have put it aside when fighting Carter.

The small Viking turned toward Yggdrasil and raised the spear. "I am Gudmund, son of Svien, and I am now Odin! May all true warriors die with a weapon in their hands, so that they may join us one day here, in Valhalla!"

To Carter's astonishment, the dead men lying on the ground stirred. Some of them struggled to sit up. As men got to their feet, they went to their fallen fellows and helped them get up, supporting them with shoulders under their arms until they were steady enough to stand on their own. No new blood poured from their wounds. The man with the split skull looked completely different. His skull had restored itself, with a crimson mark that looked like a birthmark, which gradually faded as Carter watched. Still, the men looked were a sorry sight, with ripped clothes and dried blood caked on them. Two ravens came down from the sky and swooped around Gudmund, cawing harshly before perching themselves on the roof of the great hall.

Gudmund came over to the two Americans. "Welcome to Asgard, strangers. You fought well, with courage, as we would expect. From your uniforms I see that you are soldiers."

Carter translated the old Norse for Napier, then said to Gudmund, "We appreciate your welcome. I see that you fought to the last man, except for us."

"Yes, it is what we do every day. Though now that the sun is up all day, we have to make our own days. We fight until only one stands and that man becomes Odin for the day. I am Odin now. Tomorrow, I may still be Odin, but it will be the last man standing."

"Who are you and why are you here?" Carter asked.

Gudmund laughed. Ragnar walked up and joined in the laughter. "Isn't it obvious? We're Norsemen, from the land of fiords. We are waiting for Ragnarök, the great battle at the end of the world, and then we will be released."

Ragnar punched Carter on the shoulder. "You fought well for a man who wasn't sure what to do with a sword."

Carter wanted to object that he knew how to fence, but fencing was a sport of dilettantes compared to the skills of these Vikings.

"Come to our hall and feast with us," Gudmund said. "Just leave your weapons, the Valkyries will take care of them."

CHAPTER FORTY-SEVEN

Long-haired women clad in shining coats of mail descended from the skies like angels, so bright and full of light. But angels were founts of wisdom from God, while the voluptuous beauty of the Valkyries provoked a yearning in Carter that ran deep in his bones. As the weary Vikings trudged back to their home, Carter kept watching the women. They alighted onto the ground, as if from the last step of a stairway, and began gathering up the weapons.

He hurried to catch up with the men, still taking quick glances backwards. Inside the great hall other Valkyries had already lit four fires where boars on spits slowly roasted. Other light came in through openings set high in the walls and through the smoke holes. Even though his body told him it was night and everyone else acted as if evening had come, the bright light of the sun scratched at the perception in a disconcerting way.

Carter saw that giant spears formed the roof of Valhalla. Benches made of roughly-hewn wood formed circles around each of the fires. Along the walls were sleeping platforms, some of them covered by curtains made of skins.

Gudmund and Ragnar led the Americans to one of the fires and encouraged them to sit. Valkyries brought them cups dipped from nearby open barrels.

"What's this?" Napier asked.

"I suspect it's mead." Carter took a sip. Tasted sweet, not like beer or wine, with an aftertaste that reminded him of bark. "Yep, it's mead. Brewed of honey and yeast, and water of course."

Napier took a sip, then a longer drink.

Valkyries cut slabs of wild boar and served it up on wooden platters. Carter burned his fingers and lips on the greasy meat, but after days of sausage and frozen bread, the meat tasted wonderful.

Ragnar held forth, telling stories of his childhood, battles won, enemies vanquished, and defeats suffered. He sounded like a braggart at the pub, but Carter knew that telling stories of their feats at the fire was a traditional way for Vikings to bond with each other.

Carter noticed that while Gudmund and Ragnar stayed at his and Napier's sides, the other Vikings came and went from their fire. After some observation, he realized that the Vikings were rotating around, each taking their turn to watch and listen to the strangers. Their arrival was probably the most exciting event for the Vikings in the last five or six hundred years.

During a break in the stories, as Ragnar caught his breath, Carter asked, "How did you know that we are soldiers?"

"We have the ravens," Gudmund said. "They wander the world as our eyes, showing whoever is Odin what they have seen. We have even seen you before, in the land of the Germans, at the temple that they built to us."

Carter remembered the ravens at Krohn's temple. "And what do you think of that temple?" he asked, not sure if he wanted to know the answer.

"The sacrifices mean nothing to us," Ragnar said. "They don't make us stronger or weaker, and we certainly don't help the Germans. They attacked our homelands, conquered our peoples, and fight without warrior honor."

"Seeing those terrified girls reminds me of my sisters," Gudmund said. "We have been so long without women, other than the Valkyries, that we have come to see women in a different light. We want to protect them, not use them; to be loved by them, not hated by them; and to have them cherish us in our old age, but we will never grow old. It is our curse."

"Gudmund is our poet," Ragnar said. "And he speaks truly."

"Why are you cursed?"

"We all came to this land together, in a boat," Ragnar said. "I was our leader. We had lost a war and were looking for the green valley that legend had told us was here. The great ice was smaller back then and in summer one could sail close enough. Once we got here, one of the Seekers told us that the fruit of Yggdrasil would grant any wish. I think of that Seeker as Loki, tempting us with the fruit of the gods. I was a fool, certain that my deepest desire would be to return to Norge and triumph in our war. So I took the largest fruit that I could find, cut it into small pieces, and we all ate of the fruit."

"It is not all Ragnar's fault," Gudmund said. "We all wanted to eat the fruit, and as Viking warriors we all had but one great desire."

"To go to Valhalla," Ragnar said. "The greatest desire of any true warrior."

"Then what happened?" Carter asked.

"We immediately found ourselves in this place. It was not here before, we had already explored the whole valley. Then the hall was here and so were the Valkyries. We have been fighting ever since."

"I read an account of a man by the name of Einar who talked about this valley," Carter said.

"My son," Ragnar said, looking into his cup of mead. "He built a boat and left us and made it back. We watched with the ravens. He died the long death as a peasant, without sword in hand, not the short death that takes warriors to Valhalla."

"I think that he had already spent enough time in Valhalla," Gudmund said.

Ragnar took a long drink. "I still miss him," he said.

"And I envy him," Gudmund said.

"If he had died with a sword, perhaps he would go to the real Valhalla," Ragnar said.

"You don't think this is the real Valhalla?" Carter asked.

"We are the only ones here. Surely there have been many other warriors worthy to join us," Ragnar said. "Perhaps somewhere else is the real Asgard, where there are warriors who died with swords in their hands and now await Ragnarök. We never died as warriors. The fruit made us who we are. This is a mockery of our beliefs, a curse that we must bear every day."

"Yggdrasil is here," Carter said. "How can there be more than one world tree? This must be Asgard."

"Or maybe Asgard doesn't even exist," Ragnar said. "I just don't know."

Carter blinked in surprise. An agnostic Viking: what a strange thought.

"All we know is what we experience here and now," Ragnar said. "You are the first people to ever visit us, except for an occasional Seeker. And they are not really visiting. They are just passing through and they never say anything."

"This is a place of Odin, all snow and ice," Gudmund said. "Thor never comes here. We have not heard thunder or seen lightning or felt rain ever since we came. The gods are content to watch us fight, and we are tired of fighting."

"You said that you are waiting for Ragnarök," Carter said. "What if it never happens?"

"We have watched the world," Gudmund said. "In those many hundreds of years we have seen the Christ-believers stamp out our Nordic beliefs. And now even many of the Christ-believers no longer believe. We have seen wonderful machines created. And we have seen many wars. Now that the great war that you are fighting is ending, perhaps Ragnarök will come. Your country is building a super weapon, a single bomb that can destroy a whole city. Maybe that will bring Ragnarök."

"We want it to happen," Ragnar said. "We just want everything to end."

The feasting continued, the mead flowed freely, and some of the men took Valkyries behind the curtains in the alcoves along the sides of the hall. Carter watched everything with fascinated eyes, as he felt the mead warming his body, making him ever more drowsy. Napier had already fallen asleep, slumped in on himself as he continued to sit on the bench, and Carter wanted to do the same. His body ached from too much running and fighting.

Who would have thought? Real Vikings in the Arctic; yet these Vikings were depressed with their lot in life, finding the fulfillment of their myths hollow.

CHAPTER FORTY-EIGHT

Fritz saw one of the Seeker women walking by the *Himmler*, so enticing in that simple tunic that they all wore, showing bare arms and shoulders and revealing her legs all the way up to her lower thighs. But how much she showed was quite irrelevant. She was a woman and not declared forbidden by Colonel Krohn.

He followed her into the woods, growing ever more eager with each passing moment. She heard him behind her and turned and he rushed forward and grabbed her. She made no effort to escape, did not even cry out before he clamped his hand over her mouth.

Then nothing went right. He could not get aroused, no matter what he tried. In his frustration, he beat her, and she did not resist, taking the blows like a limp doll. He left her crumpled on the forest floor and went back to his brother at the dirigible, confused and humiliated.

"Is it my turn?" his twin asked.

"It will never be any of our turns ever again," Fritz said, surprised and dismayed as the words of prophecy left his mouth.

An hour later, the Seeker walked by the dirigible, retracing her steps, her tunic torn at the shoulder, hair in disarray, bruised and scraped. Fritz followed her with his eyes, smoldering at her taunting walk, even though she never looked his way. He had thought that he had hurt her more than that, but the injuries seemed much less than what he had felt through his fists.

Krohn sat in the cabin that Captain Trott had set aside for him. The four bunks normally held petty officers. By virtue of his rank, he could have taken the captain's cabin, but one look at the number of books and diagrams crammed into Trott's quarters convinced him that it wasn't worth the effort. A small section of the bulkhead lowered to form a table. On it was a typewritten order just brought in from the radio room. The message had been sent out as an encrypted stream of gibberish, of course, and the typewriter-shaped Enigma machine in the radio room had been used to decrypt it. It was authentic.

The order was not for Unternehmen Nordkap. Krohn doubted that more than a handful of Nazis still alive knew about Operation North Pole. Admiral Dönitz, the brilliant man who had orchestrated the devastating U-boat campaign against the British and Americans, had been selected by Hitler to assume command upon his death. And now Dönitz had issued orders to the German troops in Norway to surrender. No doubt other orders had gone out to other pockets of German forces. And no doubt the Germans in Norway would obey the orders. Germans were good at obeying orders—a wonderful trait when good orders were issued, but a bad trait when the fight should go on.

The whole idea of a Festung Norwegen, a Fortress Norway, was dead.

He calmly picked up the paper and ripped it in half. He was the last hope. Laid out on the bunk behind him were his priest's robes, all white, with a large black swastika on the front and dozens of small runes woven directly into the cloth. On the table was the knife, stolen from a museum in Sweden. This knife had been used in the temple of Odin at Gamla Uppsala, near the ancient home of the kings of Sweden, and cared for during the centuries, polished and oiled to keep off rust, not like most knifes or swords from that time, turned into rusted and pitted mockeries of their former selves. The sagas recorded that the god Freyr built the temple and that human beings were sacrificed to the great idols of Odin, Thor, and Freyr. The temple had probably been destroyed in 1087 by King Ingold I during one of the last battles between the old pagan believers and the new Christian believers.

Krohn had not eaten or drunk during the last twenty-four hours. He had already walked over to the base of Yggdrasil twice and seen that Alder had the construction of the altar well in hand.

He looked at his watch. It was morning. He stood, held his robes up to admire them one last time, and began to dress.

CHAPTER FORTY-NINE

"I will not be going with you to take part in this savage ritual," Captain Trott said, standing at the hatch to the bridge. "Besides, someone must stay with the dirigible."

Krohn stood in his robes, with the twins flanking him, each dressed in their best uniform. Professor Alder had also donned robes. The five prisoners stood in a line. Their foot bonds had been replaced by a rope strung from prisoner to prisoner at their hands. The two women led the way. The aircrew stood in two lines, bringing up the rear of the planned procession; six carried rifles, the standard bolt-action Mauser Karabiner 98 Kurz, with five rounds in an internal clip, while the rest had pistols on their hips.

Krohn felt serene in the face of Trott's rebellion. He didn't need another unbeliever at the ceremony. Many of the aircrew were probably unbelievers, but they were all Aryans, and their presence was more of an advantage than a disadvantage. All in all, these were not the people he would have chosen to be at the most important event in Aryan history, but one worked with the material at hand.

The high priest of Odin waved his hand dismissively. "It's your choice, captain."

The procession set off with Krohn in the lead. Two of the aircrew carried Nazi flags on poles, black swastikas in circles of white on fields of red. Not the visual power of a Nuremberg rally, but good enough for this task.

As the procession walked through the grass, they came

across a group of nine Seekers, all alike with their white hair and multicolored tunics. Krohn was stunned to see a dark-skinned African among them. Clearly the Seekers were not an advanced form of Aryans. After the procession passed, the Seekers followed them.

"I have never seen so many of the Seekers together," Alder said.

"Do you think that they will interfere?" Krohn asked.

"No, they are too passive," Alder said. "I think that they will just watch, out of curiosity."

Krohn led the procession into the land of mushrooms and boulders, approaching ever closer to Yggdrasil, ready to bend destiny to his will. The altar was just ahead, about a meter high, built of small logs cut from the local trees, held together by wire and nails, and filled with a pile of rocks gathered from nearby. Not the elegant architecture that he would have preferred; in fact, it looked like something that children had built.

To Krohn's complete astonishment, a Viking in full costume stood up in front of him, stepping from behind a boulder where he had been crouching. He was not a big man, but carried a sword and an ornate spear, with a simple helmet on his head, like a inverted bowl that come down to his ears.

Krohn concentrated on the spear. It was made of wood and covered with runes. That is exactly what Odin's spear, called Gungnir and forged by a dwarf, would look like. Was this Odin? Come to watch the sacrifice? But surely Odin would not be a small man, but a Viking larger than life.

Another Viking appeared off to his left. This man was large, wearing a helmet with eyelets that made him look like a cat. A fringe of mail hung from the back of his helmet, like long hair, to protect the back of his neck. He carried a battle-axe, its metal gleaming from fresh oil. Someone had taken care of that weapon.

The second Viking looked like Odin, but why didn't he have the spear?

More Vikings stepped from behind boulders, on both sides

of the procession. Krohn looked back and saw even more Vikings behind them. They were surrounded and the procession had bunched up. The prisoners were only a step away, and the aircrew had broken their formation and moved close in, as if safety could be found in a crowd and not alone.

All of the Vikings were armed, a few with bows, arrows already nocked and ready. Had Odin brought his entire retinue? Then Krohn saw two men among the Vikings who didn't belong. Those two Americans, still in their rumpled uniforms, the officer holding a sword and a small axe in the hand of the sergeant.

One of the Vikings released an arrow. The feathered shaft made a *phtt* sound as it flew to its target. Karl fell down onto his side with the arrow embedded in his chest. Krohn gaped at the soldier, who still breathed, his eyes growing glassy.

The moment of betrayed surprise gave way to chaos. The Vikings screamed their battle cries, rushing in to kill. Fritz opened up with his assault rifle, which sounded like a machine gun until his clip ran empty, dropping the two Vikings in front of Krohn. The spear called Gungnir tumbled to the ground, as if it had no power.

From behind Krohn came the sharper report of the pistols and the louder reports of the rifles. The aircrew were fighting back.

Krohn lifted his robes, like a woman raising her dress, his fingers scrambling for his pistol. As he pulled the pistol from its holster, a blow from the back sent him tumbling, flinging the pistol out away from him. From the corner of his vision, he saw that Alder had drawn his own pistol just in time to shoot a Viking who had almost reached him. Another Viking came from a different angle and rammed his sword into the scholar. Professor Alder collapsed to the ground and his killer fell on top of him, red splotches blooming across his mail shirt. Fritz had replaced his clip and was dealing death with his modern weapon.

Krohn twisted around to see who had knocked him down.

The red-haired Irish virgin stood over him, a triumphant look in her eyes. She also had a small knife in her hands. As he watched, she cut through the rope holding her to the other prisoners. He saw more of his Germans falling, and the Vikings too.

Fritz's assault rifle fell silent again, drawing a quick look from Krohn. His loyal soldier lay near him, two feathered shafts protruding from his chest and another from his neck.

Everything was going wrong. Only quick action could preserve the goal. Krohn drew his sacrificial knife, scrambled to his feet, and lunged at the girl. If he could slay one of them—a sloppy sacrifice to be sure—then get to the fruit, he could still save the day.

The girl screamed and stumbled back. As Krohn drove the knife towards her, one of the other prisoners pushed himself in front of her and the knife went into his chest, buried almost to the hilt. Krohn tried to pull the knife out, but the prisoner's hands had closed over it, holding it in his chest in a death grip. Somehow the Jew had gotten his hands free. Krohn looked into the eyes of the Jewish prisoner from only a few centimeters away and saw the vermin grimace in triumph.

No!

He would not be denied. Leaving the knife and sacrificial victims behind, he ran for Yggdrasil. As he passed around the altar, he chanced a look back. No more Germans stood. Vikings lay sprawled around the area and among the fallen Germans. The prisoners were kneeling around their fallen mate—all but one. John Carter, the American officer, was chasing Krohn, a sword in his hand.

Krohn hitched up his robes and ran as fast as he could. Up there, a branch laden with grey fruit, within reach. He leaped and grabbed one of the fruit, falling with it in his hand. He rolled over and saw that the American was almost upon him. With his free hand he grabbed hold of the Thor's hammer around his neck.

The Nazi bit into the fruit.

CHAPTER FIFTY

Carter stopped.

SS Colonel Krohn looked at the American for a frozen moment, the fruit in the colonel's hand, the bite in his mouth, then a look of puzzlement crossed the German's features.

A whirlwind knocked Carter to the ground. The roar of the wind pounded at his ears. He dropped his sword and shielded his eyes with his hands, squinting to see what was happening.

The wind lifted the colonel in the air, shifted him into an upright position, and ripped his clothes into tatters. The pieces of the cloth flew away, leaving a naked man.

The roaring abated, but Krohn remained in the air. The look on his face, with closed eyes and slack mouth, was pure euphoria. Still suspended in mid-air, he drifted over to the tree, and was pressed up against the bark of its trunk.

Two limbs sprouted from Yggdrasil, quickly stabbing through his shoulders, circling back on themselves to secure the man tightly to the tree. Krohn's eyes flew open and he gasped. Blood trickled down from the wounds. His eyes fluttered for a few moments, then closed, as if he was going to sleep. His body went limp.

The Nazi officer hung there.

"Just like Odin," Rice said, coming up to stand next to Carter.

"What happened?" Carter asked.

"If I'm not mistaken, our Colonel Krohn assumed that his greatest desire was to preserve the Third Reich," Carter said. "I think that his *real* desire was the same desire that Odin had, to learn wisdom and knowledge. This was the final result of his intellectual quest."

"Will he be cut down after nine days, as Odin was?"

Rice looked at Carter. "Odin was a god. Colonel Krohn is just a man. A god can learn everything in nine days and a man can never learn everything. We lack the brain capacity. I think that he will remain there forever."

"I would have preferred to kill him," Carter said.

Rice smiled. "Let's go back to the others."

Near the altar, they came upon Napier and a Viking. Carter did not recognize the man who held a bow in one hand. Viking sagas record that bowstrings were actually made of women's hair spun into a string; in this case, Carter had been told that Valkyrie hair had been used. The Viking clutched his knife in his other hand and was weeping, Old Norse bubbling out of his lips. The sergeant looked bewildered.

"What does he want, sir?" Napier asked.

Carter listened. "He says that he is the only one left. He does not want to be alone. He is asking that you kill him while he holds his knife in his hand. He wants to die with his friends—the long death, not the short death."

"You mean that he won't be resurrected?" Napier asked.

Carter looked around at the dead Vikings. None were stirring, and only one Viking remained. The Valkyries had not come. Persuading the Vikings to help had been easy. He had told them that two innocent women were about to be murdered and that had been enough, a worthy cause to compel them to leave Valhalla. They knew that leaving their small valley might condemn them to the long death, but everyone seemed to think that this was an added advantage. This party of Vikings had been so tired of living, always dying the short death.

"They are all dead, the real death, I think," Carter said. "This man wants the long death."

Napier looked shocked. "I can't do that, sir."

Carter raised his sword. "He won't take his own life and we are alive because of him and his friends."

Napier put his hand on Carter's arm. "Wait...I'll do it, sir. Let me get a gun. It's easier that way."

The sergeant returned with a Luger taken from the dead professor. He slipped in a new clip and looked at the Viking. "Any last words?"

The Viking gripped the Thor's hammer around his neck in one hand and his knife in the other. How many hundreds of thousands of times had he died? Carter wondered. And now it was the long death.

Carson Napier shot the Viking in the heart.

Back among the corpses, the two women each held one of the hands of Rosenberg, while Mann sat on the ground with the man's head cradled in his lap. Aoife stroked his arm, her face shiny with tears.

The three others came up and knelt, completing a circle around the fallen man. The knife lay on the ground and blood bubbled from the wound with every labored breath. His ashen skin and slack mouth told the rest of the story.

"Can we save him?" Carter asked Rice.

"It's obvious that one of his lungs has been punctured, perhaps even collapsed. And I think that his heart was cut," Rice said. "His only hope is to eat the fruit."

Napier was up and racing away before anyone could say anything.

With a trembling hand, Rosenberg reached into his pants pocket. He pulled out several sheets of paper with small, neat writing on them. He thrust the papers at Carter.

"Those stories I told you...every one of them is true." He coughed and pink froth bubbled out of his lips. "The stories did not happen to me...they happened to other people."

Napier skidded in the dirt on his return and thrust one of the tree's fruits at the Jew. "Eat this," he said.

The dying man shook his head. "No...I think that Eve...and Adam...showed us the folly of that idea...besides...I really want to die."

"No!" Aoife cried.

A shudder ran through Abe Rosenberg and life passed from him. Angela closed his eyes and Mann gently laid him on the ground. Rice took the jacket off of one of the dead aircrew and placed it over the Jew's face.

Aoife was the last to let go of him, breaking out of her daze by springing to her feet as if a hot iron had been placed on her skin. "He died to save me," she blurted.

Napier went to her and wrapped his arms around her. "It's a good way to die," he said.

"I don't want him to die," she cried.

"None of us wanted him to die."

She wailed, a ragged keening that set one's teeth on edge. Abruptly gasping for breath, she sobbed, "I want to get away from all this death."

"We can come back later to bury the dead," Rice said. "Aoife, where's the keys for your handcuffs?"

Angela answered for her. "One of the soldiers had them."

Carter searched the pockets of the twins and found the key in the second man's front pocket. It was soaked in urine. As so many people do, he had pissed himself as he died.

Carter unlocked her manacles.

"There's a stream towards the big hole," Carter said. "I think that we all need to wash."

The six survivors walked away. Carter looked back and saw that a party of Seekers was watching them. He felt no threat from them.

"What time is it?" Carter asked.

Rice felt for his pocket watch. "I don't know, they took my watch."

"What day is it?" Carter asked. "I've lost track."

"May 8th, I believe," said Rice.

CHAPTER FIFTY-ONE

All around the world, save in Japan, people celebrated May 8, 1945 as VE-Day. A nightmare that began in 1939 ended with the unconditional surrender of Germany. Unknown to them all, the last battle was fought in the mystical land of Asgard, far from the eyes of reporters or the analysis of historians.

Strangers hugged on sidewalks and in town squares. Hastily arranged parades crowded the streets of cities great and small. People danced with each other. In London, two women frolicked in a public fountain with two sailors, and while many passersby disapproved, the police let them be.

At Buckingham Palace, the Royal Family stood on a balcony and waved to the revelers. Seven times that day, George VI and his family would appear. The king also spoke on the radio at six o'clock in the evening. The two princesses, always high-spirited, broke the rule and slipped out with only two Guards officers as escorts to join the crowds in the streets.

Winston Churchill stood on a balcony at Whitehall with his ministers, raised his arms with two outstretched fingers in his famous V for Victory salute, and spoke to the large crowd gathered outside. Afterwards he went out among the crowds in his car, stopping frequently to get on the roof and take in the exuberant joy. Even though eight out of ten Britons admired how he had led them through the war, only two months later, his Conservative party lost the election and the Labour Party swept into power.

In some English neighborhoods, the streets were blocked off, tables and chairs brought out, best china retrieved from display cases, and children treated to the finest meal they had eaten in their lives. Housewives left the factories, using hoarded sugar and flour to make cakes and sweets that the children hadn't seen for years; and for younger children they were the stuff of stories, not experience. A month's worth of ration coupons were splurged in a day. Now that the war was over, certainly rationing would end, but prosperity did not return so quickly. The first winter of peace was as hard as any of the winters of war, except the Germans were no longer sending rockets over to randomly kill people.

Many couples got carried away with exuberance and found themselves in bed, or in an alley, or in the bushes. Many regretted it afterwards, others didn't. Stories were invented to explain why a child arrived nine months later and, occasionally, who the father might be.

When night fell, enterprising souls lit bonfires in the streets. No one wanted the first party after six years of war to end prematurely. The fires were not necessary for warmth, since the night was unseasonably warm, more like midsummer than late spring. But by common assent, everyone agreed that the blackout restrictions that had been the rule at night for so long were no longer needed. No German bombers would ever come again. Big Ben in London was lit with floodlights. The city looked alive in a way that brought back memories of times before the war.

Some villages chose to not celebrate—not while hundreds of thousands of men still fought against Japan in the Far East. When Japan surrendered, they decided, then they would celebrate. And other people stayed in their homes, mourning the recent loss of a brother, a son, a father, or a lover.

In Prague, the city streets were still filled with over a thousand barricades. The population had risen up to claim their freedom; the fight had lasted for two days. The city celebrated the end of the war the next day.

In Tel Aviv, the Jewish city in Palestine, fifty thousand

people paraded through the streets. Zionist flags were draped in black borders, remembering the victims of the Holocaust. New schemes to get surviving Jews to Palestine were hatched and plans for the founding of Israel came closer to fruition. Never again would Jews be without a homeland, a refuge to seek when anti-Semitism turned deadly.

Even in Germany, many felt a sense of relief. Some diehard Nazis committed suicide, while others scrambled to find ways to hide their crimes. Millions of refugees still struggled to flee the Soviet army and their rapacious soldiers to find refuge in the West. The millions of Soviet men who had been captured in the war faced an uncertain future when they were repatriated to their homelands. Stalin had kept his paranoia at bay during the war, but now anyone tainted by exposure to the West, even as a prisoner, was sent straight to the Siberian gulag.

In the United States and Canada, school classes were canceled and people celebrated with parades, though not with the crazed exuberance of the English. The Americans and Canadians had known the sorrow of their men dying in distant lands, but their own homelands had not been touched by destruction, and their economies had prospered during the war.

All across Europe the corpses of millions remained—some in graves, some in ashes, and many left where they fell. Perhaps they celebrated in heaven, or in hell, or other places unknown to myth and religion. They had paid the price, often without being offered a choice.

In Norway, Albert Rediess sat in a command bunker on a country estate. He wore his best uniform, his decorations arrayed across his chest. He was proudest of his Iron Cross, Second Class, at his neck, awarded by Himmler himself. The final letters had been written, money left in a Swiss account for his family, and the bunker planted with dynamite.

There had been no word from Unternehmen Nordkap. No supernatural force had descended from the north to save National Socialism.

It was all over. The Dönitz government had signed the instruments of surrender yesterday, and the fighting would officially end tomorrow at 11:01 PM, May 8, 1945—a day much darker than the humiliating end of the Great War, on the eleventh hour of the eleventh day of the eleventh month, 1918. The other commanders in Norway had abandoned the plan for Festung Norwegen, having lost their appetite for continuing the fight. Even if they had sought to hold out, their troops wouldn't have followed them once they heard the announcement from the new German government.

Admiral Dönitz had tried to arrange a separate peace with the Western allies and continue to fight the eastern hordes, but Truman and Churchill failed to see their higher duty to their race and continued to side with the Slavs. Already the German command in Norway had surrendered to Prince Olav and the British. Norwegian troops had landed from Britain and crossed the border from Sweden, occupying the country without any opposition.

SS-Gruppenführer Albert Rediess placed the pistol in his mouth and joined his Führer.

CHAPTER FIFTY-TWO

All the streams in the green valley of Asgard flowed inwards, from the rim wall down to the great hole. The six people shivered as they rubbed their hands in the water and scrubbed their faces. Afterwards they sat on the grass, letting the Arctic sun warm them.

"We can take showers back at the airship," Angela said.

"I don't want to go back there yet," Aoife said. "This is a nice place. It's nice to be in the sun and to be free."

"What did Abe give you?" Angela asked Carter.

The major took the papers out his pocket and looked at them. "I don't know this language."

"Let me see." Rice held out his hand.

"How many languages do you know?" Carter asked with an undercurrent of envy, offering up the papers.

"Dozens," Rice said. "You live long enough and travel enough, you just accumulate them. After a while, they are all variations on themes." He looked through the papers, scanning them quickly. "It's written in Polish. I think that everyone will want to hear this. I will translate."

My name is Abe Rosenberg and I was born in Warsaw in 1912 and raised in Kraków. I married Hena Demska in 1938. We were married in a civil ceremony because even though we were Jews, we agreed that we did not believe in God. We had a son, Amos, in 1939, just a week before Hitler invaded Poland. I was an Army reservist and was called up the day before Amos was born, so I didn't see him for five months. The war was short for me. My unit was surrounded and surrendered just six days into the war. I was sent to a prisoner of war camp. The camp guards separated the Jews from the other Poles and we lived in tents, instead of barracks, and received much less food. I lost ten kilos in four months and I hadn't had a lot of weight to start with.

When they asked for factory workers to return to Poland, I jumped at the chance. I was a trained machinist and was sent to a factory near Warsaw. Hena bribed a Polish policeman to get a pass and came to visit. I held Amos in my arms for the first time and wept. When they herded us all into ghettos, I managed to arrange to be transferred to Kraków's ghetto in March 1941. On the second day in my new factory job, I hurt my hand and could no longer run the machines, so I joined the Jewish police. We reported to the Jewish council, which ran the ghetto for the Nazis. These were not collaborators, but leading men of the community who tried to make the best of a bad situation.

I joined the Jewish police for purely selfish reasons. I wanted to save my family and I thought that if I was useful to the Nazis that they would protect me. All of us in the police, though we never talked about it, thought that if we gave up a few Jews, it would protect the rest of our people. Sometimes evil is stupid and banal, and there were plenty of Nazis like that, and sometimes it is cunning. The Nazis who ran the Final Solution were cunning, and in May 1942, they began their insidious work in Kraków. At first they asked us to just round up the older people, so they could be sent to another city where it was easier to take care of them. I helped round them up and put them on the train. Not a cattle train, but a real train, with seats. I even took my own grandparents down to the station. They trusted me, but made sure that they weren't taking any valuables with them, like coins or jewelry. Grandma even left her wedding ring behind, which had been in the family for three generations. They left all these things for the family to use to buy food.

We never heard from them again. We told ourselves that it was because the Nazis were restricting mail delivery. Of course, that wasn't true. They were taken to one of the extermination camps. My grandparents went to Treblinka, though Birkenau and other camps were closer. I guess all those other camps were too busy. These camps were not like the concentration camps or work camps; extermination camps had only one industry and I am sure that my grandparents, Ari and Lucia Rosenberg, died quickly.

On February 6, 1943, a day that was bitterly cold, the Nazis came and cleaned out our apartment building. They herded everyone down to the train station. I was not there. The families of six Jewish policemen lived in that building and all six of us had been assigned to guard a food warehouse on the other side of the city. We should have known something was wrong, because the Nazis never used us outside of the ghetto. Someone managed to get a message to us and we all deserted our posts. We got to the train station just as a cattle train was being loaded. Fences had been set up to keep the victims under control, as if they were a herd of cattle. I found Hena and Amos. There were two makeshift fences between us and a good ten meters of distance. SS guards patrolled between the fences. Amos was crying and so was Hena. My parents and her parents were there, and my aunt Lena and my cousins Dov and Eitan. I called out to her not get on the train and that I would find a way to get them out.

My last sight of them was them waiting with desperate hope in their eyes. I rushed back to the Jewish council chamber, but no one could help. I rushed over to the German headquarters and the bastard sergeant laughed when I explained that there had been a mistake, I was a Jewish policeman, and my family was not supposed to be taken. They should be released. I remembered his name—Rudi Brandauer.

I ran back to the apartment. The Nazis had ripped the place apart, but they failed to find our money stash, which was hidden underneath a tile in the bathroom. I had to move the cast-iron tub to get to the tile, a heavy beast that usually took all the men and boys to lift. Such was my fear that I was able to push it aside and get to the money.

I intended to bribe the guards to let my family go, but by the time that I got back to the train station, the train had gone. The fenced area was empty of people, but there were bags and clothes and other personal belongings scattered around. The guards had forced the Jews to leave it all behind so that they could cram more people into the cattle cars. Jewish policeman were gathering up the belongings under the watchful eyes of SS guards.

One of the other five policemen in my building managed to get his wife and daughter back and we hated him for it because it reminded us of our failure. Two of the policemen took poison. I thought about that, but I am a coward. I couldn't even kill myself.

Why didn't we attack and save our families? We had no guns, no weapons, no way to fight back.

I took off my uniform, put on my best clothes, bought before the war, took off my yellow star, and sneaked out of the ghetto. I had enough money to buy a revolver from a criminal. Then I waited in the cold and sleet until Rudi Brandauer left the ghetto to return to his lodgings. I made sure that the sergeant saw me and knew who I was before I shot him in the face.

The partisans had formed units in the forest. When I asked to join, they asked if I was a Jew, and I told them no, because I knew that the partisans disliked Jews. The Poles had no problem with the Germans killing us off, though some Poles were good people and tried to help.

In the forest I heard about the end of the ghetto. On March 12, 1943, the Nazis finished cleaning out the ghetto, shooting everyone that they didn't take to the factories. The German factory owner Oskar Schindler saved some of the Jews from our ghetto—hundreds, maybe even a thousand—but it was too late for my family.

After the Russians conquered Poland, I left the partisans. I found other Jews like me, who had survived and wanted to kill Nazis. We called ourselves Avengers. I liked our job. Any Nazi that had killed Jews was fair game in our hunt. I was captured by German troops, who thought I was just a Jew, and sent with the others to Belsen. After the British liberated our camp I returned to being an Avenger.

I still don't believe in God, but I do believe in hell, because I will always live there.

CHAPTER FIFTY-THREE

"A sober letter," Rice said.

"This war has wounded many of us." Angela wiped at her eyes. "And many of the wounds are inside, where other people can't see them."

There were murmurs of agreement. Angela assumed that the others were like her, each with their own thoughts, many of them experiencing complex emotions that had not risen to a conscious enough level of coherence to be articulated. She had not had to make hard choices like Abe Rosenberg had been force to make, but she felt scarred by knowing that other people had been forced to make such choices.

By unspoken assent, the group of survivors began to walk, heading downhill towards the great hole. She saw some deer in the distance, but they were the size of dogs, not the deer of her native Midwest. The sight prompted her to pay more attention. She noticed gnats and bugs in the grass, and a great many birds—mostly small, but noisy, in shades of brown and grey, and a few all white, like miniature doves. She supposed that it was not surprising to see so many birds; they did have the world's largest tree as their home.

Angela noticed that Aoife and Carson held hands—a stalwart miner turned solider and an Irish maiden. The simple act looked so right, something that she wanted. Angela stepped up next to John and gently grasped his hand with her fingers. The cast prevented completely enclosing his hand, but it was enough. He looked at her with a rise of his eyebrows and a quizzical twist of his lips.

She squeezed his fingers. He smiled and squeezed back.

"I know that we've only been here for a few days, but I really miss sunsets," Angela said.

"I agree," Carter said. "We could really use a sunset right now. A sunset would be nice and predictable, a good way to have the day end."

Warm air from the interior of the Earth brushed against Angela's face as they drew closer to the giant hole, its grandeur trimmed by the grey cliffs and waterfalls.

The sight of the hole evoked a different sensation than the sight of Yggdrasil, a feeling that Angela Wright recognized. While a teenager, she had gone with her parents on a trip to Niagara Falls. Seeing that much water, flowing implacably over the cliff, the spray coming up in wet clouds, and the throbbing of the very air even before she reached the falls, all made her feel small in the presence of the true power of nature. This hole made her feel little, in awe of what God had wrought.

The six people stood there on top of the world, on the lip of the gateway to the inner world: a Seeker thousands of years old, two American soldiers grateful that their war had ended, a pilot without an airplane, a Cree Indian who kept his promise to not join the military, yet had still been able to participate in the adventure of a lifetime, and a young Irish woman, heir to the legacy of witches.

The Earth breathed.

AFTERWORD

When I was about twelve years old, visiting my grandmother's, I discovered a small bookcase full of paperback novels. As a voracious reader, I was intrigued. These novels belonged to my uncle, who had died in a car accident at the age of seventeen a decade earlier. I borrowed a dozen or so and took them home. Gradually all of the novels moved to my house, with a promise that I would take care of them. A promise I have kept. I think that my grandmother had always wanted to read them as a homage to her youngest child, but her tastes in fiction ran more to westerns and romances.

Many of the novels were by Edgar Rice Burroughs. Burroughs is best known for his Tarzan novels, which I enjoyed, but I found his science fiction much more interesting. What Burroughs wrote was called scientific romance, because it really didn't meet the modern definition of science fiction. I will not go into what science fiction is, mainly because I would never be able to climb out of that argument. Burroughs had started publishing in 1912, long before the term "scientifiction" was coined by Hugo Gernsback in 1929, and died in 1950, over a quarter century before I started reading him.

The world of John Carter of Barsoom thrilled me, with adventures on a Mars where canals existed and a dying civilization struggled for survival. The story was a combination of swordplay, daring heroics, rescuing the princess and other damsels, and futuristic marvels. When the novels were written, the idea that Mars was a sister world to Earth, with canals on it, was still scientifically acceptable.

I also enjoyed the Carson of Venus novels, set on a jungle planet that thrived under the mysterious clouds that blanketed the planet nearest to us. The idea that such a environment existed was quite plausible until the 1960s, when American and Soviet spacecraft passed by or landed on the planet. We discovered not the steamy tropics, but a hellish furnace with temperatures over 800 degrees Fahrenheit and a surface pressure ninety times Earth normal caused by a run-away greenhouse effect.

His Caspak trilogy, beginning with *The Land That Time Forgot*, written in 1918, told of a green valley in the Antarctica, heated by volcanism, where the different stages of evolution were played out the further one walked up the valley. Antarctica at that time was still a mysterious place.

The science behind Pellucidar, the land inside the hollow Earth, was discredited long before Burroughs created his stories, but they were a compelling read for me anyhow. A whole new world, only miles below my feet, provided hours of enjoyment. Other Burroughs novels such as *The Moon Maid* and *The Mad King* also excited my youthful desire for vicarious adventure. Burroughs wrote about one hundred novels in his life and I calculate that I read about a third of them. I also read other science fiction and fantasy novels in my uncle's collection, such as the *Time Trader* series of Andre Norton.

The novels of Burroughs are probably the one author that I regularly read repeatedly as a youth, other than the novel *Swiss Family Robinson*. By my later teens, I could no longer read Burroughs. The plots were too predictable, the characters too pulpy, and my tastes had changed. Burroughs was a man of his times, and for modern sensibilities, he is racist, ethnocentric, sexist; a whole host of negative -ism's. Burroughs was financially successful, and incredibly influential on the science fiction and fantasy fields emerging out of the pulps in the 1930s and 1940s. The importance of Burroughs in the field of science fiction can hardly be overstated and one can say without quali- fication that he was the best-selling science fiction and fantasy author of the twentieth century.

The curious result of reading my uncle's books is that I was introduced to science fiction as if I had been twenty years further back in the past, and as my reading habits changed, they recapitulated the history of speculative fiction. As a scholar interested in the history of the genre, this is an invaluable background.

It has been observed one can read older science fiction stories and novels and still enjoy them by considering them to be a form of alternative history. Just remember what was known about science at that time and enjoy the story for what it was, not condemn it for what it got wrong.

ABOUT THE AUTHOR

ERIC G. SWEDIN is an Associate Professor in History at Weber State University. His publications include numerous articles, six history books, several science fiction novels, and an historical mystery novel. His *When Angels Wept: A What-If History of the Cuban Mystery Crisis* earned the 2010 Sidewise Award in Alternate History. Eric lives with his family in a house built in 1881. His website is:

http://www.swedin.org/